PRAISE FOR BESTSELLING AUTHOR DIANE CAPRI

"Full of thrills and tension, but smart and human, too. Kim Otto is a great, great character. I love her."
Lee Child, #1 *New York Times* Bestselling Author of Jack Reacher Thrillers

"[A] welcome surprise...[W]orks from the first page to 'The End.'"
Larry King

"Swift pacing and ongoing suspense are always present...[L]ikable protagonist who uses her political connections for a good cause... Readers should eagerly anticipate the next [book]."
Top Pick, *Romantic Times*

"...offers tense legal drama with courtroom overtones, twisty plot, and loads of Florida atmosphere. Recommended."
Library Journal

"[A] fast-paced legal thriller...energetic prose...an appealing heroine... clever and capable supporting cast...[that will] keep readers waiting for the next [book]."
Publishers Weekly

"Expertise shines on every page."
Margaret Maron, Edgar, Anthony, Agatha and Macavity
MWA Past President

ALSO BY DIANE CAPRI

For a complete list of Diane Capri Books visit DianeCapri.com

DON'T KNOW JACK

DIANE CAPRI

A POST HILL PRESS BOOK
ISBN: 978-1-68261-397-9

Post Hill Press
New York • Nashville
posthillpress.com

Published in the United States of America

For Lee Child, with unrelenting gratitude.

CAST OF PRIMARY CHARACTERS

Kim L. Otto
Carlos M. Gaspar

Charles Cooper
Lamont Finlay

Beverly Roscoe
Jacqueline Roscoe

Sylvia Black
Harry Black
Michael Hale
Marion Wallace
Archie Leach
Jim Leach

and
Jack Reacher

CHAPTER ONE

Monday, November 1
4:00 a.m.
Detroit, Michigan

JUST THE FACTS. And not many of them, either. Jack Reacher's file was too stale and too thin to be credible. No human could be as invisible as Reacher appeared to be, whether he was currently above the ground or under it. Either the file had been sanitized, or Reacher was the most off-the-grid paranoid Kim Otto had ever heard of.

What had she missed?

At four in the morning the untraceable cell phone had vibrated on her bedside table. She had slept barely a hundred minutes. She cleared her throat, grabbed the phone, flipped it open, swung her legs out of bed, and said, "FBI Special Agent Kim Otto."

The man said, "I'm sorry to call you so early, Otto."

She recognized the voice, even though she hadn't heard it for many years. He was still polite. Still undemanding. He didn't need to be demanding. His every request was always granted. No one thwarted him in any way for any reason. Ever.

She said, "I was awake." She was lying, and she knew he knew it, and she knew he didn't care. He was the boss. And she owed him.

She walked across the bedroom and flipped on the bathroom light. It was harsh. She grimaced at herself in the mirror and splashed cold water on her face. She felt like she'd tossed back a dozen tequila shots last night, and she was glad that she hadn't.

The voice asked, "Can you be at the airport for the 5:30 flight to Atlanta?"

"Of course." Kim answered automatically, and set her mind to making it happen.

Showered, dressed, and seated on a plane in ninety minutes? Easy. Her apartment stood ten blocks from the FBI's Detroit Field Office, where a helicopter waited, ever ready. She picked up her personal cell and began texting the duty pilot to meet her at the helipad in twenty. From the pad to the airport was a quick fifteen. She'd have time to spare.

But as if he could hear her clicking the silent keys, he said, "No helicopter. Keep this under the radar. Until we know what we're dealing with, that is."

The direct order surprised her. Too blunt. No wiggle room. Uncharacteristic. Coming from anyone lower down the food chain, the order might have been illegal too.

"Of course," Kim said again. "I understand. Under the radar. No problem." She hit the delete button on the half-finished text. He hadn't said undercover.

The FBI operated in the glare of every possible spotlight. Keeping something under the radar added layers of complication. Under the radar meant no official recognition. No help, either. Off the books. She didn't have to hide, but she'd need to be careful what she revealed and to whom. Agents died during operations under the radar. Careers were killed there too. So Otto heeded her internal warning system and placed herself on security alert, level red. She didn't ask to whom she'd report because she already knew. He wouldn't have called her directly if he intended her to report through normal channels. Instead, she turned her mind to solving the problem at hand.

How could she possibly make a commercial flight scheduled to depart—she glanced at the bedside clock—in eighty-nine minutes? There was no reliable subway or other public transportation in the Motor City. A car was the only option, through traffic and construction. Most days it took ninety minutes, door to door, just to reach the airport.

She now had eighty-eight.

And she was still standing naked in her bathroom.

Only one solution. There was a filthy hot sheets motel three blocks away specializing in hourly racks for prostitutes and drug dealers. Her office handled surveillance of terrorists who stopped there after crossing the Canadian border from Windsor. Gunfire was a nightly occurrence. But a line of cabs always stood outside, engines running, because tips there were good. One of those cabs might get her to the flight on time. She shivered.

"Agent Otto?" His tone was calm. "Can you make it? Or do we need to hold the plane?"

She heard her mother's voice deep in her reptile brain: *When there's only one choice, it's the right choice.*

"I'll be out the door in ten minutes," she told him, staring down her anxiety in the mirror.

"Then I'll call you back in eleven."

She waited for dead air. When it came, she grabbed her toothbrush and stepped into shower water pumped directly out of the icy Detroit River. The cold spray warmed her frigid skin.

Seven minutes later—out of breath, heart pounding—she was belted into the back seat of a filthy taxi. The driver was an Arab. She told him she'd pay double if they reached the Delta terminal in under an hour.

"Yes, of course, miss," he replied, as if the request was standard for his enterprise, which it probably was.

She cracked the window. Petroleum-heavy air hit her face and entered her lungs and chased away the more noxious odors inside the cab. She patted her sweatsuit pocket to settle the cell phone more comfortably against her hip.

Twenty past four in the morning, Eastern Daylight Time. Three hours before sunrise. The moon was not bright enough to lighten the blackness, but the street lamps helped. Outbound traffic crawled steadily. Night construction crews would be knocking off in forty minutes. No tie-ups, maybe. God willing.

Before the phone vibrated again three minutes later, she'd twisted her damp black hair into a low chignon, swiped her lashes with mascara and her lips with gloss, dabbed blush on her cheeks, and fastened a black leather watch-band onto her left wrist. She needed another few minutes to finish dressing. Instead, she pulled the cell from her pocket. While she remained inside the cab, she reasoned, he couldn't see she was wearing only a sweatsuit, clogs, and no underwear.

This time, she didn't identify herself when she answered and kept her responses brief. Taxi drivers could be exactly what they seemed, but Kim Otto didn't take unnecessary risks, especially on alert level red.

She took a moment to steady her breathing before she answered calmly, "Yes."

"Agent Otto?" he asked, to be sure, perhaps.

"Yes, sir."

"They'll hold the plane. No boarding pass required. Flash your badge through security. A TSA officer named Kaminsky is expecting you."

"Yes, sir." She couldn't count the number of laws she'd be breaking. The paperwork alone required to justify boarding a flight in the manner he had just ordered would have buried her for days. Then she smiled. No paperwork this time. The idea lightened her mood. She could grow to like under the radar work.

He said, "You need to be at your destination on time. Not later than eleven thirty this morning. Can you make that happen?"

She thought of everything that could go wrong. The possibilities were endless. They both knew she couldn't avoid them all. Still, she answered, "Yes, sir, of course."

"You have your laptop?"

"Yes, sir, I do." She glanced at the case to confirm once more that she hadn't left it behind when she rushed out of her apartment.

"I've sent you an encrypted file. Scrambled signal. Download it now, before you reach monitored airport communication space."

"Yes, sir."

There was a short pause, and then he said, "Eleven thirty, remember. Don't be late."

She interpreted urgency in his repetition. She said, "Right, sir." She waited for dead air again before she closed the phone and returned it to her pocket. Then she lifted her Bureau computer from the floor and pressed the power switch. It booted up in fourteen seconds, which was one fewer than the government had spent a lot of money to guarantee.

The computer found the secure satellite, and she downloaded the encrypted file. She moved it to a folder misleadingly labeled

Non-work Miscellaneous and closed the laptop. No time to read now. She noticed her foot tapping on the cab's sticky floor. She couldn't be late. No excuses.

Late for what?

CHAPTER TWO

AT PRECISELY 5:15 a.m. the cab driver stopped in front of Delta departures at McNamara terminal. Fifty-five minutes, door to door. So far, so good, but she wasn't on the plane yet.

She paid the driver double in cash, as promised. She ignored the cold November wind and pulled her bags from the car and jogged inside as quickly as she dared. Running made airport officials nervous. Airports were touchy places in America these days, particularly those close to known arrival and departure points for terrorists. Detroit-Wayne Metro had two strategic advantages for the bad guys. Proximity to the Canadian border allowed rapid deployment once they entered the country, and they could easily blend in. Greater Detroit was home to more people of Arabic descent than any city outside the Middle East. Which was the very reason Otto had requested the Detroit deployment: more opportunity for advancement on the front lines.

Right then she thought she would have been better off somewhere else.

She slowed to a walk. There were cameras everywhere. She was under the radar, but she wasn't invisible.

She approached the checkpoint and looked for her contact. She saw a man with *Kaminsky* on his nameplate, manning the crew line, putting each crew member through the same screens as the regular passengers. He was focused intently on his work.

Come on, come on, come on.

She willed him to notice her. When he did, she ducked under the rope and walked up to where he stood. She said, "You're expecting me."

He said, "Correct."

He glanced at her credentials and passed her along, with her bags, and her electronics, and her gun, around the outside of the metal detector hoop. Behind her a passenger called out, "Hey! What's so special about her?"

She thought: *Shit. Now someone will remember me if they're asked, for sure.* She didn't glance back to give the guy another look at her face. She just jogged the last hundred yards to the gate, where another TSA agent waited, blocking the entrance. She flashed her ID. He nodded and stepped aside. The moment she crossed the threshold, he closed and locked the door behind her. She rushed through the tunnel and stepped onto the plane. The flight attendant closed and sealed the door behind her, the jetway retreated, and the plane backed away. The pilot had only a ten-minute delay to cover up.

Should anyone ask.

She found her seat in first class. The seat next to hers was empty, as was the seat across the aisle. Probably not by chance. She stowed her bags and buckled her seatbelt low and tight. She laid her head back and closed her eyes. She gripped the armrests until her fingers hurt.

God, she hated flying.

Experts said fear of flying was irrational. They were fools. Kim knew too much to believe that nonsense. Planes made powerful weapons and they were no match for Mother Nature. And she was in a bad way to start with. The acid in her stomach had boiled up the night before, when the untraceable cell phone had arrived. She unclenched one hand long enough to slide an antacid between her lips. She pressed it with her tongue to the roof of her mouth, and as it dissolved, she tried to calm her racing pulse. She kept her eyes closed until the plane was safely in the air and she could breathe again. She asked for black coffee and opened her laptop to find out why the hell she was headed to Atlanta.

She had two hours and thirty-eight minutes to learn everything she needed to know.

The encrypted file she had downloaded in the taxi was zipped. Inside, she found five separate documents. The first contained a short memo explaining her assignment. The other four files were identified by unfamiliar names: first, Carlos Marco Gaspar; second, Beverly Roscoe (Trent); third, Lamont Finlay, Ph. D.; and fourth, Jack Reacher.

Jack Reacher's file was the largest, and it ended fifteen years ago. The other three were brief résumés.

She started reading.

The assignment seemed straightforward enough: Complete background investigation on potential candidate Jack-none-Reacher. She'd handled dozens of these since she'd joined the Special Personnel Task Force. But this assignment was different in every respect. There was no indication of the job for which Reacher was being considered. Nor did the assignment memo explain the secrecy, the haste. Or why the boss was involved. Everything about it felt wrong.

She was instructed to begin in Margrave, Georgia. Nothing further.

The second document was brief but normal. It contained limited data on FBI Special Agent Carlos Marco Gaspar, her partner on this assignment. She'd never met Gaspar and the file told her very little about him. He was forty-four years old, married with four children, and he was currently posted to the Miami Field Office.

The only odd note was the explicit direction that she was to take the lead, even though Gaspar was ten years more experienced.

She'd never acted as lead on a SPTF assignment. Was this a test of her leadership ability? Was she being considered for promotion? No. Too soon. What, then? Another secret. She hated secrets unless she was the one keeping them. She popped another antacid and studied Gaspar's official ID photograph, learning his face. Then she spent the next two hours reading, analyzing, and memorizing the limited information contained in the remaining three files.

The more she read, the less comfortable she became, but she was already on security alert level red, and there were no higher levels in her system.

She began with the candidate. His file was simply too thin. In her line of work, less was definitely not more. Where were Reacher's tax returns? Credit card files? Property records? Criminal records? Had Reacher never bought a car? Rented an apartment? Owned a cell phone? Surfed the Internet? Been arrested? What about banking records? Where did he get his walking-around money?

There had to be more documentary evidence on Jack-none-Reacher, but she'd been allowed no time to do her own thorough preparation using the extensive tools available to the FBI. And she couldn't call and ask for assistance. She was under the radar. Only two people were authorized to help her: one she hadn't met yet, and one she couldn't ask.

She closed her eyes again.

CHAPTER THREE

EVENTUALLY, AND RELUCTANTLY, Special Agent Kim Otto reached the only possible conclusion: Reacher's file was deliberately thin. There had to be more. The rest was being withheld.

Which made her nervous. What always made her nervous were the things she didn't know. What you didn't know could kill you. She could handle anything, but only if she saw it coming. Two antacids this time, washed down with the cold coffee she hadn't touched. She pushed the button for the flight attendant to refill her cup. Then she copied and stored the limited data on Reacher to her own encrypted files. When she had access to the satellite again, she would send her private files to secure storage.

Because too many people had access to FBI files. She had been burned before when confidential reports were acquired by unintended recipients who lived to tell about it. She never made the same mistake twice. In the field, she relied on memory alone. Her formal reports were carefully drafted and filed according to protocol, but her private records remained her own. It was impossible to be too careful.

She copied the Roscoe and Finlay files too. Straightforward information there, a bit unusual but nothing mysterious. None of it explained why Roscoe and Finlay had been selected as interview subjects, except one point of possible connection: Margrave, Georgia.

Today's destination.

Fifteen years ago, Roscoe and Finlay had been present in Margrave. Reacher's honorable discharge from the army was six months fresh back then. Whether Reacher had been in Margrave, and whether they'd all met there, and what had happened between them, were just three of the thousand questions Kim would need to answer. But something had happened. The boss wouldn't send her there otherwise.

She glanced at her watch. There was still time before landing. She ran through the Reacher material one more time.

Birth certificate (West Berlin 1960); education record showing attendance on military bases around the world, including one year in Saigon, Viet Nam. Kim read that fact for the tenth time before the Taser charge she'd felt the first nine times lessened. Kim's mother was Vietnamese; her father served in the U.S. Army in Viet Nam. No connection to Reacher back then, right?

No. Reacher was a kid when Kim's parents left the country; Reacher's father was a Marine; Army and Marines hadn't mixed much in Viet Nam. There couldn't be any connection between them. But was Viet Nam the reason the boss had chosen her to lead this assignment?

She pushed that new worry aside. No time to deal with it now and nothing she could do about it from 35,000 feet anyway.

Reacher had graduated from the U.S. Military Academy at West Point (1984). Parents deceased (father 1988; mother 1990). One brother, also deceased (1997).

At West Point and afterward, until he was honorably discharged, the file contained the usual batch of military forms crafted in army-speak. Uninitiated readers would need an interpreter to decipher the batch of acronyms. When Kim copied the contents of

Reacher's file into her own private documents, she included the full phrases and definitions, and studied them carefully, testing herself, building her knowledge. She'd labeled the section "Accomplishments," but the title was far too benign when you knew what each entry meant. Reacher had investigated, arrested, subdued, and otherwise dealt with some of the most highly trained soldiers on earth, all of them capable of extreme violence.

He had done it by matching their violence with his own.

He was a killer.

So what did the FBI want from him now?

He'd been decorated several times, each for some form of extraordinary heroism or outstanding service or extreme military achievement. He had been wounded in combat and been given a Purple Heart. He'd been trained and won awards as a sniper. Summary: Reacher had handled whatever had come his way. He'd faced the enemy and come out alive. More than once. Kim imagined the type. He'd be confident, hard to persuade, manipulate or overpower. In no way like any other candidate she'd investigated before.

No wonder the project was under the radar.

And how the hell would she accomplish it?

The pilot announced the initial descent into Atlanta. Not much time left for electronic devices. She kept on working. Reacher's file contained no details on the situations he'd handled as a military cop. Those would have been filed separately at the time the investigations took place. Kim made a note to find them. The search wouldn't be easy, but the years Reacher spent doing his job were the last that would have clear and complete records, and those records would be the only clues to his current activities or location. Understanding how he'd performed back then would teach her the man and his methods. And scare her out of her wits, probably, if she had any wits left by then.

The file ended with Reacher's army discharge papers, followed by a short memo stating that he'd been off the grid for more than fifteen years. No one knew where he was. FBI files, Homeland Security files, all were empty of references to Major Jack (none) Reacher, U.S. Army, Retired.

No way, she'd typed into her notes. *Can't happen.*

Was he dead? In prison? Witness protection? Classified assignment? At a minimum, either Reacher himself or someone else didn't want him found.

Maybe he was unfindable.

And maybe that was the good news.

Twenty minutes from Atlanta the plane started to bounce around like a steer on cocaine. Clear air turbulence, the pilot called it, but Kim didn't believe him. More likely a fatal mechanical fault. She pulled her seatbelt as tight as possible. The belt failed to hold her securely in the wide seat. She would have some odd bruises tomorrow. If there was a tomorrow. Not that anyone would see her bruises. The Danish she'd eaten threatened to come back up. She wanted to grab the airsickness bag, but she'd have to crack her fingers away from the armrests to reach for it.

Then the plane's wheels bounced twice on the tarmac and skidded a long, loud, smoky distance before grabbing the runway hard enough to jerk her head off the seat and slam it back again. She breathed out and felt stupid, as always. Then her embarrassment doubled when she looked down at her lap and realized she'd never finished getting dressed.

Kim waited curbside behind the wheel of a rented Chevy Traverse. She took a look at the airline's web site flight tracking data on her personal smart phone. "Terrorist.com," she called it, because constant flight status updates on any commercial flight were quick and easy to find. Agent Gaspar's flight from Miami had just landed. He'd be with her soon. She ate the last antacid in the roll. When it melted, she washed the chalky taste away with a swig of black coffee.

Then she opened her computer and stared one more time at Jack Reacher's face, critically analyzing the full photo, committing every pixel to memory. The Army's black and white regulation headshot suggested but didn't confirm Reacher's height, which was recorded at six-five, or his hair color, described elsewhere as fair, or his eye color, which was blue, or his enormous build, listed at two hundred and fifty pounds.

Kim shuddered. On the inside she was one hundred percent lithe, lanky, formidable German, like her father. But on the outside, she was exactly 5'0" tall, like her mother, and she weighed 100 pounds on her fat days. Reacher was more than twice her size; she hoped she was more than twice as smart. Brains, not brawn, would have to be her weapon.

Therefore, she needed a better photo. An army photo wouldn't do the job. People would remember Reacher. He wasn't just memorable. More like unforgettable. But no doubt patriotism was still alive and well in Margrave, Georgia. Locals would say nothing negative about a man dressed in army green and gold and sporting a chest full of medals. Witnesses might even deny knowing him, even though it was a federal crime to lie to an FBI agent in the course of an investigation.

Kim had been trained to observe witness reactions to photographs. Witnesses found it difficult to deny recognition, and harder still to lie effectively when confronted with a picture. People had trouble remembering names, but faces were imprinted in a different area of the brain, more easily recalled. So she would know if a witness recognized Reacher, even if they lied. She'd be able to tell. But failure was not an option, so she needed a different picture.

She switched to the altered headshot she had created on the plane. She had cropped out Reacher's army uniform and removed his hat in this version. Was her photo editing good enough to deny Reacher his unfair advantage?

Then knuckles rapped hard on the Traverse's side window. Kim closed her computer and looked at the inquiring face only inches from her own. She pressed the button to lower the window. Before she had a chance to speak, Special Agent Carlos Gaspar said, "Sorry, didn't mean to startle you. I tried to open the hatch, but it's locked. Give me the key. I'll toss my bags in and we can get on the road."

"Sure," she said. She turned off the ignition, handed him the keys and stepped out of the truck. She met him at the rear of the vehicle, watching as he moved her bag out, placed his on the bottom, and then put hers back on top.

A considerate guy.

Very proper.

She extended her hand in greeting and said, "Kim Otto."

"Carlos Gaspar," he said, taking her hand in a firm grasp, neither too hard or too soft. A respectful handshake. Not at all macho. She liked him already.

He said, "It's about an hour to Margrave. I've been there before. I'll drive."

"Actually, I prefer to drive," she said. She felt uncomfortable with anyone else behind the wheel. Particularly someone she didn't know and had never traveled with before. She had no idea what kind of driver he was. Her queasy stomach might not survive, and there was no way she was going to throw up in front of this guy. Not now. Not ever.

"I'm a good driver," he said. "And I'll be faster, because I know where we're going."

He opened the driver's door and moved the seat back, for his longer legs.

Maybe not so proper or respectful.

Maybe he was going to be one of those overbearing Latino males.

He was all the way inside the car now. He stuck his head out the window and asked, "Are you coming or not? We'll have to hustle to get there on time as it is."

When there's only one choice, it's the right choice.

She got into the passenger seat and Gaspar accelerated the second she closed the door.

CHAPTER FOUR

CARLOS GASPAR WAS hurting, but that was nothing new. Inside and out, mentally and physically, he lived with pain. He had slept badly and given up on it before three in the morning. He had crept out of the bedroom and holed up in the kitchen and started his day with Tylenol and coffee, like he always did. Nothing stronger, although God knew he was tempted. But that way lay ruin, and he knew he couldn't afford to get any more ruined than he already was. He had a wife and four children and twenty years to go before he could relax.

He showered and shaved and dressed in a tan poplin suit from Banana Republic, which would have gotten him killed in D.C., but which was the standard uniform in the Miami field office. He went back to the kitchen and ate more Tylenol and drank more coffee and sat still and imagined he could hear his family breathing.

His phone rang at three minutes past four in the morning. Not his regular phone. Not his personal phone, either, but a plain Motorola that had been bubble-wrapped and delivered to him through the Bureau's internal mail service. He knew who had sent it. He had fired it up and noted its number and run it through the databases. It didn't exist.

He answered it and a voice asked, "Gaspar?"

He said, "Yes, sir," quietly, so as not to wake his family, and because a low tone seemed to be appropriate for this guy.

The voice said, "There are files for you in your inbox. Read them on the plane. You're going to Atlanta."

"When, sir?"

"Now."

"Okay."

Then there was a pause. Just a beat, but Gaspar heard it. The voice said, "You're going to be the number two on this. Your lead will be Otto, out of Detroit. *No reflection on you.*"

Which was bullshit, of course. Everything was a reflection on him. Although maybe this guy Otto was a big deal. People who were referred to by their first name only usually were. Gaspar wondered whether he was supposed to have heard of him. But he hadn't. He had never worked in Detroit. Knew nothing about the office or the city, except that they used to make cars there.

He said, "No problem," but he said it to nobody, because the voice was already gone. He put the phone in his bag, which was permanently packed and ready to go, laptop, shirt, underwear, Tylenol. The bag was made by the same people that made Swiss Army knives, which was okay, but it had wheels and a handle, which wasn't. Trundling a bag around was one step from being in a wheelchair.

It was what it was.

He drove himself to the airport in his Bureau car, which was a blue Crown Vic with government plates. He could park it anywhere. He propped his laptop on the passenger seat and drove one-handed and stabbed at the keys and brought up his e-mail, not commercial wireless, but a secure satellite connection. One new message, as expected. One attached file, zipped and encrypted. No accompanying text. No hello, no best wishes. Par for the course.

He dumped the file to his desktop and closed the laptop's lid. Ten minutes later he was wheeling his hated bag into the terminal.

A TSA supervisor met him and gave him a boarding pass and fed him through the crew channel. An airside supervisor took him onward from there. The plane was waiting for him. The cabin door closed right behind him. He was in seat 1A, which was the seat airlines usually saved for late bookings. He hated 1A. You had to put your bag in the overhead, which he absolutely couldn't do. He couldn't lift it over his head. But 1A-type passengers were used to a certain standard of service, so he took his laptop out and left his bag in the aisle, and a stewardess bustled up behind him and dealt with it.

Then he eased himself into his seat. He had been shot twice, once in the right side and once in the right leg, and the wound in his side had collapsed the network of muscles there, and sitting was painful. The weight of his upper body crushed his organs, literally, like his ribs and his pelvis were the jaws of a vise. His doctors weren't concerned. They were like mechanics who had rebuilt a totaled car, and they weren't about to listen to complaints about a tiny scratch in the paint.

His leg wound had been dismissed as trivial. The bullet had hit the shinbone and hadn't even broken it. But day to day it was far worse to deal with than his side. It ached constantly, like someone was in there with a drill from the Home Depot. Hence the Tylenol.

He ate two more from his pocket and waited respectfully until the plane was in the air and the road warriors all around him started firing up their approved electronic devices. He opened his laptop and the screen came to life and he leaned to his left, partly to relieve the pressure on his right side, and partly to keep the screen away from his seatmate. He asked the software to decode the text and unzip the files.

Five documents. Four of them routine, one of them a big surprise.

The four routine files were the assignment, a target and two sources. Some guy named Jack Reacher was the target, and Beverly Trent née Roscoe and Lamont Finlay were the sources.

No big deal.

The big deal was the surprise file. Otto was not some famous agent's first name. He was not a Bureau legend. He wasn't even a he. He was a she. Kim Otto, younger than Gaspar, newer, less experienced. His leader.

No reflection on you.

Which, he supposed, way deep down, was true. Once or twice, back in the day, he had led older agents. He had no objection in principle. And even if he had, it would have been disqualified immediately, by the Bureau of course, and by himself. He had woken up in the ICU and his first thought had been: *what the hell do I do now?* He had a wife and four children and twenty years to go. Then his Special Agent in Charge had visited, and told him that he still had a job, and always would. Modified duty, of course, mostly behind a desk, not the same as before. But a job. Gaspar had been flooded with gratitude, simple as that, and he kept that gratitude in his mind the way people keep lucky charms in their pockets, and he touched it often, to console himself, to reassure himself. Number two? Hell, he would fetch the coffee.

He read all four files. There were photographs. Kim Otto was cute as anything. Asian and tiny. Reacher was a shadowy ex-military psychopath. A perfect prospect, all things considered. Trent née Roscoe and Finlay had been cops in a place in Georgia, probably where Reacher had first shown up again on the official radar after leaving the army. That place was a town south of Atlanta called Margrave, which was a place Gaspar had been before, which was maybe why he had gotten the assignment, not that the man who had mailed the phantom phone had a huge labor pool to pick from.

Gaspar tried to read more, but there was a headwind out of the north, and the engines were straining a little, and the vibration was making him sleepy. A precious gift, to which he yielded happily, his head on the window to his left, his right side for once mercifully uncompressed.

CHAPTER FIVE

CARLOS GASPAR WOKE up when the stewardess fussed at him about shutting his computer down before landing, but then she made up for it by hauling his bag down for him when they made the gate. He wheeled the bag for what seemed like a mile and then he stopped and telescoped the handle and picked the bag up like a regular guy when he saw the sidewalk ahead of him. He figured Otto would be waiting on the curb in a rental, and he didn't want to make a bad first impression. He found her pretty quickly, in a Chevy Traverse. Her head was down. She was reading. An A-student. Asian too. Maybe her first lead assignment. She wanted to be ready.

He tried the tailgate, but it was locked. He knocked on her window. She glanced up. She looked about eighteen. No more than five feet, no more than a hundred pounds, maybe less. She got out and he lifted his bag in and kept the pain out of his face. He offered to drive, which she seemed a little unsure about at first, but hey, she was number one and he was number two. Number two drove, simple as that. It was what it was. And they were already late. No time for a big discussion. He got in and she got in on his right and he took off.

Margrave was one hour and about a hundred years south of Atlanta. As always, traffic was bad at first and then it got easier. Strip malls changed to agriculture. Red earth, peanuts, the whole nine yards.

Georgia, for Christ's sake.

Gaspar asked, "You tired?"

Kim Otto said, "A little."

"Let me guess. He called you at four o'clock exactly."

"How do you know that?"

"Because he called me at three minutes past."

"Were you okay with that?"

"I was already awake."

Otto said, "I mean, are you okay with being number two?"

Gaspar said, "I'm okay with being number anything."

"Really?"

Gaspar smiled to himself. Asian, a woman, ambitious. She wanted to go all the way. She wanted to be the Director. He wondered how she would deal with being a cripple. A charity case. Her head would explode, probably.

He said, "You know his name?"

"Whose name?"

"You know whose name. The guy who called you at four o'clock and the guy who called me at three minutes past."

"Yes," she said. "I know his name. Do you?"

"Yes," he said. "You going to say it out loud?"

"No."

"Me neither."

She asked, "Did you read the files?"

"I looked at the pictures."

"Is that all?"

"No, of course I read them."

"And?"

Audition time. First duty of a number two was to make his number one feel confident in his competence. Second duty was to get a little competition going. He said, "I'm not sure why we got the call at four in the morning. Seven would have been okay. Flights into Atlanta from other major U.S. cities are not rare. So what's the rush? And the target file asks more questions than it answers. No IRS, nothing from the banks, no debts or loans or liens, no titles to houses or cars or boats or trailers, no arrest record, no convictions major or minor, no rent rolls, no landline or cell, ever, no ISP data, and he's not in prison. He's not in witness protection or undercover for any of the other three-letter agencies, or why would we be looking for him? We'd already know where he is. So either his file is mostly redacted, or he's the most under-the-radar guy who ever lived."

Otto was quiet for a moment. *Bull's-eye,* Gaspar thought. *Home run.* He'd seen everything she had. He'd missed nothing.

"I'm not sure I like him," she said.

"We don't have to like him."

They drove onward into the heartland. The Traverse was an underpowered piece of shit, and the tires were all wrong for concrete. Gaspar wished Otto had asked for a sedan. He would have.

She asked, "Can a person be so far under the radar?"

He said, "It's difficult. But if you put your mind to it, I imagine it's possible."

"You think he's a good candidate?"

"Ideal. Otherwise we wouldn't be here."

"I'm not sure I like that either."

"Above our pay grade," Gaspar said.

He came off the Interstate, down the ramp, around the cloverleaf. Fourteen miles to town. On the right, a burned-out warehouse. It had been that way for years, for as long as Gaspar could remember. Then on the left, much later, a diner. Then the police station, rebuilt quick and dirty after a fire. He pulled in and parked. They went inside. There was a sergeant behind a desk. Gaspar stepped up and said, "We need to speak with Chief Roscoe. Or Trent. I'm not sure what she goes by now."

Behind him, Otto tapped her foot. Quietly, but he heard it. She was annoyed. She had wanted to speak first. But tough shit. It was the number two's job to clear the way. Everyone knew that.

The guy behind the desk asked, "Who are you?"

Gaspar said, "FBI." He pulled his badge and held it out.

The guy behind the desk said, "Down the hall, second on the right."

CHAPTER SIX

KIM OTTO WATCHED Carlos Gaspar's retreating back as he hustled toward Chief Roscoe's office, widening the physical distance between them. The big clock on the wall above the sergeant's head showed ten past eleven. Their first objective had been precise: arrive in Roscoe's office before 11:30 a.m. Done. With twenty minutes to spare.

So now what? Build the Reacher file, obviously, but aside from the boss's order to start with Roscoe, they didn't know what they were looking for, or how they might find it, and it was always a mistake to get ahead of the intel. But given Reacher's talent for trouble, it was likely Chief Roscoe possessed not only relevant but potentially important knowledge about him, which she might reveal in a well conducted personal interview, but not otherwise. These things needed patience. And thought. But long before Kim even reached the office door, Gaspar rapped his knuckles on the wood and opened it without waiting for a reply.

"Chief Roscoe? Sorry to barge in," he said, as he barreled across the threshold sounding not the least bit sorry. "I'm Carlos Gaspar, FBI."

Kim got there just as Margrave Police Chief Beverly Roscoe was rising from the oversized brown leather chair behind her desk. She was taller than Kim, but then, who wasn't? And she was more attractive than the headshot in her file, but again, who wasn't? She was slim and not at all flat-chested. She had a caramel complexion. She had dark curly hair cut with a big-city style, falling all over her face. She had remarkable dark eyes. They were accented like a child's drawing of the sun by whiter skin dashing out toward her temples. Maybe some Native American or African-American heritage. Roscoe's family was said to have lived in north Georgia for more than a hundred years; either ethnicity was plausible.

Kim said, "I'm FBI Special Agent Otto." She handed over her ID. "We'd appreciate a few minutes of your time if you can spare them, Chief Roscoe."

"Okay," Roscoe said. She took Kim's wallet and waited while Gaspar dug his out. She examined both sets of credentials carefully and used her phone to summon the sergeant from the front desk. He came in and she said, "Brent, make copies of these and bring them back to me."

The sergeant said, "Yes, ma'am," and closed the door behind him. Roscoe waved Kim and Gaspar toward two green leather chairs across the desk. Roscoe pushed her chair back and crossed her legs. She rested both forearms on one knee, hands loosely clasped. She was wearing a platinum wedding ring. Fourteen years married, her file said. The ceremony had taken place the year after Reacher presumably passed through Margrave.

"How can I help you?" she asked.

The words were appropriate but the vibe was part annoyance, part worry. No small town police chief appreciated a surprise visit from the FBI, especially on a Monday morning. Agents in her office meant unexpected trouble on the way, or maybe right there in her jurisdiction already. Neither the FBI nor the trouble was welcome at any time, but especially not on Mondays.

"We won't take up too much of your day, Chief," Gaspar said, a long sentence, spoken slowly. He was stalling. He didn't know what they were looking for any more than Kim did.

Roscoe said, "I'm busy. This is a small shop and my day sergeant didn't show up this morning. Sergeant Brent is on overtime as it is."

"When Sergeant Brent gets back, we'll get started," Gaspar said. "We don't want to be interrupted."

Still stalling.

Roscoe looked at the round-faced silver watch on her left wrist. It had numbers big enough to read from Kim's position on the opposite side of the desk. It showed 11:15 a.m.

"How late is he?" Gaspar asked.

"Who?" Roscoe asked.

"Your sergeant who didn't come in today. What time did his shift start?"

"Seven thirty this morning. My budget being what it is, I don't have a backup. So I really don't have a lot of time to spare. Let's risk the interruption. What's up?"

Gaspar didn't reply to that. Neither did Kim. Something about the office was nagging at her. Something odd. What was it? She scanned the room, unobtrusively, observing each detail.

She noticed the scents first. A familiar but faded memory. *Ahhh.* Lingering traces of Old Spice and the faint wisp of Irish Spring bath soap. Both from the private bathroom in the corner behind the door. The office smelled like her father's den, a dark-paneled man-cave. In fact, everything about Roscoe's home away from home screamed Boston Brahmin instead of Margrave Top Cop.

Not just odd, Kim decided. *Downright weird.*

In the man's world of law enforcement's upper ranks, females in the top spot were as scarce as an innocent felon. Even in small towns like Margrave close to big cities like Atlanta. Roscoe had no doubt achieved her status through years of hard work and sheer grit. She'd never have made it otherwise. Roscoe had every right to be proud of herself.

Yet, she'd owned the office for *eight years* without making it hers? Under the same circumstances, Kim would have redecorated in eight minutes. Of course, Kim wouldn't have stayed in any job for eight years, either. Up or out was a better career strategy. Yet Roscoe was still here. Had she topped out?

Kim double-checked. Scanned the entire room again. Confirmed she'd been right the first time. The room contained nothing personal except one photograph of a younger Roscoe with a Navy man in uniform. The husband, probably. No pictures of her kids. The file said she had a girl of fourteen and a boy of eleven.

The rest of the photo wall was all grip-and-grins: Roscoe with the Governor; Roscoe with the current Mayor of Atlanta and the prior one as well; Roscoe with Jimmy Carter. But the last one was the money shot: Roscoe with a large, attractive black guy dressed in a tweed sport-coat and sweater vest.

Bingo.

Kim recognized him immediately, from his file photo: Lamont Finlay, Ph.D. Interview subject number two. A Harvard man. The guy who had decorated this office, clearly. Roscoe's predecessor as chief. Maybe her mentor too. Were they still connected? Such that she couldn't bear to erase his presence?

Weird, but good to know. A possible angle. Kim hadn't pegged Roscoe as the sentimental type. A clearer picture of the woman was emerging.

She said, "Nice office, Chief Roscoe."

"Thank you," Roscoe said. She didn't invite Kim to dispense with the formal title.

Sergeant Brent came back with the ID wallets. He was lanky, with red hair and a freckled face. He seemed young for his job. He put the photocopies on Roscoe's desk and handed the originals back to their owners. His forearms below his uniform shirt's short sleeves were covered by a wild tangle of red hair. Even his fingers were freckled.

"Any chance we could get a cup of coffee?" Gaspar asked him.

Brent looked to his boss. Roscoe nodded.

"How do you like it?" Brent asked.

"Four sugars," Gaspar said.

Brent looked horrified, as if no real man, let alone an FBI Special Agent, would so pollute a cup of joe.

"What?" Gaspar said. "I have a sweet tooth. Something wrong with that?"

Brent seemed to realize Gaspar was baiting him. He grinned, and Gaspar added, "And maybe a couple of jelly donuts?"

Brent laughed out loud. Roscoe sat quiet. Brent turned to Kim for her order. She said, "You wouldn't have chicory coffee, would you?"

His freckled face reflected genuine sorrow. "I wish we did, ma'am," he said. "I haven't had chicory since my Louisiana grandma died."

"Don't worry. Regular black will be fine for me."

As if to compensate for his chicory failure, Brent asked, "Want a jelly donut too?"

"You're a bad influence, I can tell," she said. He bowed his head shyly. He was just a kid. Early twenties, max. She said, "But if only all men were so thoughtful," and shot a mock glare at Gaspar.

"You're killing me, boss," Gaspar said.

Brent left, and Roscoe said, "Okay, you made a friend there. Mission accomplished. Nicely done. But I'm older and wiser. How can I help you?"

No one spoke, and Brent brought the coffee and donuts and left again, closing the door quietly behind him. Kim lifted her mug and took a deep, appreciative whiff before she sipped and held on for a second sip.

"How can I help you?" Roscoe asked again.

"This is great coffee," Kim said, still stalling. She flashed through what she knew about Roscoe, searching for a non-threatening opening.

Gaspar picked the wrong one.

He asked, "You got kids?"

The question pushed Roscoe's hot button. Kim saw it happen. Roscoe's carotid pulse thumped hard on the side of her neck. Kim counted twenty-five beats in ten seconds, 150 beats a minute. Fast, like she was sprinting toward a fire.

Professional tone steady, Roscoe said, "Look, if you're going to be in town a while, you can take me out for a drink after work one day and try your very best bonding techniques. But until then, I'm busy, as I believe I mentioned. So don't try to butter me up. If you've got some bad news, just hop right to it, okay?"

Kim responded before Gaspar could jump the rails again. She said, "This is not a law enforcement visit, Chief. We're hoping you can give us some direction, that's all. Because we don't know where to start, actually. We're looking for information."

As bland as possible, just a favor, one officer to another.

Roscoe asked, "What kind of information do you need?"

Kim saw wariness in those big, dark eyes. Pulse still pounding. But tone not so hostile. Maybe a little progress.

"Agent Gaspar and I are assigned to the FBI Specialized Personnel Task Force."

"Which is what?"

Roscoe's pulse slowed a few beats. Kim counted twenty in ten seconds. Still rapid, but better. Like calming any wild thing, Kim sought to lull through non-threatening routine. Since 9/11, law enforcement personnel never resisted any halfway plausible FBI request, whether they understood its basis or not. Few outside the agency knew its inner workings or expected transparency in the relentless war on terror.

"We conduct candidate background investigations. It's our job to build the file. Supplement sketchy records. Get a clear picture. So the folks upstairs can make informed decisions."

"I was asking what kind of specialized personnel you're dealing with."

Still wary. Had this woman been burned before? Kim counted fifteen pulse beats in ten seconds. Better.

"Potential candidates to serve in situations where no current FBI expertise exists."

"Such as?"

Roscoe was pressing harder than cops usually did. Kim might have done the same, but only if she had something to hide. She said, "I can't speak for the entire SPTF, but I've worked up files for interpreters of uncommon languages, for example. Or forensic accountants in niche businesses. Or scientists who can identify obscure chemicals. Things that don't require permanent expertise inside the bureau."

"Routine, then."

"Mostly."

Roscoe nodded. She didn't ask why the FBI had failed to make an appointment to see her. There should have been an appointment, if the meeting were routine. Instead she said, "I gather these candidates don't have security clearances already?"

Which was an astute question. Reacher had a security clearance once, according to his file. Beverly Roscoe and Lamont Finlay had one too. As did Daniel Trent, Roscoe's husband, for that matter.

"Usually not," Kim replied. She watched the pulse in Roscoe's neck now at a steady five to six beats in ten seconds. Resting pulse rate lower than fifty-five under normal conditions. Good for a woman of Roscoe's age.

As a test, Kim added, "When an existing security clearance is available, it makes our job easier, of course. Then all we need to do is update."

The pulse jumped to one-twenty again. Whatever Roscoe concealed burrowed deep into its hiding place, but it didn't feel safe there.

"As I said, I'm happy to help if I can," Roscoe said. Then she hesitated, just slightly, but Kim noticed the held breath before the question. "Who is it you're interested in?"

Kim glanced at Gaspar. He signaled agreement with a slight nod. They'd get nowhere with Chief Roscoe today unless they could shake her loose a little. If they had to come back another time, she'd have her answers sanded to smooth uselessness.

Now or never.

"We've been asked to conduct a background check on an army veteran," Kim said, slowly, watching Roscoe's demeanor closely. Almost like the children's game of hot, hot, cold, but the method depended less on what Roscoe said and more on how she reacted. Standard interview techniques Kim had applied a thousand times. If

Roscoe was worried about anyone not an army veteran, she should relax a bit.

But she didn't relax.

Gaspar bluffed. "We know he came to Margrave about fifteen years ago. Maybe he lives here now. Law enforcement might have had some contact with him."

Pulse elevated and steady at one-twenty. Something Gaspar had said had alarmed Chief Roscoe further. Good.

Roscoe said, "Our population has grown quite a bit because of sprawl out of Atlanta. But I'd know anyone who's lived here more than a few months. What's his name?"

The way she inquired, the tension she carried in her eyes and shoulders, the timing, her failure to breathe. Pulse at one-twenty-five. Very concerned. But the greater Atlanta area boasted a significant veteran population. She could be worried about someone else entirely.

But Kim had noted that fifteen men were referenced in the materials received from the boss. And only two women: Reacher's mother, now dead two decades.

And the first source: Beverly Roscoe.

Not identified by her married name, either. Roscoe, not Trent. The name she had when Reacher swept through Margrave. The name she still used on every official record. In an old-fashioned small town where everybody knew she was Mrs. Trent.

Kim set her coffee mug on the table between her chair and Gaspar's. She wiped her hands. She reached into her pocket for the photograph.

"Here, let me show you," Kim said, as she lifted her gaze directly to Roscoe's face, watching for nuanced micro movements, lowering her voice to focus Roscoe's full attention while she revealed the photo, and she said, "The man's name is Jack Reacher."

Roscoe's face aged instantly. The formal smile she'd worn a moment before vanished along with all vitality from those enormous eyes. Her expression became both vacant and horrified.

A full second passed. Maybe two. Roscoe continued to stare at the altered photo of Jack Reacher. Her pulse was erratic, racing.

And then she started to cry.

CHAPTER SEVEN

TEARS FLOODED ROSCOE'S eyes. One rolled down her cheek before she grabbed a tissue. The tears kept on coming. Her chin quivered. She took a deep ragged breath, and another. Still the tears fell. She swiveled her chair around, turning her back on Kim and Gaspar, hiding her face. They could hear her rhythmic breathing, struggling to regain control.

She was like the hundreds of crime victims Kim had interviewed after unimaginable, tragic, deeply personal disasters. What the hell had Reacher done to her? Nothing in Reacher's file reflected violence against women, although he was certainly capable of it. *The bastard.* Why hadn't she considered that Reacher might have hurt this woman?

Kim glanced toward Gaspar. Blatant emotion had not been on his list of expected reactions, either. What should they do now? Gaspar didn't seem to have a clue.

Roscoe's deep breaths continued a minute or two until she finally composed herself and turned around to face them once again. Her eyes were clear and her chin was strong. She smiled weakly and took a sip of coffee, stalling, maybe steadying her voice.

"I'm sorry," Roscoe said, a little catch in her tone. She sipped and swallowed again, and regained her self-control.

"No, Chief Roscoe, I'm the one who's sorry," Kim said. "I didn't know. Truly. I had no idea Reacher's photograph would upset you so much. I sincerely apologize."

Roscoe's brows arched and she tilted her head and jutted her chin, like a dog identifying the source of a distant sound. Her lips lifted slightly at one corner, amused.

She's laughing at me now? Kim felt played. But she didn't understand the game. Heat rose in her chest.

Roscoe said, "Reacher's not here. You've wasted your time, I'm afraid."

Gaspar said, "It's been a long time since I've seen a cop cry when shown a missing persons photo, Chief Roscoe. In fact, I think this is a first for me. How about you, Agent Otto?"

"A first for me too," Kim snapped.

Roscoe replied with a little sarcasm of her own. "Sorry. Really shocking, my behavior. Seeing as how you've been so upfront with me. So I should definitely have been more helpful."

Gaspar didn't let up. "So you're refusing to cooperate with an FBI investigation?"

Roscoe's back was up now too. "Look, you barge into my town, into my office. Unannounced. Unexpected. Lie to me. You knew Reacher wasn't here when you asked me, didn't you? I don't owe you anything."

Quietly, Kim asked, "What caused you to cry? What did Reacher do to you?"

Roscoe took a breath, and another, and said, "Not that it's any of your business, but I got emotional because, well, I was ... relieved."

"I'm lost," Gaspar said. "Some guy assaults you, or worse, and you're *relieved* that we think he might be back in your jurisdiction?"

Roscoe said, "He didn't assault me. And I'm relieved because the FBI thinks he's still alive. I haven't heard from him since he left Margrave."

"You expected to hear from him?" Kim asked.

Gaspar seemed to get it too. "You knew him well, then?"

Roscoe hesitated too long.

Kim could almost see her rejecting one reply after another. Why so much concern over what to say about a drifter who passed through her jurisdiction briefly more than a decade ago?

Finally, Roscoe offered a weak, "I knew him well enough."

Which made perfect sense and no sense at all. *So that's the way it was.* Followed swiftly by, *But how could that be true?*

"Where did you meet him?" Gaspar asked.

Roscoe's pleasant expression returned. She'd collected her poise once again. Kim felt the momentum shift to Roscoe. She would cooperate, but only on her terms. Whatever those terms might be.

"In the interview room across the hall in the old station." Roscoe tilted her head in that direction. She grinned. "I took his fingerprints and his mug shot after he was arrested."

Gaspar looked surprised. "Our files don't contain any arrest records."

"No arrest records?" Roscoe's desk phone rang. "Hard to believe the FBI missed something like that." She glanced down to see where the call came from and then ignored it.

"We'll need copies," Gaspar said. "Can we get them now, while we're here?"

Roscoe feigned chagrin. "Afraid not. We had a fire. The station and everything in it was destroyed, unfortunately."

Gaspar ran his hand through his hair. He looked as peeved as Kim had felt a few moments before. "What was he arrested for?"

"Something he didn't do."

Not likely, Kim thought. If Reacher was arrested for anything, he'd done ten times worse and not been caught. Reacher was the kind of guy who solved all problems as permanently as possible.

Roscoe's phone kept on ringing. A low, insistent buzz. Two, three, four, five times.

Gaspar pressed on. "What didn't he do?"

The phone kept buzzing. Someone really wanted Chief Roscoe to pick up that receiver.

"Murder," Roscoe said.

Kim wasn't surprised. An army-trained expert killer prowling under all available radar for fifteen solid years, invisible even to the mighty FBI. What else had Reacher been doing besides murder? That was the relevant question. Gaspar looked equally skeptical. He'd read the same file Kim had. No way would he believe Reacher innocent of murder, either.

Maybe disappointed in their reaction, Roscoe offered something that did astonish. "And then he saved my life too."

Roscoe smiled at their surprise. Finally, she picked up her phone. She said, "Yes, Brent?" And then her smile died. She said, "What?" All business now. Short concise questions, longer periods of listening. Controlled. No tears. "He's sure? When?" Concentration, closed eyes, deep furrows in her brow. "Okay, call crime scene, paramedics and medical examiner too. Phones only. Keep listeners out as long as we can."

Roscoe stood up, rested the receiver against her shoulder with her chin to free her hands, patted her waist in two places, one where her gun would be holstered and the other where her badge would likely rest. She said, "Good plan. Both in the air?" She looked around for a cell phone, found it, picked it up, and dropped it into her jacket pocket. She put the phone down and picked up her car keys. She glanced across the desk and said, "My sergeant, the one who didn't come in today? He's been killed." Her voice was soft, but the rest of her behavior was purely professional. "So can we pick this up later?" she asked, on her way to the door.

Gaspar moved fast. "We could ride along, like a couple of extra hands. If you like. Purely informal."

Roscoe hesitated, pinched the bridge of her nose between her eyes again, breathed deep. Then she said, "Yes, that would be great."

Before Kim had a chance to say anything at all, Gaspar headed out, Traverse keys in hand. "I'll drive. You can brief us as we go. Have Brent bring your car out."

Roscoe followed close behind, issuing instructions to Brent along the way.

Kim remained seated in the abandoned man-cave. She checked her watch again to confirm the timing. She collected Reacher's photo from Roscoe's desk and looked around to be sure she hadn't forgotten anything.

No reason to rush. Plenty of reasons not to. For the first time in eight hours she felt she finally understood where this assignment was going.

CHAPTER EIGHT

ROSCOE AND GASPAR were already belted into the front seats of the Traverse. The engine was running, the air conditioning was blasting, and the left rear door was open. Kim stepped up into the backseat half a second before Gaspar took off. She didn't fall out, so maybe she was getting used to his style. He drove as fast as he could without a bubble light to clear traffic, straight back the way they had come less than an hour ago. They'd reach the interstate in about fourteen minutes.

"The deceased is Sergeant Harry Black," Gaspar said, glancing into the rearview mirror to meet her eyes, catching her up on what he'd heard while waiting. "Shot and killed at home. With his own gun. By his wife, Sylvia."

"Did you know him well?" Kim asked Roscoe.

"Since we were kids," Roscoe said. "Harry Black grew up here. He's worked in our department about five years, I guess. Second marriage. Sylvia worked as a secretary in our shop a while. That's how they met. Married three years or so."

"So what happened today?" Gaspar asked.

"You were there when I took the call. I have limited data. Sylvia called nine-one-one at eleven twenty-eight a.m. I haven't heard the tape yet. At some point, we'll get a copy and a transcript. I'm told she said, quote, 'I shot him. He's dead. I just couldn't take him anymore.' The operator asked her all the appropriate questions, and Sylvia just repeated those three sentences over and over again. She hasn't uttered another word."

"Anybody at the scene?" Gaspar asked.

"At the time of the shooting? I don't know. But now, yes. The nine-one-one service here is routed through Atlanta. The operator called Georgia Highway Patrol first. Maybe not sure who had jurisdiction out at Harry's. Could have been the County Sheriff. Both of us are at least twenty miles away. GHP had a car fairly close. They called us."

Roscoe's voice had a slight edge to it, Kim thought.

Gaspar asked, "Something wrong with calling the GHP?"

"Not by itself, no."

"What, then?" Kim asked.

Roscoe turned around in her seat. She met Kim's gaze with a steady stare. She said, "GHP is a professional organization. They've got good officers and good training. Just like the FBI, I'm sure."

"But?"

"But their jurisdiction is mostly crime on the highway system. You should know that's different from murder of a small-town cop. And they ride one man per car, so they have to call in for backup. And they use radio to communicate. And people listen in and show up. Which causes problems. Things can get out of hand in terms of crowd control."

Kim nodded. She'd handled more than her share of homicides, gang violence, domestic assaults. Law enforcement was a dangerous job everywhere, especially for women. The last thing Roscoe needed was chaos at the crime scene.

Gaspar asked, "How soon would you have heard if the nine-one-one dispatcher had called you first?"

"Within a couple of minutes, probably."

"Literally?"

"More or less," Roscoe said. "Two minutes would have done it."

"Eleven twenty-eight plus two is eleven thirty exactly," Gaspar said, and he met his partner's reflected gaze again. Kim nodded back. Gaspar saw it too.

The Black Road intersection was about two miles shy of the interstate. Roscoe told Gaspar to turn left, southwest, onto the dirt road. About fifty feet in the road became a mess of washboard grading, dust, and previous washouts. Gaspar slowed the Traverse to forty, which still bounced them around more than Kim found comfortable. She asked, "What did the GHP officer find when he arrived at the crime scene?"

Roscoe said, "Sylvia came out onto the porch with her hands on her head before the GHP guy got out of his car. She didn't say anything to him."

"Textbook," Gaspar said. "For a perp, I mean."

"She worked with us a while and her husband was a cop. She knew what to do." Roscoe peered ahead down the narrow alley between the Georgia pines. Kim could see nothing worth the stare.

Gaspar asked, "And then?"

"The GHP guy put her in handcuffs, confirmed Harry was dead, called for backup, medical examiner, crime scene, and paramedics."

"And then he called Officer Brent," Gaspar said.

"All using the radio," Kim said.

"Right."

"Anybody question Mrs. Black since GHP arrived?" Kim asked.

"She's not talking. We'll arrest her, take her back to our station. And go from there. Once we see what's going on."

Gaspar concentrated on navigating the deserted country road around its multiple hazards. All three of them were bounced around in their seats. Gaspar said, "I remember Margrave as a pretty well maintained place for a rural community. Lots of newer buildings and fresh paint when I was here last."

"Things change," Roscoe said, a little coldly.

"Just asking. Nothing personal."

Roscoe didn't smile. She just stared on down the dusty road. Looking for what, Kim didn't know. There was nothing to see. Piney woods either side of the road hid everything beyond its ditches.

Kim asked, "What did Sylvia mean by not being able to take him anymore? Is she claiming abuse and self-defense?"

Roscoe said, "Hard to say before I talk to her. Crazy talk, possibly."

Gaspar glanced back again and met Kim's gaze with a look that confirmed Kim's impression. Harry was abusive. Kim had no use for a wife-beater. None. Even less use for friends and co-workers who covered up. She wondered whether Harry was a drunken abuser or just a power tripper control freak. And whether battered spouse defense was a legal excuse for murder in Georgia.

Roscoe said, "About five more miles, I think. Harry's family owned this land for generations. He built the house himself about twenty-five years ago. He liked being away from people. He said the quiet was restful."

Gaspar looked back at Kim again. She wondered if he was thinking the same thing: *Rest in Hell, Harry. You sick bastard.*

CHAPTER NINE

THEY DROVE ON. The car bounced and lurched, hitting potholes with regularity. Kim said, "Chief, we need to know about Reacher. Whatever you can tell us. Whatever you know. We need to find him. It's important."

It seemed to take Roscoe a couple of seconds to switch her mind back to Reacher. She asked, "What do you want him for?"

"He's a potentially valuable asset. The FBI is telling you it needs him. Whose side are you on?"

Roscoe turned and stared a long time directly into Kim's face. Still wary. Maybe searching for some hint that Kim could be trusted. The Traverse hit a big pothole. Roscoe smacked her head on the roof. She raised her hand to rub the sore spot, and glanced out the back window and realized where they were.

"Back up," she said to Gaspar, and she pointed to a mailbox so obscured by weeds and kudzu only a previous visitor could find it. "The house is about a mile down that driveway you just passed."

Deep dents marred every surface of the mailbox. Once painted white, now veined with rusty cracks, it dangled from its thick re-rod pole, held by a single remaining U-bolt and the grasping kudzu. The door to the mailbox was missing completely. "It wasn't like that the last time I was here," Roscoe said.

"When was that?" Kim asked.

"Couple of years ago, I guess. Maybe longer. Before they were married, I think."

"Looks like extreme mailbox baseball," Gaspar said. "Kids in a car with a bat. Vandalism, in other words. A federal crime, actually. If memory serves, two-hundred-fifty-thousand dollar fine and three years in prison for each offense. And each blow counts as a separate offense."

Kim asked Roscoe, "Was Black targeted in some way? Kids would have to be pretty determined to come all the way out here just to beat the snot out of a mailbox for the fun of it."

"I didn't hear anything about it," Roscoe said. "I don't know."

The Traverse's tires bounced from one hole to the next. Dead skunk perfume came in through the air vents. Kim held her breath. Then she saw a good-sized dirt lot and a pea-gravel driveway full of two GHP cruisers, two marked Margrave squad cars, an unmarked sedan with a portable bubble light on the dash, and a county ambulance. A coat of red dust already covered them all.

Kim asked, "Anything special you want us to do?"

Roscoe paused a moment and said, "Do whatever you think you should, I guess. I'll catch up with you inside. Check in before you leave and we'll see where we are."

Then she said, "We'll talk more about Reacher later. After I get this situation sorted out. Okay?"

Kim watched as Roscoe followed a line of cracked sandstone slate pavers by taking a little hop from one to the next and over the dirt between them, like she was crossing stones in a running stream. Withered plants filled cracked red-dirt beds along each side of the pavers. Uncut yard weeds thrived, impersonating a lawn. Thirty feet ahead a frame shotgun style house rested on a cement block foundation. Its metal roof reflected the glare of the sun. Between the roof and the foundation were four windows cut into the walls, all grimy. A porch ran the twenty-foot width of the house. On one end, a gray weathered bench swing hung crooked on a rusty chain, and on the other end sat two white plastic dollar-store rockers with an overflowing ashtray between them.

Roscoe stepped over the last weed gap, up the single plank step to the porch, and entered the house through the open front door.

Kim stayed where she was.

Gaspar, too, seemed momentarily transfixed.

"What a hole," he said. "My wife would never have moved out here in a million years. What kind of woman lives like this?"

"The killing kind, apparently," Kim said. She reached into her bag and found her camera. Then she opened her door and stepped onto the hard, red ground.

The first thing she noticed was the quiet noonday, bizarrely still. She was a city girl. Noise was normal; quiet was not.

Out in the woods, no one can hear you scream.

"Did you know?" she asked.

"Know what?" Gaspar said.

"Why he gave us the eleven thirty deadline. Why he put us in that room at that time."

"You don't trust me, do you?"

"He wanted us to be there when the call came in. He wanted us out here at the crime scene. That how you read it?"

"Yes," Gaspar said.

"What about Reacher?"

"Reacher's irrelevant."

"To what? This homicide? Or is the whole assignment bogus?"

He shrugged. "You're number one. You figure it out."

She could feel sweat above her lip. She couldn't figure it out. She hated that. She said, "Take pictures, okay? And don't be obvious about it."

If Gaspar resented her orders, he didn't show it. He just turned back to the Traverse and got his own camera. She watched him from behind her sunglasses.

Was he limping? FBI field agents didn't limp. Physical fitness was one of the basic requirements of the job. Definitely no limping allowed. She reached up and dabbed the sweat from her lip, and then she headed for the house, matching Gaspar's longer stride step for step. As they walked his limp became less pronounced. Maybe it was just a cramp.

Maybe she could rely on him.

Only one choice.

CHAPTER TEN

INSIDE THE HOUSE the tiny hallway was full of people and full of familiar muted crime scene sounds. Then one guy moved right and another moved left and Kim got a clear line of sight into a messy bedroom. Time stood still, like a single freeze frame in a video.

Harry Black's body was face down on bloody sheets, right where his faithful bride had shot him seven times less than two hours ago.

Not a chance.

Complete bullshit.

Kim smelled him even over the skunk perfume. She saw the rigor and the lividity from all the way across the room. Every professional in the house had to know Harry Black had been dead a lot longer than two hours. The GHP trooper must have known when he called in the homicide.

People shifted again, blocking her view. The freeze frame ended. The video moved on. Gaspar looked at her and nodded. He had seen it too. The interior of the building matched its exterior for bleakness. There were four rooms. A total of maybe 800 square feet. Lots of pine, lots of gaps and warps. The living room had two worn recliners and a 60-inch flat screen TV. There were fashion magazines on a folding table. The windows were opaque with dirt.

Gaspar had moved farther into the house, observing everything, just as she was. He was taking pictures from time to time.

Of what?

Am I missing something?

Kim recalled Gaspar's question. What kind of woman had chosen to live in this place? She glanced toward the kitchen and saw the answer right there.

Mrs. Sylvia Black sat on one of the two kitchen chairs, head down. Cuffed hands hung between her knees. She held her palms together, rhythmically opening and closing each set of matched fingers, one set at a time, like a metronome, counting.

Counting what?

She had a recent manicure. She had perfectly shaped nails, quite short, painted pastel pink. She had a large, square onyx ring with a silver cable around it on her right index finger, and a smaller turquoise ring by the same designer on her right pinky. She was wearing the kind of black patent sandals that fashionable women covet, and she had a fresh pedicure. Her toenails were polished deep purple. Her yellow silk blouse had a pink and green designer's monogram. Dark silk slacks tapered smartly down her calf, where an ankle bracelet sat near a yellow rose tattoo.

Then someone made a noise and Sylvia's head snapped up, eyes darted wildly. Kim saw dark beauty, enhanced by skillful makeup. Sylvia's eyes met Kim's, and then she lowered her gaze to the floor and began her finger tapping again.

Kim reached into her pocket and pulled out her camera. She framed the shot and said, "Sylvia?"

The woman looked up and saw the camera. She squared her shoulders, raised her chin, and smiled, revealing bright white teeth offset by shimmering pink lip gloss.

She was posing.

Kim switched the camera to video mode and followed her gut.

"I love your shoes," she said. "Jimmy Choos, right? They look great on you."

Girlfriends.

"Thank you," Sylvia replied, holding her leg out in front, the better to display her stylish footwear. "These are my favorites." She looked up into Kim's face again. "Want to try them? Your foot's really tiny, though."

"I'd better not," Kim said, as if the refusal cost her a lot. "They wouldn't like it."

They.

Us and them.

Girlfriends.

Sylvia pressed her lips into a firm line, nodded as if to say she understood, and lowered her head again.

Kim asked, "So what happened here?"

Sylvia looked up again. Unsmiling this time, but not distraught. Not like she'd just killed a man whose body still lay in her marriage bed. "I'm not supposed to talk about it. I shot him. I couldn't take him anymore. That's all I'm allowed to say."

"Who told you that?"

"I'm not allowed to say."

"Well, aside from his horrible taste in interior design, what was wrong with him?"

Sylvia smiled. She didn't seem to grasp her situation. Maybe there was something wrong with her. Mentally. "I'm not allowed to say," she repeated, smiling sadly now, as if she had much more she wanted to say, if only she was allowed to, which she wasn't.

"Did he hurt you? Do something to you?" Kim continued to record. Sylvia knew she was being filmed, but didn't seem to mind. She didn't ask for a lawyer or object to the questions. But she didn't offer any information, either.

"I'm sorry," she said.

Was that a confession? Remorse generally followed when wives killed their husbands, in Kim's experience.

"About what?" Kim asked.

"That I'm not allowed to say anything."

Kim heard another car outside. "When do you think you'll be able to tell us what happened?"

Sylvia asked a question of her own. "What time is it?"

Kim looked at her watch. "It's one o'clock, give or take."

"Maybe later this afternoon," Sylvia said.

"Why then?" Kim saw Sergeant Brent and another Margrave cop come in.

"I'm just not allowed to say." Sylvia returned her gaze to the floor, and began her finger tapping again. Kim filmed the ritual for a full minute, but Sylvia didn't look up again.

"I'll catch up with you later," Kim said.

No response.

Kim slipped into the bedroom for a closer look. The master suite contained two rooms. She checked them quickly before focusing on the body. Both were lined in rough pine planks like the rest of the house. There was a small bathroom on one side, and a small closet on the other. The closet was open. It held three empty wire hangers on the rod, and two men's sneaker boxes on the shelf above, and dry cleaning bags and paper shoulder covers on the floor.

The bathroom was barely large enough for a shower stall, a sink, and a toilet. The shower curtain was moldy and stained by iron-rich water. The toilet was running, porcelain cracked. The bedroom itself had a fourteen-inch oval mirror hung too high for Sylvia Black. A ceiling fan hung in the middle of the room, not turning. One jalousie window with frosted panes provided weak natural light.

But the bed itself was the main attraction. It filled most of the room. It was just a queen mattress on a box spring. No headboard or footboard. There was about two feet of space all the way around the bed. There was a beige cotton blanket tangled up in sheets that might have been white once. There were three pillows with cases in the same yellowed percale as the sheets. There was not as much blood as there might have been.

Kim noticed everything: the blood, the smell, Black's pallor, and the blue bruises unmistakably creeping up his sides from where he lay on his stomach, rigid with full rigor. She was certain he'd been dead more than ten hours. Probably closer to fifteen. But absolutely, positively, most definitely more than two.

She memorized his position. She'd need a recent photograph to know anything about his face. The bullets had gone right through. They were buried in the wall planks. Kim thought about the difficulty of removing them for evidence.

Black's left arm was bent at the elbow, his hand resting near his face. A thin gold band encircled his ring finger. Not a symbol of love and fidelity in his case, clearly. His right arm was bent palm up. His legs were splayed.

Kim counted the entry wounds: seven visible. Two in his head. One in each of his four limbs at the elbow and knee joints, and the seventh at the base of his spine.

Out in the woods, no one can hear you scream.

Next Kim checked the kitchen and noted the camper stove, the small refrigerator, and the dirty sink. She opened the cabinets and saw plastic dishes and plastic glasses that might have been yard sale bargains ten years ago. One cabinet held canned food, mostly soup and beans, with a few cans of sausage. Stuff that would last a good long while, she guessed.

The refrigerator was just as sparsely stocked. Three bottles of beer, some orange cheese, some yellow mustard. Some catsup, half a jar of sweet pickles. Nothing that would sustain a human soul.

Kim found Gaspar waiting on the porch.

"Now what, number one?" he asked.

She said, "Did you know that a hummingbird consumes more than four times its weight in food every day?"

"What?"

"Try and keep up, okay? We tiny Asian women eat like birds."

One beat. Two. Then he got it. He grinned.

"You see all that and still want to eat?" he said. "You're cool."

Home run.

She said, "I saw a diner on the county road. Maybe they'll have something that won't give us a disease. But let's walk around the house, first. Outside. I don't want to miss anything. I'm hoping I never have to come back here again."

"I hear ya, sister."

They stepped down off the porch together and walked the outside perimeter. The side and back lawns were in the same condition as the front. Cracked, dried, mostly bare red dirt, a few dead weeds for color. There was one outbuilding in the rear yard, clearly constructed by the same inept craftsman as the house. The outbuilding had never been painted and weather had grayed the pine boards. It was nothing but a three-sided box with a wall from back to front that divided port from starboard. On the left side was a clothes washer and a dryer probably purchased when Reagan was president. On the right side was a ten-year-old Ford Taurus, sun-faded, beat-up, run-down. The driver's door was slightly ajar.

Kim used her jacket sleeve and pushed the door fully open. The dome light came on inside. A bell warned that a key was in the ignition. The odometer showed 156,324 miles. On the passenger seat was an expensive designer handbag. Gaspar whistled, low and appreciative.

"Look at that, would you?" he said. "That thing's worth way more than the car. More than the house. Hell, more than the land, too, I'll bet."

"How do you know so much about handbags, Agent Gaspar?"

"I've got a wife and four daughters. I mentioned that, right?" He grinned at her. "Did I also mention we're all big soccer fans? You know who David Beckham is?"

Beckham wasn't one of the top ten most wanted terrorists this week, so no, she didn't recognize the name. But she didn't say that.

"The soccer genius with the gorgeous wife, Victoria?"

Kim shook her head.

"Victoria Beckham is a very beautiful and fashionable woman and a huge fan of all things Hermès. She has quite a collection. To the tune of about $2 million worth, according to my oldest daughter. Including a birthday present in the same style as this one here, that her husband reportedly purchased for north of $150,000."

"Assuming it's not fake," Kim said.

"Even a fake would cost more than I'll bring home this week after Uncle Sam takes his cut." He opened the glove box and pushed a yellow button. The trunk lid released.

Kim walked around to the back of the car and used her jacket sleeve to push the trunk lid up. "So, if the handbag is worth so much, how much do you suppose these four pieces of matching luggage would set you back?"

Gaspar said nothing. Just took pictures of the luggage. Maybe to show his daughter, Kim thought. Then from behind them Chief Roscoe said, "I'd appreciate copies of those pictures. Unless you'd prefer to hand over the camera."

Gaspar slipped the camera into his pocket. Kim didn't look up. She said, "Sure. No problem. We may want to look at your evidence too. We can exchange when it's convenient for you."

Roscoe didn't back down. "I assume this trunk lid was already open when you got here and you haven't violated anybody's rights by opening it without a warrant."

"I love a cat fight," Gaspar said, loud enough only for Kim to hear.

Kim looked at Roscoe, square in the eye, and said, "I'm guessing this luggage and the other contents of this vehicle belong to your suspect. I didn't know Harry Black, but he doesn't seem like the luxury leather goods type to me."

"No," Roscoe said. "He wasn't. You're right."

"Or rich."

"He wasn't that either."

"And the way it looks is that Mrs. Black was packed, dressed, and ready to go. She waited until her husband was asleep. And then she shot and killed him. The question is why she didn't go ahead and leave at that point. Why did she call 911 and turn herself in? That doesn't make any sense. She's maybe a little crazy, maybe out of touch with reality somewhat, but she's well oriented to time and place, as the psychiatrists say."

"How do you know?" Roscoe said.

"I talked to her."

Gaspar said, "And she didn't kill him a couple of hours before we got here, either. Based on the lividity and rigor and the smell of decomp, I'm guessing he'd been dead eight hours or more when we arrived. There could be a federal crime here. We could call Atlanta, if you want. We could get some agents out here to take over."

"Or not," Kim said. "It's up to you. You can take Sylvia Black as a murdering wife and process her for homicide and use this evidence of flight to support premeditation and we can get back to our assignment."

Roscoe was considering her options. Kim recognized the signs. Eventually Roscoe said, "We'll take it from here. We need to finish up with the scene and then I'd like to talk to you. Tonight. Or tomorrow. How can I reach you?"

"We're going to eat," Kim said. "Our cell numbers are on the business cards we gave you earlier. Call us when you're finished here and we'll meet you at your office or somewhere else in town. How's that?"

"Sounds good," Roscoe said, offering the firm, cool handshake she'd extended previously, but this time she offered it with more sincerity. "I appreciate the help. We're a small department. We don't get a lot of trouble. Some drugs. Meth mostly. A few robberies to finance the drugs. Some domestic battery on Saturday nights. And that's about it. We're a little out of our depth today."

Kim appreciated the effort to make nice, even though Roscoe was more than just a little out of her depth and she knew it. That fact was obvious to the least sophisticated observer. But Kim would never have made such an admission in Roscoe's shoes. Or any other shoes.

"It's going to rain," Roscoe said, and walked away.

"She'll call us," Gaspar said. "Right after she checks us out with Atlanta."

"That's what I would do," Kim said. "Wouldn't you?"

Gaspar grinned. "Of course I would."

Kim's stomach growled. "Good thing Asian women don't weigh much. If I don't get real food pretty soon, you may have to carry me when I faint."

"Then we'd better hurry. We Cubans are not that chivalrous," he said, as fat raindrops started to fall.

CHAPTER ELEVEN

A SOLID WALL of rain overwhelmed the Traverse all the way down the country road. Gaspar turned the wipers to their fastest speed, but they didn't do much. Headlights on bright showed nothing but a curtain of water dead ahead.

"There," Kim said, pointing at a dull gleam of aluminum. A sun-faded sign out front of the place said *Eno's Diner* in letters the size of garbage cans.

"Got it, boss." She saw exhaustion around his eyes and pain in the lines that etched his face. He pulled the Traverse into the lot. The only other vehicle was a green Saturn. He drove as close to the door as he could get and turned off the engine. They sat for a moment listening to the rain hammering on the roof.

Then they ran. She got there first. *Was he still limping?* She wrenched the door open, and they fell inside and back in time about sixty years.

Eno's Diner resembled a converted railroad car. Retro. Like *American Graffiti*. There should have been tableside jukeboxes in the booths loaded with Elvis and Jerry Lee Lewis records. Maybe Ray Charles singing Georgia, or even that sad old dude, Blind Blake, considering the location.

The place was narrow, with a long counter on one side, and booths lining the opposite wall, and a kitchen off the back. The doorway was in the center where one of the booths had been removed. A small sign posted at the cash register immediately ahead said, "Please be seated." The entrance aisle formed a T intersection from the front door and required a right or left turn to choose a table. Gaspar turned right, walked fifteen feet on checkerboard black and white tile and chose a booth. He sat down hard on the red vinyl upholstered bench, facing the door. Predictable.

Kim headed straight for the restroom, feeling her shoes squeak as each step pressed water through the soles. Noxious fumes from a pine scented air freshener assaulted her when she pushed the door open. She flipped on the harsh overhead florescent and a roaring fan started up. She performed her tasks briskly while forcing herself to ignore the rust stains and broken toilet seat. She pulled a bit of toilet paper to protect her fingers when she flushed and held the handle down, as the note taped to the tank instructed.

Then she checked her reflection in the cracked mirror over the sink. "You're hopeless," she told the face. "Be careful or you'll scare small children." She pressed the water out of her hair with her hands and washed without touching the nasty soap cake and refused to use the wrinkled pull-down cloth towel hanging from its dispenser near the door. She shook her hands by her sides to dry them as best she could, and then drew her fingers up inside her sleeve and pulled the door open to escape.

She slid onto the bench opposite Gaspar. He was full-on focused watching the diner, the parking lot, everything, like a predatory bird. God, she was tired. What she wouldn't give for eight hours solid sleep. She'd be a new woman. But food first. She pulled napkins from a chrome holder and used them to dry her hands and pat the rain off her face. There was a two-foot round mirror on the opposite wall. It gave her a decent view of the room behind her. By moving her head slightly, she could see the entrance too. Not perfect. But good enough for government work.

A waitress walked over and put two laminated menus with curled corners down on the red plastic tabletop and asked, "Can I bring y'all some coffee while you decide what you want?"

"Absolutely," Kim said, without looking up from the menu. One page with pictures of all-American diner food on both sides. Breakfast, lunch, desserts, and drinks. No dinner. No alcohol. No pre-packaged food. Ptomaine, she decided, was a real possibility.

"Wide selection here," Gaspar said. "We can get our burgers with or without cheese. Or our cheese with or without burgers."

"I didn't take you for a vegetarian," Kim said, and the waitress returned with the coffee. "What do you recommend, Mary? And can you leave the pot?"

Mary's name was embroidered on her breast pocket. She seemed pleased that Kim had noticed and made the effort. She set the coffee pot down. She said, "I'd have the burger with cheese, lettuce, tomato, and mayo. Fries are good, if you like the crispy thin ones. Dill pickles."

"Sold," Kim said.

"Make it two," Gaspar said.

"Be about fifteen minutes while I get it ready," Mary told them, taking their menus and heading back to the kitchen to do the cooking.

"Low margin operation," Gaspar said. He took the sugar jar and tipped it to pour about two ounces of sugar into the eight-ounce cup. Kim wondered how he was going to get half a cup of cream in there too. She took out her personal smart phone and saw a surprisingly strong signal, considering their location. She brought up a search engine. Typed "Major Jack Reacher" with one thumb. Waited for the search to complete.

"Figured it out yet?" Gaspar asked.

"Figured what out?"

"When exactly Black was shot."

"Have you?"

"He's not God. He doesn't know everything."

She blinked, shook her head quickly as if to clear the fog inside. "What?"

"How fast does the boss think?"

"Pretty damn fast," Kim said.

"Exactly. Therefore, Black was killed around three this morning. The boss put a plan in place and called us at four, so we'd be here when the call came in."

"How did he delay the nine-one-one?"

"I don't know."

"Why did he need us here at all?"

"I don't know. You tell me. You're the brains of the outfit. I thought we had established that already."

Kim's smart phone pinged. She looked at the screen for the results of her search. Nothing. She tried "Jack Reacher, U.S. Army," and pressed search again.

She asked, "What else do you know?"

He shrugged. "Nothing. I know what you know. I got a call. Told to fly to Atlanta, meet you, drive to Margrave. I got encrypted files identical to the four you got, I think, but you're welcome to read them for yourself. The last one is about you. Name, rank, and serial number. And I'm guessing your last one is the same about me. The assignment is build the Reacher file for some secret project and keep it under the radar. I'm number two, you're number one. Interview Chief Roscoe first, get to her before eleven thirty a.m. Met you at the airport. We've been together ever since. That's it."

Her phone pinged again. Still no results. She tried one more time, "Reacher, Jack," and the phone pinged once more. No results. Reacher was a ghost. He didn't exist. Or her equipment was faulty. She thought about it a couple of seconds and tried a name belonging to an actual flesh and blood person she had seen with her own eyes: *Beverly Roscoe.*

She asked, "So is this whole Reacher thing a distraction?"

"It would be a very elaborate decoy, wouldn't you say? Four files, and a guy we actually can't find?"

"And the dead cop? The one with the killer-pretty wife wearing designer duds and packing pricey luggage? Is he the elaborate decoy instead?"

"He can't be."

"So how are they connected, Einstein?"

"I'd say 'you tell me,' but given the Vietnamese Inquisition here, I'm guessing you don't know either. Right?"

She'd pushed, he shoved. Best defense is strong offense. Typical man. Good. Reactions she understood made her trust him a little more. She'd have been pissed off in his place, but she'd have concealed her anger, which was much more sensible.

Mary chose that moment to deliver two overflowing blue melamine platters. Kim felt the heat of the food rise up to her face and the mouth-watering aroma started her stomach growling again. "This looks amazing," she said.

Mary stood by while Kim and Gaspar examined their meals. Kim pressed the bun, delighted by its freshness. Mary might have just baked it. Burgers juicy, lettuce crisp, ripe tomato as thick as a slice of bread, and a thick raw onion slice she'd remove when Mary turned her back. Plenty of calories to sustain Kim for a week.

64

"I added the Vidalia. You would have ordered it if you were from around here. You can take it off, but after you taste it, you won't want to," Mary told them, displaying obvious pride in her creation. "Try mustard on the fries. That's the way I like 'em. Save room for pie. Lemon ice box. Made it this morning. Can I freshen your coffee?"

Once she had them settled with their food to her satisfaction, Mary said, "I'm sorry to say this, but we close at three." She pointed to a round clock above the soda machine behind the counter. It was showing 2:40. "Normally I could stay later, but I've got to pick up my boy this afternoon. His daddy can't make it and I can't leave him by himself. I don't mean to rush you, though. Y'all let me know if you need anything else."

"We'll do that," Gaspar said.

Kim watched Mary's reflection as she retreated to her stool near the kitchen where she pulled a yellow pencil from behind her ear and returned to her newspaper puzzle.

"German inquisition," she said.

Gaspar looked up from his food. "What?"

"I'm no more Vietnamese than you are."

"Have you looked in the mirror lately?"

"Born and raised right here in the U.S. of A. One hundred percent American."

"Me too. So what? I'm still Cuban. And proud of it."

"Sure. I get that. That's my point. I'm still German. Too bad for you. Germans are a lot more stubborn than Vietnamese. We're more focused too."

"I noticed."

She said, "Mary's right about the Vidalia onion, though. Fair warning: I'm eating it."

"Me too," he said, and shrugged, as if they were stuck with each other and might as well make the best of it. Mary came back with two slices of lemon pie, a fresh pot of coffee and a new set of issues. "I'm sorry about the rush. If I could stay, I'd do it, really I would. But I just can't. I brought you the pie on the house to make up for being so rude. And I brought cups if you want to take the coffee to go. Here's your check," she said. "I wouldn't even charge you, but I'd get fired if my boss found out. I hope y'all don't mind." Mary's apology, like everything else about her, was excessive but genuine.

"No worries," Kim said. "Really. We've got to get on the road, anyway."

Gaspar pulled his wallet from his hip pocket. Number Two pays and keeps the expense records. More paperwork Kim didn't have to do. She was getting to like being Number One. Gaspar rooted around and unearthed a damp, tri-folded hundred from under the billfold flap.

He said, "I'm sorry. I thought I had something smaller, but my kids must have raided my wallet again." He flattened the hundred, laid it on top of the check, and handed both to Mary. "It's old, but it's still good. I hope you have change?"

Mary stared at the Franklin as if he'd handed her a dead frog or maybe a live snake. Her face transformed from apologetic to confused to shocked. She squinted out the window checking the parking lot. Only two vehicles were there: the Traverse they'd arrived in and the green Saturn, presumably hers. Both were engulfed in the continuing monsoon.

"Something wrong?" Gaspar asked.

"I'm not supposed to make change for a hundred," Mary said so quietly Kim could barely hear her.

"I can give you a credit card if you want, but it seems silly to do that for a twelve dollar lunch tab." His voice trailed off when he, too, noticed Mary was close to panic.

What the hell?

Kim wiped the mustard and salt off her fingers with her napkin, reached into her pocket, and took out a twenty she'd gotten from the ATM in Atlanta. She handed it to Mary. "Here. Use this. He can pay me back later."

"That's great. I'll be right back." Mary took the twenty, pinching both bills and the check between thumb and forefinger, and rushed off to the kitchen.

"What do you suppose that was about?" Gaspar asked.

"Maybe she closed the register already. It's 2:58, according to their clock." Kim drank coffee while they waited for Mary's return with the change. Gaspar remained alert. For what, Kim couldn't say.

Mary didn't come back.

Gaspar said quietly, "There's something happening here."

Kim looked up, saw nothing new in the mirror. "Where?"

"GHP cruiser in the lot. Two guys inside, not one. Roscoe said GHP rides one to a car unless they need back up."

Kim looked outside and watched the GHP car park between the Traverse and the diner's door. "Maybe they don't know the place closes at three."

Both officers exited the car. Burly. At least 6'3" and 250 pounds each. Either end of any decent college football team was smaller. They moved through the rain side by side like they had a purpose. Each one held a shotgun.

Gaspar said, "I'm guessing they're not here for the Vidalia onions."

"Probably not."

"Less than ten seconds. Are you ready?" Gaspar asked.

She set her cup down. Wiped her hands. Put her napkin on the table. She noticed she'd never picked up her phone after the last Internet search and she couldn't remember whether she'd checked the results. No time for that now. She positioned the phone in the breast pocket of her jacket and pressed the application button to record and send video to the remote FBI server, just in case.

"I'll lead. I'd rather not shoot anybody today," she said, looking out the window. The twin towers seemed to glide through the rain curtain as if a moving sidewalk carried them relentlessly forward instead of their feet.

Gaspar placed both of his hands on the tabletop, in full view. She did the same. He asked, "Have you ever shot anybody?"

Kim didn't answer. She lifted her gaze to the mirror. Only the trick of reflection and perspective made them seem to grow larger with each step, right?

The two men entered the diner single file out of necessity. No way two sets of those shoulders could pass through the door frame at the same time, even without the shotguns.

At the T, they peeled off. One moved toward the kitchen; the other approached, shotgun raised and ready. He stopped across the tile directly parallel to their table, set his legs shoulder width apart as if he was bracing to shoot. He stood out of reach, but left space for Kim and Gaspar to exit the booth and stand. Which they did. Slowly. Hands in the air, palms out. Before being asked.

"Officer...Leach," Kim said, facing him because of the camera in her pocket, reading his name plate for the audio, like she'd been trained. "Do you know who we are?"

Leach said nothing, which was not normal law enforcement procedure anywhere.

"I've got I.D. in my pocket," Kim said. "I'm going to pull it out and show it to you. Okay?" The guy nodded. Once. Kim said, "I'll take that as a yes. Don't shoot me." She kept her left hand raised, and reached slowly into her pocket with her right and pulled out her ID wallet. She showed him her badge and her photograph.

He looked. Said nothing. Kept the shotgun steady.

"I'm FBI Special Agent Otto," Kim said. "This is my partner, FBI Special Agent Gaspar. Would you like to see his ID too?"

Leach nodded once. Gaspar repeated Kim's actions. Leach repeated his.

"What's this about?" Kim asked him.

He said nothing.

"You are holding a federal officer at gunpoint, sir. You realize that? What you're doing is a federal crime. Do you understand?"

Leach kept his eyes open, his mouth shut, and his shotgun pointed.

What the hell?

Kim looked over at Gaspar and he shrugged as if to say, "Now what?"

According to the diner's clock, four minutes had passed since Gaspar noticed the GHP unit in the lot outside. Her arms were tired. She'd never actually been ordered to raise them, so she lowered them again. Gaspar did the same thing. Leach showed no reaction. He just stood there, braced, shotgun pointed, staring, silent. Everybody waited. For what, she didn't know.

Six minutes later, the second GHP officer emerged from the kitchen and strode down the aisle. He stopped two steps north of the first guy. His name tag said Leach too. Brothers?

The second one did the talking.

He said, "Can I see your identification, please?"

"What is this about, Officer Leach?" Kim asked him. When he didn't reply immediately, to make a clear audio record at the very least, she said, "We are FBI agents. Why are you holding us at gunpoint? What is going on here?"

He stood with his hand out, palm up. They handed the wallets to him. He took them, read them, refolded them. "If my dispatch says you check out, you can be on your way. It'll take a minute, if you want to sit down."

"What's this about?" Kim asked, and was ignored, for the third time.

"Finish your pie. Mary makes great pie." He took the ID wallets and returned to the cruiser. Rain settled on the brim of his hat while he opened the driver's door, before pouring onto the ground when he ducked his mass to enter the vehicle. He left the cruiser's door open while he used the radio.

The first Officer Leach remained in position, shotgun pointed. Looked like a Browning A-5, weighing about eight pounds. Even if he could bench press 80% of his body weight, his arms had to be getting fatigued by now. Yet the shotgun didn't waver.

No one sat. No one ate pie. They waited. About ten minutes later, the second Officer Leach returned. He handed their ID wallets back.

"It's okay," he said to his partner. "You can put the gun down."

The first Officer Leach lowered the shotgun.

"Will you tell us what's going on now?" Kim asked again.

The second Officer Leach's manner was professional and matter-of-fact. "Everything checks out with you two. GHP is aware of you now. We've got your rental in the system. We'll be able to find you, wherever you are. You understand?"

"Mary needs to close up," Leach continued. "She's already late for her boy. She'll feel better if we wait for her. So you two run along now."

"Sure, no problem," Gaspar said, hostility apparent. He gestured for Kim to precede him. They exited the diner, made it to the Traverse through the ceaseless rain. Gaspar unlocked the doors and settled behind the wheel and started the ignition. Kim bent inside the vehicle, reached into her bag and pulled out her camera. She ignored the deluge to snap pictures of the GHP cruiser, its plate, and both Officer Leaches. The burly brothers were braced side by side, facing the parking lot, watching through the windows. Mary stood dwarfed between them.

Before Kim entered the Traverse, she opened the hatch and pulled out her laptop case. She stowed it on the front floor, then climbed into the navigator's seat.

"What the hell do you suppose all of that was about?" Gaspar spoke first, after he flipped on the heat, and pointed the Traverse's nose toward the exit.

"You're asking me?" she said, teeth chattering with cold and receding adrenaline. "I'm thinking this entire day is a crazy nightmare caused by too much schnapps."

"Yeah, well, easy for you to say. You're not out a hundred bucks."

"Plus the eight dollars change from my twenty, that's the best tip Mary's had this week, I'm sure."

He scowled at her. At the driveway's exit, he asked, "Which way, Ace? Margrave or Atlanta?"

"I'm pretty tired of Margrave right at the moment. How about you?"

"I was hoping you'd say that." He turned the Traverse north and headed for the Interstate. Their wet clothes coupled with the Traverse's blasting heat put fog on every inside window. Gaspar reached over to flip on the defroster. Cold air blew hard across the windshield and Kim started to shiver again.

"You could have asked for your hundred back, you know," she told him, huddled into her wet jacket as far away from the blasting defroster as she could move.

"Oh, I'll get my hundred back. Don't you worry. Cubans are not as harmless as we look."

"Drugs," Gaspar said, after they'd put ten minutes of pavement behind them. "Meth, most likely. Black must have been dealing, at least. Maybe cooking too."

Kim took her phone out to check she'd terminated the recording application, and remembered her aborted internet search.

Gaspar said, "They've had a couple of big drug busts around here. I told you I'd been to Margrave before. I was on two busts that took down some Mexican cartel cocaine. Meth is a big problem in rural areas too. More likely to be meth."

"Makes sense." Kim pulled out her laptop. She didn't need a secure connection now. Just normal service would do it. She opened a search engine, typed in "Beverly Roscoe," and waited.

"Am I boring you?"

"Germans can do two things at once, Agent Gaspar," she said. He laughed and some of the tension in her shoulders melted. "Drugs; meth; cooking; dealing. See? I was listening."

"The place was too empty. Roscoe said Black had lived there twenty-five years. Even the most diligent minimalist would accumulate more stuff than that place had in it over that length of time."

"You're thinking someone ripped him off? Took everything out of the house before we got there?" The signal was weak and intermittent at first. She lost the connection a couple of times before one caught and held.

Gaspar continued, almost as if he was thinking aloud. "The guy who beat the crap out of that mailbox was having some fit of rage. Could have been a meth head. Hard to work up that level of frenzy otherwise."

"True." The search engine returned a surprisingly long list of articles containing Roscoe's name. Several pages. Each page had to load individually, and the loading was slow.

After a while, Gaspar said, "And Mrs. Black."

"What about her?" The connection was lost again. Kim tried four times before it reestablished.

"Way too hot for that house. And way, way, way too hot for that dude."

Kim laughed for the first time since Officer Leach had pointed his shotgun at her. "Leave it to you to notice."

He looked over, raised his right eyebrow, and adopted a fake Spanish accent. "The phrase 'Latin Lover' mean anything to you, Helga? Did I mention that I have four daughters, and a pregnant wife?"

"I got that, Casanova."

"Damn straight."

"Yeah, yeah. You're irresistible, even to the murderously hot babes. What else?" The long list of entries for her search terms was organized by the LIFO method: last in, first out. The articles at the top were shorter pieces with very little useful content. She flipped through the pages as quickly as the intermittent connection allowed.

"Besides the obvious, you mean?"

"One man's obvious is another woman's obtuse." She was on page ten of the list. Nothing helpful so far, but she kept reading, hoping for a glimmer of something.

Kim felt the Traverse's speed slow. Flashing lights proclaimed road construction ahead. Outbound traffic from Atlanta was barely moving. Inbound traffic moved slightly faster.

Then it stopped altogether.

"Okay, including the obvious, then." Gaspar slid the transmission into park and moved his right leg as if cramping had returned. Again, Kim would have asked about the leg, but she didn't want to go down another contentious road.

Gaspar said, "Whoever shot Mr. Black knew where to put the bullets. The two shots to the head would have done the job. The other five were pure vengeance."

She looked up from the screen. "For what?"

He considered the question for awhile. Finally he said, "Now that's the sixty-four dollar question, isn't it?"

"That, and why the Leach brothers ran us out of town."

"You think the two are related?"

"The Leach brothers?"

He shot her the *Oh please* look he'd learned from his teenagers. "Black's murder and our close encounter with the Leach brothers."

"You think they're not?"

"I see what you mean about being obtuse," he said.

Traffic began to move again, but barely. Kim's Internet connection remained strong for five miles. Long enough to download four large articles before she lost the signal again. She scanned the pieces quickly, seeking new facts.

When the construction zone ended, the road widened to four lanes again, and Gaspar punched the Traverse back to eighty miles an hour. The cell signal cut out. Kim barely noticed, so engrossed was she in the *Atlanta Constitution* article she'd pulled up.

"Are you reading a novel over there or what?"

"Strictly non-fiction," she said.

"Interesting?"

"Well, I think I know why Mary the waitress freaked out when you gave her that hundred dollar bill."

CHAPTER TWELVE

THEY HEADED FOR Hartsfield Airport, south of the city. Gaspar chose a Renaissance Hotel and parked the Traverse within easy sprinting distance of a side entrance. He said, "Is this okay? They've got a bar and a restaurant, which most of these airport racks don't have. We wouldn't need to go out again tonight."

The rain had stopped about fifteen miles earlier, but the air was still heavy with moisture and small lakes had collected in every low spot. The temperature had dropped after the storm too. Kim was exhausted. Gaspar looked as bad as she felt.

"Sure," she said. "Perfect."

He got out of the Traverse and limped to the back and lifted the hatch. They pulled out their bags. She wheeled hers inside, but he carried his. Macho man. She sighed, too tired to deal with him.

They registered, and they requested and received second floor billets close to the emergency stairwell nearest the Traverse. Then they went up in the elevator to adjacent rooms.

"Let's meet for dinner," Kim said. She checked her watch. Six o'clock now. "Maybe eight thirty?"

She wanted a nap, and a shower, and then some time to work. She'd acquired a lot of data.

"I'll knock on your door at eight thirty," he said.

"Perfect." But almost before she got the word out, she felt the boss's cell phone vibrating in her front pocket. After three tries, she swiped her key correctly and released the lock. She pushed the door open with her hip, wheeled her bags inside, closed the door, and lifted the phone to her ear. By then it had vibrated seven times.

"Otto," she said, breathless. Out of habit she walked through to the bathroom and pulled back the shower curtain. No crawly bugs. No surveillance. No ambush.

"I didn't expect you to be back in Atlanta so soon."

The implied question stopped her room inspection cold. And at first it confused her. Then she realized the cell phone must have an active GPS monitoring chip in it. She wasn't surprised, exactly. She was used to being monitored while on duty. Knowing someone was watching her had always made her feel safer. Serious things could happen to agents out of electronic range. Unfixable things.

But she didn't feel reassured right then. She felt unsettled. Mostly because she hadn't worked out what she would tell him and what she wouldn't yet. She looked at herself in the bathroom's vanity mirror. Did she sound as bedraggled as she appeared?

She stood up straight, squared her shoulders, looked her reflection in the eye. She imagined that he was on the other side of the mirror, watching her; that he saw what she saw as they talked. She tried to create a positive impression.

He asked, "You're making good progress, then?"

"Just the opposite, I'm afraid." She'd stick to the fiction he'd given her about this assignment until he tasked her otherwise. Or until she figured out his real agenda. And the truth was that she'd learned almost nothing about Reacher that she hadn't known before she arrived in Margrave.

"How so?" he asked.

"Chief Roscoe was called to a homicide, so our interview was cut short. We're going back tomorrow."

"Was she cooperative?"

Translation: he'd known Roscoe wouldn't be cooperative.

"She didn't have time to tell us much. She said Reacher had been arrested and charged with murder back then. She was the intake officer. That's how she met him. She said he wasn't guilty. She said he saved her life."

"Does she know where he is?"

"She said not."

"You believe her?"

Kim thought about Roscoe's reaction to Reacher's photograph, to learning he was alive. Roscoe wasn't faking then, Kim was certain. "I do believe her. Yes."

She listened to a few moments of silence; waited for him to state his pleasure.

"Who died?"

"Sorry?"

"Roscoe's homicide."

Had she been wrong? Did he truly not know? She tamed her puzzled mind, now persuaded he was testing her. But immediately wondered: testing her for what?

"Margrave Police Sergeant Harry Black."

"Who killed him?"

Kim thought about the question on its merits and his motivation for asking. She decided she was too tired to think along two tracks at once. "I'm not sure."

"Why?"

She took a deep breath. She hadn't meant to reveal her assumptions until she'd been over everything and settled it in her own mind. But there was no possibility of evading him, even if she'd wanted to.

He knew where she'd been. The cell had been in her pocket from the time she left her apartment. He'd monitored her movements, and Gaspar's too. And, if she was right, he'd sent her to Margrave to be his eyes on the ground at that homicide scene. This was really what he wanted to know. Failure was not an option. She had to deliver. But deliver what?

"I haven't been able to go over the evidence yet."

"What evidence?"

"We took photos while we were there. We made observations."

"Why?"

What should she say? Because she believed he'd sent her there to do exactly that? Because she was ambitious and wanted to impress him, to get promoted, to have his job and go beyond it one day? Scratch that. What was she thinking? She shook the cobwebs out of her mind.

"Roscoe asked us to help, and we were trying to gain her trust, so she would answer our questions about Reacher. She was short-handed. She needed the help." Not precisely true, but not much of a lie, either.

As if he was actually watching her through a one-way mirror, could see her expressions, gauge her veracity, he offered only silence for too long. Was her fanciful idea true? Could he see her right now? If he knew she was there, had he arranged her room assignment in order to watch her? Anxiety crept up from somewhere, raising her internal security alert level to red again. No. That was not even possible. Was it? And what was he thinking?

She said, "Black's wife claims she killed him. Shot him with his service weapon. Seven times. While he slept."

"You think otherwise?"

"I don't know."

"What's bothering you about her confession?"

So he didn't know everything. A better question: what *wasn't* bothering her about Sylvia Black's confession?

She didn't want to screw up. This case was the biggest test of her career so far. She wanted, needed, to handle it perfectly. She didn't want to jump to conclusions based on her gut. FBI Special Agents don't operate based on vibes. And they didn't get promoted for shooting their mouths off, either. Especially if they were wrong.

"I'd feel better if you let me look at my photos before I answer that. I can call you back with more solid intel."

"It feels wrong. The confession. Is that what you're saying, Agent Otto?" As if *feels wrong* was objective forensics they could use in court. Was he mocking her? Had she already blown it?

"Not only that," Kim told him.

"But partly that? What else? Any support for those assumptions?"

She gave up her efforts to stall him until she felt more secure. *Take a risk, Otto.* If she was wrong, she'd just have to deal with that later. That's why they put erasers on pencils. So she told him the obvious things Gaspar hadn't noticed. Or hadn't mentioned. She wasn't sure which.

"The crime scene was unlike any domestic homicide I've ever covered. No signs of violence. No injuries to the widow. Husband shot in his sleep. Seven times. Deliberate placement of the bullets. The first two shots to the head killed him. Blew his face off along with most of his head. The other five were placed specifically and only after he died."

"How long after?"

"I'm guessing at least thirty minutes."

"Could be less?"

"Not much less."

Silence again for a longer while. Kim waited.

"Examine your evidence. Talk things over with Gaspar. Send me your report before ten tonight. Include the photos. I want to see them."

Ten tonight? He wanted a full encrypted report in four hours? "Yes, sir."

"You're booked on a ten thirty Delta flight to Kennedy. Same security set up as this morning. Your second subject is only available tonight. Someone will meet you at the gate and take you to him. Sorry for the short notice."

"Yes, sir."

Six minutes later Gaspar knocked on the door.

CHAPTER THIRTEEN

New York, NY
JFK Airport Hudson Hotel
November 2, 2:00 a.m.

KIM ROLLED HER shoulders and stretched her neck, seeking to relieve the unremitting tension. For twenty-four hours, she'd been running on her standard triple As: ambition, adrenaline, and anxiety. Add two gut-wrenching plane rides on less than two hours sleep and her nerves, like her muscles, were screaming. None of this, she knew, was visible even to the keenest observer. And she meant to keep it that way.

Sixty-five minutes ago, she'd arrived in the luxury suite of the JFK Hudson Hotel excited and fully armed with her well-crafted approach. Allotted ninety minutes, she'd planned to complete the Reacher file through this single interview. She would make a powerful ally, learn everything she needed to know, write a perfect report, and wrap. From start to finish in less than twenty-four hours. Record success in record time, even for her. The boss would be pleased. She'd go home in triumph, sleep for a week, and never go back to Margrave again.

That was then.

Her optimism had dimmed as her time expired. She was forced to revise, cut, refocus, and revise her plan again and again. Now she had only twenty-five minutes to complete the mission. Not enough time. Not even close.

"You're looking a little silly up there on the ceiling," Gaspar said, without opening his eyes. He rested on the edge of his seat, legs stretched out, ankles crossed, head supported by the narrow wood across the chair back, hands folded like a corpse.

"Whatever do you mean, Gumby?" she said, haughty, as if he'd missed the mark completely.

"This is total bullshit. You didn't cause it and you certainly can't fix it. You might as well relax until he shows up." He grinned. "I'll let you know when it's time to panic."

"You're too kind."

"It's a gift."

"A curse, you mean."

"Suit yourself. Wake me up when his royal highness appears."

He wasn't fooling her. She saw the white knuckles on his clasped hands. He'd been slouching like that since they arrived, but he hadn't actually slept a second.

"Don't worry, Quixote. You'll hear the trumpets."

She'd run the revised plan through her head a hundred times, but it never got any better. All available accounts proclaimed Finlay an honorable man whose integrity equaled his superior competence. Which had to mean the negatives had been removed from his records and the complainants silenced. Nobody got as high up the ladder as this guy without making enemies.

She needed leverage and she simply didn't have any.

His title was Special Assistant to the President for Strategy. What did that mean? The precise nature of his job was nowhere described. Which was more than enough to shove her internal threat-level against the top of the red zone and hold it there.

He'd been selected by the highest-ranking civilian responsible for Homeland Security and Counterterrorism, and placed one heartbeat away from the U.S. Commander in Chief. No watchdog kept tabs on him. He reported seldom and only through verbal briefing. No paper trail so much as named the missions he'd undertaken. Process, performance, results, also absent from the record.

Casualties, of course, never acknowledged. She'd heard rumors. Unconfirmed.

Everything she'd learned about Finlay marked him as dangerous. He deployed unspecified unique skills in service to her country on unidentified missions. Like nuclear power, when properly harnessed he might be useful. But she'd found nothing restraining him; not even his own word.

Was he friend or foe? Wiser to assume the worst.

She heard a door swish over carpet in the suite's anteroom. The noise charged her nervous system like a cartoon character's finger plugged into a light socket, an image she'd never found remotely funny. She'd been Tasered. She knew how it felt.

"He's here," she said. Her voice sounded calm. No tremors, good cadence, low octave. So far, so good.

"Finally." Gaspar's scowl had become a permanent groove in his forehead. "Who does the guy think he is? Jennifer Lopez? Now there's someone worth waiting for."

She knew what he meant. Worthy leaders never disrespected subordinates. Loyalty was a two-way street in her book too.

Gaspar had decided Finlay's tardiness was deliberately dismissive. Kim wanted to believe he'd been unavoidably detained, even as her stomach acid said Gaspar was right.

She warned Gaspar again, "Our time is his time."

"Yeah. I got that. Remember me? I'm the one with four kids to put through college." He stood up, stretched. Kim pretended not to watch him stroll awkwardly around the room. She saw the pain on his face too. At some point, she'd ask him about the leg. But not now. She had more immediate things to worry about.

Maybe the interview wouldn't be a disaster. A glimmer of her initial excitement remained. She'd been given this rare chance to impress a powerful man who could and did advance women on the job. Finlay had a proven track record on that score: Roscoe.

Would Roscoe have become Margrave Police Chief without Finlay's support? Hardly.

"He could have a good reason for being late, you know," she said.

Twenty-two minutes left. She strained to hear the voices in the anteroom. But the suite was near soundproof; she couldn't quite capture the words being exchanged, which might be okay. Or not. Depended on what the words actually were, didn't it?

Three or four men were talking. One was the aide who had escorted them from their arrival gate. She hoped one was their subject. If so, the other two could be his protection detail. A lot of firepower for a friendly conversation with two FBI agents.

She heard footsteps. She stood up. Lamont Finlay, Ph.D., pushed the door open and crossed the threshold as if he owned the room and everything in it.

Even at two o'clock in the morning, he looked like a spokesman for financial services. Tall, straight, solid; close cropped hair slightly gray at the temples. Clean shaven. Well dressed. Everything polished to high gloss. Distinguished. Experienced.

Intimidating.

A black man, but his ethnicity was not African-American. The file said his grandparents had emigrated from Trinidad to New York before settling in Boston, where he'd been educated at Harvard. The Boston accent had faded but Kim could hear it.

"Mr. Gaspar, Ms. Otto," he said, shaking hands with both of them in turn. His paw felt as big as a catcher's mitt. She could have made a fist with both hands inside his grip. "I'm sorry to keep you waiting. Please, sit, sit. Have your needs been adequately attended to?"

"Yes, thank you, sir," Kim said. A tray delivered more than an hour ago still rested on the tabletop. The silver coffee carafe with sides of sweeteners and cream, bone china cups and saucers, silver spoons, crystal glasses, linen napkins, and four green eight-ounce bottles of bubbly French water consumed the flat surface. Sparkled lamplight danced from a cut crystal pitcher as if fairies filled the room.

Finlay was their host. This was his turf, his agenda. He displayed no concern. He had one knee crossed over the other. He had pinched the fabric to reset the sharp crease in his dark trousers. He had revealed bench-made cap-toe shoes and dark hose, not mere socks. Superior livery for a man with a government salary, Kim noted. She felt actual chest pain when she attempted to breathe, like an asthmatic.

Stress.

That's all.

Finlay waited, unconcerned. Both arms were folded across his lap. No rings on his capable fingers. A watch, for surely he wore one, hid under crisp white shirt cuffs. Cufflinks glinted with each spare movement. Even before seeing Finlay's enduring influence on Chief Roscoe, Kim had formed a clear mental portrait of a competent man. Rumor suggested violence and fatal consequences for those who crossed him. His presence cemented every impression of the absolute power she'd imagined. She'd expected ruthless entitlement as well. He was all of that and more.

In short, he scared Kim to death. Gaspar should be afraid too. They were in way over their heads. They had eighteen minutes.

And then they caught a break. Two breaks, really, in quick succession. First, Finlay spoke when he should have waited. He smiled and said, "I realize we don't have as much time as you'd hoped. So let's get right to it, okay?"

But, second, he directed his question to Gaspar. He'd assumed that Gaspar was lead. He wasn't fully briefed.

Was that good or bad?

"Of course," she said, projecting her voice past her closed throat. "We certainly don't want to waste your time."

His eyes opened a fraction when he realized his mistake. He corrected swiftly and directed his attention to her, as if he'd never erred at all.

Ah, she thought, *you're one of those.* But before she could integrate this new piece of data, he seized the advantage.

"I understand you're building a file on Jack Reacher for the Specialized Personnel Task Force. What job are you considering him for?"

His question knocked her back. Finlay knew why they were here. So was he briefed, or not?

"Reacher's proposed use is unknown at this time, sir," Kim said. She sounded more deferential than she'd intended. She sat up straighter and leaned slightly forward.

"Hard for me to hit the target in the dark," Finlay said.

She didn't believe he was in the dark. Smarter not to believe him.

"We came directly from Margrave after speaking with Chief Roscoe," she said, watching closely. No reaction. Unclear whether he already knew that too. "Frankly, we didn't have as much time with her as we'd hoped and we're just getting started. Whatever you can add is more than we've got at the moment."

"You want me to fill in the blanks?" He seemed to relax a bit more, as if the mission was less than expected. "The Margrave files are comprehensive. Not much missing, is there?"

Margrave files? What Margrave files?

"We don't have all the documents yet," Kim said, covering as well as she could.

Finlay pushed his starched cuff back with one finger and looked at the slender platinum timepiece on his left wrist. She'd guessed right about the watch at least.

He said, "It would take several hours to brief you. Quickly, ask me your most pressing questions."

Several hours? Strike three. How could there be several *hours* worth of missing data?

She couldn't think about that now. She had a million questions based on the little bit she *did* know. Literally. Which topic was the most important? She needed to know what made Reacher tick. Could he be counted on when his country needed him? What was his particular expertise? Why had he been off the grid all these years? What was he doing? What was he running from? Had Reacher assaulted Roscoe? Was he violent? Unpredictable? Crazy?

Gaspar cut directly to a question she was saving for later.

He asked, "Do you know where Reacher is now?"

Finlay said, "No."

"Do you know where he went when he left Margrave fifteen years ago?"

"No."

"Have you seen him since?"

"No."

"Is he dead or alive?"

Finlay flinched. A small flick of his right eyelid. Did it happen? Was it just a sparkle from the dancing fairies? She watched more closely.

"I don't know," Finlay said.

The flick again. Right there. She was sure.

Definitely a lie.

"Do *you* have any reason to believe Reacher's dead?" Kim asked.

"None." That was true, at least. She could tell. Then he added, "But it wouldn't surprise me. Do you have any reason to believe he's dead?"

"Only that he's too far off the grid for any man alive," Kim said.

She heard movement in the anteroom. A toilet flushed.

Finlay said, "Look at the files. You should find something."

What was he talking about? She had consumed those files. She could recite the contents by rote. *Start over. Analyze. You're good at this. You see the hidden relationships that others don't see. What does he know that you don't? He looks relaxed, but he's not. Why did he come here at all? What does he want?*

Finlay had access to information well beyond anything Kim could acquire. Both official and unofficial.

If he said there was something in the Margrave files they could use to locate Reacher, then it was there.

But Finlay wouldn't have more knowledge than the boss.

So Finlay was wrong.

Or lying.

Or testing.

Which was it?

She took a pause, a breath, and Gaspar asked, "You're saying you know how to find Reacher?"

Finlay said, "I'm saying you should look at the Margrave files and then we'll talk further. Roscoe and I testified back then. There's a lot of material. Some of it is arcane and complicated. Foreign policy. Diplomacy. Chemical analysis. We can't deal with all of that right now and it wouldn't help you if we did."

He looked at his watch. They were losing their chance. They might never be alone with him again.

Kim asked, "Do you know what Reacher's hiding from?"

"Is he hiding?" Finlay asked back.

"If he isn't hiding, why is he so far off the grid?"

"When I asked him about his lifestyle, he told me he was traveling the country simply because he hadn't seen much of it. He said he didn't work because he didn't have to. He lived off his army pension, he said. He'd been in the military, one way or another, his entire life. He told me he wanted to enjoy his freedom for a change."

"And you believed that?" Gaspar asked.

"We've all heard wilder stories. His checked out. No law requires an American male to be an upstanding husband and father of four, right? He doesn't have to hold a steady job and pay a mortgage until he dies, no matter how hard it is, and no matter how much he hates it, does he?"

Gaspar went quiet.

Finlay *had* been briefed.

Kim said, "Chief Roscoe told us Reacher was arrested for a murder he didn't commit. That's how you met him, right?"

"That's right."

"Why did you like Reacher for the crime?"

"Both the victim and Reacher were strangers we knew nothing about. Several witnesses saw Reacher walking in the vicinity of the crime scene during the relevant time frame. It made sense in context."

Kim understood. She'd been to Margrave. She realized how much a stranger like Reacher would stick out, how the coincidence would be too much to ignore. She'd have figured him as the killer, herself. In fact, Reacher was still the best suspect based on the little bit she knew. She'd held suspects on less.

"Who was the victim?" Kim asked.

Finlay hesitated. "We didn't know the name when Reacher was arrested. Victim had no ID on him and his body had been rendered unrecognizable. We identified him after we'd confirmed Reacher's alibi and released him from custody. With apologies."

Gaspar repeated the question. "Who was the victim?"

Again, the pause, but nothing with the eyelid. Kim saw Finlay didn't want to say the victim's name. But this was a guy who did what he had to.

"It was Reacher's brother," he said, quietly.

Kim stared. Finlay had arrested Jack Reacher for murdering his own brother, a crime he didn't commit, didn't even know had occurred. His only brother. A screw-up of monumental proportions. Finlay was lucky to be alive.

And maybe he knew it.

Finlay said, "I'm sorry to be in such a hurry, but I do have a plane to catch. Is there anything else you need right now?"

"Was Reacher violent?"

"Yes."

"Was he crazy?"

"I didn't think so at the time."

"Unpredictable?"

Finlay laughed. The sound was deep, resonant, and it shook the room for what seemed like a full minute. Eventually he said, "Agent

Otto, I'd say that if you looked up that word in the dictionary, you'd find nothing but a full color photo of Jack Reacher."

Then his handlers knocked on the door. Time to go. They accompanied Finlay toward the exit. He towered over Kim and he was a good four inches taller than Gaspar too. When he reached the door, he turned and reached straight out and took her phone out of her pocket. Like a magic trick. He pushed the button to stop the recording and dropped the phone back into place.

He said, "Let's go off the record now." He slid two business cards from his jacket pocket. He handed one to each of them. "I promised your boss I'd help you if I can. That's my private cell. Call me with your questions after you've read the files. Let me know if you need anything else. If I can't talk immediately, I'll get back to you."

Then with his hand on the doorknob he added, "And when you do find Jack Reacher, give him my regards, will you? Ask him to call me when he has the time. You can give him that number."

Gaspar asked, "Did you know Harry Black?"

Finlay thought and came up empty. "I don't recognize the name. Who is he?"

"Who *was* he. He's dead."

Finlay shook his head. "Should I have known him?"

"He was a Margrave cop. Killed last night. Roscoe was pretty upset about it."

There it was again. The eyelid flick. Finlay knew something. But he said, "Must have been hired after I left."

"His wife shot him, she claims." Gaspar pulled out his smart phone and showed Finlay a picture. "Sylvia Black. Do you know her?"

The flick came before the lie this time, and again afterward.

"Never saw her before," Finlay said.

"Did Reacher kill Harry Black?" Gaspar asked.

The aide knocked again, opened the door, stood aside.

"You'll have to ask him yourself," Finlay replied. He turned and walked away. His entourage followed behind him like ducklings follow their mother.

CHAPTER FOURTEEN

KIM STARED AT Finlay's business card. There was nothing on it except the phone number. No name. No title. She slapped it back and forth across her fingers. Gaspar said, "Roscoe and Finlay are both as nervous as hens in a fox house every time we ask about Reacher. They've got something to hide, and it's big enough to bury them both. Don't you think?"

Kim said, "Whatever they're hiding, it's something the boss doesn't know."

Gaspar raised his right eyebrow.

She said, "Don't give me that. You're the one who said he's not God. Obviously, he doesn't know. Think it through, Zorro."

"It's a mystery to me how your mind works, Susie Kwan." Gaspar moved over to the coffee and poured a cup for each of them before pulling out his laptop. "We've got about an hour before our flight to Atlanta. I'm not walking into Margrave again until I know everything Roscoe and Finlay are hiding. No more flailing around in the dark. I'll find the files Finlay was talking about. Should be easy enough unless they're sealed. You take Joe Reacher and Sylvia Black."

He bent his head to his task. She got her phone out. She sent the recording to her secure storage. Then she beamed a copy to her laptop. The audio would be transcribed and available on her laptop in minutes; she'd go through it again on the plane.

She asked, "You still think the Blacks are involved in the Reacher situation somehow?" She wrinkled her nose. The coffee was tepid. She liked her coffee hot.

"It would be stupid not to think so," Gaspar said.

"Agreed." And Special Agent Kim Louisa Otto would not fail because she'd been stupid. Not now, not ever. She walked to the window and pulled the heavy drapes open and gazed into the pre-dawn. Airports were fascinating places. Little cities of their own. Then she turned away from the window and rubbed the tension out of her neck and refocused.

She saw she had voice mail from Chief Roscoe's cell phone. She pressed play. Only a fragment had been recorded due to fluctuating cell tower signals. Roscoe must have been out of range or in a vehicle when she called. "—couldn't wait? I told you I would handle this. Where did you take her?—"

"Sounds like Roscoe's ticked off at us again," Kim said. She put the message on speaker and played it again. Roscoe sounded angry. Gaspar didn't look up from his screen, but he cocked his head like a wolf hearing distant threats.

Kim played the message twice more. "Makes no sense. What's she talking about? Did she call you at any point?"

He pulled his phone out to check. "Nothing. What time did she call?"

"Timer says her message came in at twelve thirty-three a.m." Kim felt herself squint, remembered the white lines around Roscoe's eyes and made an effort to stop wrinkling her face.

"I doubt she'd appreciate a call back at this hour. It's got to be after four in the morning." Gaspar worked his laptop as fast as any college kid. "I've got an ace analyst in my office. She could find this stuff in a Miami Minute."

"Which is what? Two hours?"

"Funny. The point is: I'm getting nowhere. Are you?" He ran a hand through his hair, stood briefly to stretch, and restarted.

"She's talking about Sylvia, right?"

"Who?"

"Roscoe."

"Can't imagine who else she'd be that pissed about, can you?"

"Why would we take Sylvia? Why would anyone? That's crazy, isn't it?"

Gaspar shrugged, not looking up from his work. "Our flight leaves in forty minutes."

"I haven't been this confused since I tried to learn Mandarin," she said, not joking.

"What's to learn? Little oranges in a can." He glanced at her and said, "Look up Joe Reacher's date of death. That'll give us a way to figure out the exact date Jack Reacher arrived in Margrave, right?"

Kim said, "Joe died Thursday, September 4, 1997, about midnight."

Gaspar stared at her. "Did you just pull that out of thin air?"

She shrugged. "It's in Jack Reacher's file. I've got a good memory for dates. As in: June 6, 1998, Roscoe's daughter was born. Jacqueline Roscoe Trent. Nine pounds, two ounces. Thirty inches long. Fair hair. Blue eyes."

"Big kid," Gaspar said. "My wife would've killed me if any of ours were that size."

"Beverly Roscoe and David Trent were married on Christmas Day 1997. December 25. The bride was nearly four months pregnant at the wedding."

Gaspar pointed and clicked. He said, "Finlay was promoted from Chief of Detectives to Chief of Police on September 30, 1997, after the former top cop died on September 7, 1997. He was called Morrison. Which means that Joe Reacher and this Morrison guy died within three days of each other. That can't be a coincidence."

"No, it can't," she said. "And I just found Joe Reacher's obituary."

"Interesting?"

"Born in Palo, Leyte, Philippines, August 1958, died at the age of 38 years. Parents Stan and Josephine both predeceased him, his only sibling Jack survived him. Educated on military bases around the world, then West Point, then Military Intelligence, and then Treasury."

"That's an odd trajectory."

"You bet. Military Intelligence and Treasury are about as divorced from each other as it's possible to get and still be in government service. He was killed in the line of duty. As a Treasury agent. Cremated. Ashes scattered in Margrave, Georgia. Which is weird."

"I know," Gaspar said. "He was a veteran. Why wasn't he buried at Arlington?"

"That's not what's weird. What's weird is how a Treasury agent gets killed in the line of duty in a sleepy little town like Margrave, Georgia, in September 1997? How would that happen? Why was he even there?"

"Were you even born in 1997?" Gaspar asked.

"There's no death certificate online. This is nuts. We're the FBI. The most sophisticated and best equipped and most comprehensive agency in the world. And we can't get any information from our own sources on an active investigation?"

"Welcome under the radar, baby. If it was easy, they wouldn't need high-octane talent like us, now would they?" He closed his laptop and began packing up.

"I'm calling Roscoe."

"Good luck with that."

She picked up her phone and pressed the call back button.

Gaspar stretched and limped around the room, limbering up. She noticed the limp and knew he was shaking it off. The list of things she intended to discuss with him was already long, but maybe that one should be moved to the top. She put the call on speaker while she shoved cords into her bag and pulled the zippers. Roscoe's cell rang ten times, twelve, fifteen. Then Roscoe's angry voice filled the room. It said: "You better tell me your ass is back in Margrave and you have Sylvia Black with you."

Gaspar tapped his wrist with his finger to show her time was ticking. Kim said, "Chief Roscoe, I have no idea what you're talking about."

"Save it, Agent Otto. I've got the guy's card right here in front of me. L. Mark Newton, *Esquire*. From Washington, D.C. He had a Federal Marshal with him, for God's sake. You sent them down here to pick up Sylvia. In the middle of the night when I wasn't here to stop them. You know it. I know it. And I want her back. Whatever it is you want with her, you can get in the damn line behind me."

"We don't have her."

"Save it," Roscoe said again. "Just get her back here, or I'll make you sorry. Are we clear?"

"Look, we don't have her. But we're on our way. See you before noon."

The call died.

Gaspar said, "There's one truly major flaw in that story."

"Which is?"

"L. Mark Newton died last year," he said.

"I know. I was at the funeral."

CHAPTER FIFTEEN

HALFWAY TO THE departure gate Kim felt the boss's cell phone vibrate in her front trouser pocket. She shifted her bags around to free one hand and tried to fish the phone out without slowing her stride. She couldn't do it. The phone buzzed on. It felt alive, wriggling against her abdomen. She'd have to stop. But she couldn't. The jet way door at their gate was already closed. She saw the plane through the plate glass window, still parked outside. But passengers could not be boarded after the doors were closed. Technically, the plane was gone. They'd missed the flight.

"We have to board," Kim told the gate agent, breathless.

"I'm sorry, that's not possible," the gate agent said without looking up. She was working the final documents to get the plane in the air.

Kim felt the cell phone buzz on. She'd never failed to answer the boss. She never planned to. She kept her voice calm. She said, "I need you to open the door." She put her hand in her pocket. To get the cell phone. But the gate agent misinterpreted. Her left hand darted under the counter. She hit the panic button.

Kim gave up on the cell phone and kept both hands in plain sight. She stood stock still. Where the hell was Gaspar?

He showed up three paces behind two TSA personnel. They had guns drawn. Kim kept her hands in view and said, "FBI," as calmly as possible. She reached slowly across her body with her left hand and opened her jacket to reveal her badge, clipped to her waistband.

Gaspar came up behind her and flashed his badge too.

"What's the problem?" he said.

Kim held her breath while the agents looked them both over. In the corner of her eye she saw the plane begin to move.

"You're too late," one of the TSA guys said.

"Let's pretend we're not," Kim replied.

The phone was still buzzing.

Time stood still.

Then the first agent said, "Okay, hurry."

Agent two opened the departure door wide enough to slip through. Kim ran. Gaspar followed. The door sucked shut behind them. The boss's phone bounced against Kim's hip as she ran. She turned the final corner and saw the jet way separating from the plane's open door. She stopped at the widening gap. Cold November air blew into the tunnel. The flight attendant was on the phone in the cabin. To the gate agent, presumably. She called out to the jet way engineer. The jet way stopped moving. The plane stopped moving.

Four feet of empty space.

Maybe five.

The stewardess said, "You can make it. I've done it lots of times."

Kim lifted her computer bag off the travel bag and telescoped its handle down. She grabbed one heavy bag in each hand, swung both, and tossed them over the void. The stewardess set them out of the way. Kim breathed in, breathed out, rocked back and forth like a varsity high jumper, and leapt across the empty black hole into the plane. The stewardess caught her by the arm and then they both moved out of the way to let Gaspar follow.

Gaspar had a problem.

He was right-handed. Therefore, he would want to push off from his right leg. But his right leg was the one with the limp. And even if he could push off with his left, would his right leg be sturdy enough to stick his landing?

"Can't we go back?" Kim asked.

"You don't want to know what would happen if we did that," the stewardess said.

So Kim braced her foot at the raised edge of the bulkhead doorframe. She grasped the molded handle on the inside frame with her left hand and leaned her body outside, into the frosty abyss, jutting her right arm toward him as far as she could reach.

"*Now*, Gaspar," she called.

"On my way," he called back.

In one fluid motion, as if they'd choreographed the move and practiced for decades, he backed off ten feet, and transferred his heavier bag to his left hand, and slung his computer bag over his back, and came in at a run. He got his bags swinging for momentum, he got his feet in place, and he pushed off with his right leg.

His right leg didn't hold.

No elegant arcing trajectory.

The weight of his bags jerked him onward while gravity pulled him down. Kim lunged and grabbed his left forearm in her right hand and she pulled with all her ninety-seven pounds of body weight and hauled him in. His left foot landed inside the bulkhead frame. He sprawled on the galley floor. She thought he might have said, "Thanks," with something very vulnerable in his voice. Something she didn't want to be there. Not now. Not ever. For her sake, as well as his.

But whatever, they were on the plane.

Not that being on another plane was a good thing, Kim felt.

Gaspar struggled to his feet, breathing hard, and he said, "Thanks," again.

Kim said, "From now on, we'll answer to Karl and Helen."

"What?"

"You know the Flying Wallendas are Germans, right?"

She got the grin she'd hoped for. He said, "Yeah, Gertrude. I know."

She felt better, as if equilibrium had been restored. She watched the flight attendant secure the hatch. If the hatch failed, the plane would crash. She couldn't move until the hatch was securely closed.

Her cell phone was still ringing.

She watched the attendant lock the door lever and test it. Then she moved.

Seat 1A was open.

She hated 1A.

Too much open space around 1A.

From 1A, she could see the galley and the door to the flight deck. She could hear the flight attendants talking among themselves or on the phone with the cockpit crew.

In 1A she'd be the first to know when something went wrong.

No.

She glanced back. "You take 1A," she told Gaspar, before she hurried back to 3D.

She shoved her computer bag under the seat in front of her and left her larger bag in the aisle for the attendant to heave into the overhead. She belted herself in as tightly as possible and grabbed both armrests and closed her eyes and prayed.

The cell phone had stopped ringing.

CHAPTER SIXTEEN

Atlanta, Georgia
November 2
7:45 a.m.

GASPAR PICKED A full-sized sedan at the rental counter in Atlanta. A black Crown Vic. The kind of car Kim hated because it was too big, and too low to the ground. She'd have to pull the seat all the way up to reach the pedals. Even then, she couldn't see the road beyond the long front hood. Not that she needed to worry. Gaspar wouldn't let her drive anyway.

"Much better," he said. "This is the kind of car G-men ought to drive, Tila Tequila."

"Absolutely. Unless the airbag deploys and suffocates me, the most serious problem is a seatbelt that scrapes my neck and cuts my head off."

He looked over at her scowling face and laughed. "Should I go back for a booster seat?"

She bent at the waist and scooted forward to reach her travel bag in the foot-well, and rooted around to find what she needed.

"Seriously?" Gaspar asked. "Do you want me to get a different vehicle? I'm glad to do it, but now's the time to say so."

"Not necessary." She pulled the seatbelt slack, and anchored the small alligator clamp from her bag onto the belt webbing immediately below the retractor. She settled into the seat and checked her adjustments. The shoulder harness now snugged across her body instead of her throat. She left the clamp's wings up to be sure it would fly off in a collision and allow the retractor to do its job.

"German engineering at its finest," he said.

"Precisely," she said. She tested the harness again, flattened her hand, chopped her forearm from the elbow straight ahead, and said, "Engage."

They stopped at a drive-through for coffee and greasy egg wraps, and then they joined the interstate traffic heading south. Sixty-six miles to the Margrave exit, according to the first road sign Kim noticed. The coffee was bad and the food was worse, but they were both hungry.

Gaspar chewed his eggs a while and flushed them down with the coffee before he asked, "Tell me again what Roscoe said about Sylvia Black."

"She said a U.S. Marshal and a lawyer showed up at the jail around midnight with a federal court order. The desk guy released Sylvia into their custody. Now, they can't find Sylvia, the lawyer's office doesn't answer the phone, and the Marshal's office said no order ever existed."

"So we got a dead lawyer, a phony Marshal, and a fake order, right?"

"Exactly."

"I know these small-town departments don't always put the brightest bulb on the desk at night, but Brent seemed a lot savvier than that to me. He must have believed the two strangers, right? So we must be missing something."

"I'm not sure Brent was on duty. Remember he'd worked the night before and then straight through Harry Black's shift too. Once

Brent took Sylvia back to the station and finished her intake, Roscoe might have sent him home."

"What kind of court order was it?"

"Roscoe was a little irrational during the phone call, remember," she said.

Gaspar shook his head, as if to clear out the cobwebs. "Doesn't make any sense. The desk guy's maybe new on the job, and yet he didn't call Roscoe first? Before letting a couple of strangers take his one and only inmate?"

Early morning sunlight bathed the countryside in pink and blue. Fall harvests were finished. Red dirt fields were wet mud saturated by yesterday's rainstorm. "I don't get it, either. We'll have an opportunity to ask Roscoe shortly, I'm sure."

They came up behind a grandpa poking along in an ancient wood-paneled truck loaded heavy with hogs. He was having trouble holding the truck in his lane. Maybe the truck was overloaded or maybe Gramps was just a bad driver. Regardless, his cargo's stench was unavoidable.

Kim pinched her nostrils between thumb and forefinger.

Gaspar said, "No kidding," and pulled out to pass on the left.

Gramps didn't want to be passed, though. When Gaspar got alongside him, Gramps sped up and kept pace for half a mile or so. At the higher speed the truck's random weaving was forcing Gaspar toward the median.

"Oh, for cripe sakes, Gramps, slow down," Gaspar said. "You're going to splatter that bacon all over the asphalt."

"He can't hear you, you know," Kim said.

"Sorry, bad habit. Lot of crazy drivers in Miami. Griping at them is better than shooting at them."

"Sometimes," Kim said.

"Crazy old fool," Gaspar said, but he returned the Crown Vic to a more reasonable cruising speed once Gramps was too far behind to catch up again. They ran along in the fast lane for a mile or so. Kim saw muddy fields and billboards advertising outlet malls, carpet discounts, and pecans farther down the road. Every now and then, an abandoned vehicle on the shoulder or in the median. Typical interstate. Nothing more or less. Traffic cams mounted high enough to catch traffic scenes made her feel more secure, as always.

Gaspar asked, "Should we make some calls? On the court order? Easy enough to chase that down before we get to Margrave."

"Not necessary," Kim said. "Roscoe will have done all that by the time we get there. But she won't find anything."

"Because?"

"Because there's nothing to find. There was no order. No U.S. Marshal would show up with a private lawyer in tow, or the other way around. If any part of that story was legitimate, they would have coordinated with Roscoe, at least."

"The whole thing sounds like government work, doesn't it? There are national security courts that issue secret orders. Inmates do get picked up from local jails these days. Crime doesn't happen only during business hours, either."

Kim sighed. The sun had come out and it was hurting her eyes. She didn't know where she'd put her sunglasses. "We're talking about Sylvia Black here. Not a terrorist or a spy."

"Good point. But whoever she is, Sylvia did not belong in Harry Black's house. That's for sure."

"She didn't belong anywhere in Margrave. But what reason would a national security court have to move Sylvia to federal custody? She'd have to be a fugitive or in need of protection." Kim closed her eyes against the sun's glare.

"Witness protection?"

"Unlikely. Sylvia didn't strike me as valuable enough to be living under witness protection. Even if she had been, a single U.S. Marshal wouldn't show up with a private lawyer in the middle of the night and grab her after she murdered her husband."

Traffic was backing up ahead. Gaspar lifted his foot off the accelerator and the big sedan slowed to a crawl. Kim said, "But whatever, Sylvia Black is not our case and not our problem. We're building the Reacher file, remember?"

He gave her a level stare. "Who knew you Germans were so gullible?"

He braked to a full stop. A worker with a flag was holding traffic in the fast lane to let four trucks enter the highway. Gaspar tried to move over into the right lane because traffic was still moving there, albeit slowly. Kim checked her side mirror and saw Gramps coming up in his panel truck on the right. Gramps waved and grinned as he and his pigs passed them by. She noticed he had a dog in the passenger seat too. Some kind of taupe colored hound with floppy ears and expressive eyes. Huge. Probably weighed as much as Kim did.

She said, "Slow and steady wins the race, I guess."

Gaspar laughed. Gramps continued traveling below the speed limit down the road in the slow lane, while the big Crown Vic waited for the heavy trucks to get out of the way.

"You should call Roscoe and tell her we've been delayed," Gaspar said.

Kim shook her head. "And give her another chance to bitch me out? No thanks. I'll wait. Let her get it out of her system all at once."

"Are you sure you don't have kids? That's the kind of logic I get from my teenagers."

"Forget Roscoe," she said.

"Good plan." His tone was grim.

"What did you find out about Joe Reacher's final case?"

He said, "A lot. None of it good."

"How so?"

"It must have been about money, obviously. And lots of it, judging by the mayhem. If we count from the day Joe Reacher was killed, until six government agencies swarmed into Margrave to sort it all out, it was twelve days. In those twelve days, at least twelve people died, maybe more."

Kim stared at him. "Twelve people?"

"Or more. Including Joe Reacher and Police Chief Morrison. And there were two big explosions, followed by raging fires. Several buildings were destroyed, including the firehouse, the police station, and those old warehouses."

"No wonder Finlay said we didn't have time to get the details last night."

Gaspar gave her the raised eyebrow again. "If you say so. Still think the boss didn't know about this?"

She didn't answer his question because the answer was obvious. "I saw those burned warehouses on the way in yesterday. Big area to be burned out like that. But it does explain why there are no records of Jack Reacher's arrest. They'd have been in the burned police station, right?"

Gaspar said, "That's what Roscoe claimed."

"You don't believe her?"

Gaspar took a deep breath, as if to fortify himself before he spoke. "If Roscoe and Finlay didn't know about a crime spree like that at the time it happened, then they're idiots."

"Which they're not."

"So they knew what was happening when everything went down." He looked at her to see if she was following his logic. "Agreed?"

Kim said, "You think that's what this is about? Dirty cops?"

"It's looking that way," he said. "I don't trust her. She's in this up to her neck. That's one of the reasons she's acting so odd. Not like any cop I've ever known, or you either, I'm betting. I'm telling her nothing."

Kim considered the facts. Roscoe's behavior was off, just as Gaspar said. But dirty cops didn't feel like the right answer, exactly. "Which makes me think that's not why we're here."

"Sometimes a cigar is just a cigar," he said.

They followed the four heavy trucks for six miles until the work area ended. Gaspar dumped his lead foot on the accelerator. Kim looked at her watch. They had lost thirty minutes. Roscoe would be thirty minutes more annoyed. Kim wasn't sure she cared.

Gaspar said, "There are only two possible answers here. Either Roscoe and Finlay participated in those killings or they covered up for the killer, who had to be Jack Reacher."

"I know," Kim said, too quietly.

"You know why it had to be Reacher, right?" Gaspar asked, when she'd had enough time to work it through.

"Yes."

"Are you gonna say it out loud?"

"No."

"Me, neither," Gaspar said.

But the logic was as clear as spring water. The boss knew all. He knew about Roscoe and Finlay, about the murders, the explosions, the fires, about Jack and Joe Reacher. He knew everything. He'd known yesterday when he sent them to Margrave, and he'd known for years. And let it slide. Maybe even helped with the cover-up. Why would he do that? And why change course now? And why lead them here but not tell them anything? Did he have money to burn in his covert budget like that? What was he up to?

Kim needed to work it out. The wrong move could end her world as she knew it, and Gaspar's too. She'd worked too hard to throw everything away. She wouldn't have Gaspar's career on her conscience, either. If she screwed this up, if she made accusations that weren't true, or pulled the trigger on suspicions too soon, Finlay and Roscoe would lose their careers, at least. They could go to prison. She'd need to be absolutely, stone cold, deadly certain before going down that road. The blowback would be deadly.

Gaspar said, "Live by the sword, die by the sword, as they told us at Quantico, Gretel."

"Yeah, well, what they meant was that FBI agents live in a world where kill or be killed is a daily possibility. I'm fine with that, because I've got a good chance of being on the winning end of the battle. But I'm not going to commit suicide by cop. And as long as I'm Number One on this job, you're not, either. Got it?"

Gaspar looked away and shrugged. "You're the boss."

"Exactly. For now, we'll play everything as it happens. Just like we have been. No sharing with Roscoe. Treat her like a potential suspect. I'll let you know if that plan changes."

"And when that time comes? What will we do then, Lady Boss?"

She didn't answer, because she didn't know what to say.

CHAPTER SEVENTEEN

THEY REACHED THE exit for Margrave. Somehow the livestock-toting grandpa was ahead of them again, still traveling below the speed limit, still weaving all over the road, still mostly in the right lane and on the shoulder. Gaspar had to slow down and get behind the smelly pigs. Then, Gramps exited at the cloverleaf too.

The truck leaned too far all the way around the curve, and Gramps overcorrected, sending the squealing pigs slamming into the panel on the truck's opposite side, and causing more weaving. Then the truck stopped askew at the bottom of the ramp. Stalled out. Gramps sat there without restarting for much too long.

Another old truck was abandoned on the right shoulder, blocking Gaspar's escape route. "Doesn't anybody tow these heaps outta here?" Gaspar griped. He began tapping his thumbs on the steering wheel. "Come on, Gramps. Time to turn. Only two choices. Right or left. Pick one. This is not brain surgery."

Eventually Grandpa leaned over and opened the passenger door. His big blue dog leapt out and ran around the back of the truck, right in front of the Crown Vic. When they saw the dog, the squealing pigs ratcheted up the volume to ear-splitting levels.

"Oh, man, Gramps, what are you doing?" Gaspar said.

Kim said, "Have a little patience, Speedy Gonzales. The dog had to take care of business. He'll be right back. Gramps will move along. That truck has carted a lot of pork in its day."

She leaned her head back and closed her eyes.

"I'll be right back," Gaspar said.

Kim felt the transmission shift into park and heard him unlatch his seat belt and open his door. He left the keys in the ignition, which caused the alarm bell to *chime, chime, chime.*

After the fourth annoying reminder, she opened her eyes.

Chime.

"What are you doing?"

Chime.

She saw that Gramps had exited the truck on the driver's side. Chime. He stood on the exit ramp's narrow shoulder, truck door standing open, and called to the dog.

Chime.

"Where are you going?"

Chime.

"To help the old guy find the dog so we can get on the road. If somebody comes down that ramp in a hurry, we could be slammed." *Chime.* "You might want to get out."

She watched him walk toward Gramps until the truck blocked her view. Then from the corner of her eye she saw a car, maybe fifty yards away, up above ground level. An old green Chevy, parked off the shoulder on the median weeds between the highway's fast lanes, pointing north. In the no-man's land between the southbound exit ramp and the northbound entrance ramp at the other side of the cloverleaf. The hood was up. It looked like it had been there a while. She didn't remember seeing it before. Not surprising. Old cars off the road were so commonplace they were practically invisible. She'd noticed at least ten on the drive from Atlanta. Probably more she hadn't seen.

The old man's dog had found the Chevy. The crazy hound was bouncing around like he wanted to play. With what? A car? Kim didn't know much about dogs. She knew some liked to chase cars. But what did they do when they caught one?

She called out, "Gaspar? The dog is over by that green car. I can see him from here."

If Gaspar answered, the squealing pigs drowned him out. Where was he? She got out of the Crown Vic and walked down to the truck, holding her nose because of the pigs. She saw Gramps standing with one foot on the rusted runner, the other on the ground, leaning on the open door, looking across the truck's hood toward the Chevy.

She followed his gaze and saw Gaspar up there, bent over, looking into the disabled Chevy's dim interior. The dog jumped up and down, ran around in circles, acting crazy. He barked a few times for good measure.

Kim hurried a few feet upwind from the pigs, released the grip on her nose, pulled her phone out and dialed Gaspar's number. He picked up on the first ring.

"What's going on?" she asked.

"Is this Roscoe's turf?"

Kim glanced around, didn't see any city limit signs on either side of the ramp. What was it? Maybe fifteen miles into town?

"We're a long way from the Margrave station. Why?"

Gaspar stood up and faced her across the distance. Vehicles passed between them on the southbound lanes, fast noisy blurs of color.

Gaspar said, "There's a dead man in this car."

CHAPTER EIGHTEEN

GASPAR SAID, "I hope this is Roscoe's turf, because we have to call it in to someone, and I'm not thrilled about going another round with the Georgia Highway Patrol right now. Are you?"

And right then the boss's cell phone began to vibrate in her pocket.

"Bring the dog back," she said. "Get rid of Gramps. I'll figure out who to call."

She disconnected and then opened the boss's cell and winced when it pinched her hand at the base of her thumb. She looked down and noticed a crack in the phone's case, and she wondered how she'd cracked it. She raised her thumb to her mouth to lick it, and raised the cell to her ear, and watched Gaspar take off his belt and wrap it through the dog's collar as a leash.

"Agent Otto?" her boss said.

Gaspar started back with the dog.

"Yes, sir." Traffic noise made it hard to hear him. She covered her opposite ear with her palm and tried to concentrate on his voice alone.

"Are you standing in plain sight of the Chevy?"

How did he know about the Chevy? She looked skyward as if she could locate the satellite he was using to spy on them. The traffic cam directly overhead wouldn't have been within his control, would it?

She said, "Yes, sir."

Two eighteen wheelers roared past with the whine of tires and a howl of wind. She couldn't hear her boss. Sounded like he'd said, "Get the hell out of there."

"Sir?"

"I'll take care of the traffic cam. GHP is on the way. I don't want you within ten miles of that car. You haven't been there. You haven't seen the Chevy. You haven't seen what's in it. Under any circumstances. Understand?"

"Yes, sir."

But she didn't understand why he'd tell her to leave the scene of an accident. Not at all.

"Be in Roscoe's office when they call about the Chevy. You've got less than six minutes to get out of sight. Move." He disconnected the call.

"Yes, sir," she said again, to the dead air, no chance to ask more questions.

Gaspar had covered about half the ground, pulling the gyrating dog. The dog jerked hard and Gaspar slipped on the gravel and fell to his knees. He got up again and the crazy hound jumped and pulled back toward the Chevy. Gaspar held fast to his improvised leash and kept on coming. Kim put the phone in her pocket and hustled toward the old truck. Gramps was still standing on the shoulder, watching his dog, awaiting its return. His pigs were squealing louder than ever. Kim gagged on the stench. How in God's name could Gramps stand that smell?

"Sir, I'm sorry," Kim said. Gramps cupped his hand around his ear. Kim yelled to be heard over the traffic and the squealing. "We've got an emergency here. My friend will be right back with your dog. Can we get your truck off the road here so we can get moving?"

The old guy smelled nearly as bad as his pigs. Kim gagged again. The greasy eggs she'd barely tasted an hour ago didn't want to stay down. She swallowed twice, three times. When the old man failed to budge, she yelled, "Okay?"

Gramps flashed a big, toothless grin. "Sure, honey. Anything you say. You're a cute little thing, you know that?"

For a horrified second she thought he might touch her. If he did, she'd have to burn all her clothes. She stepped back. Smiled at him. Cajoled him toward the driver's seat with gestures.

"Start your truck," she yelled.

By the time Gramps got settled and moved his truck out of the way, Gaspar had returned with the leaping dog. He placed the dog inside the cab with his appreciative owner. Kim tapped her foot while Gaspar stood with his head inside the truck's window, unable to break away from Gramps undying gratitude, wasting precious seconds. She listened for sirens; couldn't hear any. But a silent approach was more likely than a noisy one. GHP would be here any moment. They had to leave.

Kim ran back to the Crown Vic and leaned on the horn. Gaspar didn't hear it. She hopped into the driver's seat and perched on the edge and started the car. She could barely see over the dash. The hood stretched ahead forever.

Deep breath. Hands on the steering wheel at the ten-and-two position for balance. Transmission in drive, one set of toes on the accelerator and one on the brake. Braced for takeoff.

She threaded the monstrous sedan between the ditch and Gaspar's backside. She stopped. Lowered the window. Tapped the horn again. Pig squeals drowned out the sound, but Gaspar felt the big car's heat and vibration behind him. He glanced over his shoulder.

Kim screamed to be heard over the pigs, the passing traffic, and the Crown Vic's engine. "Gaspar? Get in. Right now." She waved her left palm toward the passenger side for emphasis. Gaspar looked at her as if she'd lost her last ounce of sense. He pulled back from the truck and stood upright. No hurry.

"You drive carefully now, sir," he said to the old man through the open window, and watched Gramps head off in the opposite direction. Then, satisfied with his good deed, he slipped into The Crown Vic's passenger seat.

"Where's the fire?" he asked.

Kim didn't answer. She just lifted her left toes off the brake and pressed the accelerator hard with her right. The car jumped forward into the intersection. Momentum sent Gaspar sprawling back in his seat.

Kim turned toward Margrave. The Crown Vic swallowed miles in tense, silent minutes. Then it jerked, stopped, and stalled in the Margrave Police Station parking lot.

"And you accuse me of having a lead foot," Gaspar said.

Kim pried her fingers off the steering wheel and checked the time on the dash. Amber LCDs showed 10:43 a.m. She said, "If the boss was right on the timing, GHP should be looking inside that Chevy any minute now."

Gaspar's eyes widened and then narrowed as she relayed their orders. The crease reappeared in his brow. Nostrils flared. "What the hell is that old bastard up to?"

"I don't know, *compadre*. But something tells me we're about to find out."

He put a hand on her arm to capture her full attention. She looked into his serious face. Concern slowed his speech and lowered his voice.

"Watch yourself, Susie Q. Assume you're being watched every minute too. What I didn't get the chance to tell you back there? The Chevy guy was murdered. No doubt about it. Two holes in the back of his head. Fair amount of his face missing. It's all too tidy. This whole thing doesn't pass the smell test. Not even close. Understand?"

"I understand," she said. She opened her door and pulled the keys out of the ignition and handed them over. "We're supposed to be in Roscoe's office when she gets the call. If it hasn't come in already."

CHAPTER NINETEEN

Margrave, Georgia
November 2
10:46 a.m.

KIM FOLLOWED GASPAR toward Roscoe's office. Heavenly whiffs of brewing coffee lured her into the break room first. She poured strong, black stamina into the largest mug she could find and carried it into the rosewood office.

Roscoe was showered and dressed in a crisp white blouse, sharply creased khakis, and a full equipment belt that matched her work boots for allure. She looked formidable. Kim felt worn, rumpled, and stained by comparison. Her suit looked like a cast-off the Salvation Army couldn't give away to a naked hobo. Soon, she promised herself, a shower and a clean suit. A decent meal and some shut-eye would be welcome too.

"Good morning, chief," she said, as normally as she could manage. The big round clock hanging on the wall over Roscoe's credenza showed 10:48 a.m. Five minutes since she'd parked out front, twenty minutes since she'd received her orders. Surely enough time for GHP to choose the right jurisdiction and notify first responders?

"We've been working half the day already. Where have you been?" Roscoe stood behind her desk, searching through papers in two Manila folders, preoccupied. Brightly patterned reading glasses rested at the bottom of her nose.

Gaspar slouched low in a green leather chair, eyes closed, his usual coping posture. Kim closed the door and slipped into the other chair.

"Well?" Roscoe asked, staring over the glasses directly at Kim as if she were a disobedient teen.

"Sorry?"

"You left her outside? Put her back in her cell?"

Kim said, "Whatever happened to Sylvia, we knew nothing about it until you called."

Totally true.

"Then why are you here?" Each word an accusation.

Kim said, "You know why we're here. We're building the Reacher File for the SPTF. We need to find out what happened when he was here in Margrave fifteen years ago. What he's been doing since then, and where."

"Reacher file, my ass." Said with a stare.

Kim was tired and tense, but not looking for a fight. She said, "Chief, please, that tone might get confessions from purse snatchers and cow-shooting delinquents or whatever else you get around here. But you must know it won't work with me. We know nothing about Sylvia. We left because we had to interview Finlay in New York before he left the country."

"So he said."

"When did you talk to him?"

"About ten last night." Roscoe's jaw muscles clenched. "At that point, I still thought we were all on the same team."

The same team? Who does she think she's kidding?

Roscoe studied Kim for a few moments over the top of her glasses. Silence filled the space until she shrugged and returned to her paper shuffling. "Okay, see Brent on your way out for an appointment.

Maybe we can discuss ancient Reacher history sometime in the next couple of decades. Or not."

Roscoe continued searching for a few more seconds, but she failed to find what she was looking for. She dropped the two Manila folders onto the desk, left the rosewood office and headed down the hall.

Kim turned to Gaspar, still slouched in his chair. "Any chance you could help me out here?"

"You were doing a good job without any help from me," he replied. "Tell me when you figure out what you want me to do, Boss Lady."

She reached over and grabbed the two folders off Roscoe's desk. "These are personnel files. One for Harry Black and one for Sylvia."

"Anything about either Jack or Joe Reacher? Common dates? Prior military service? Employed at Treasury?" Gaspar moved nothing but his lips.

"Not that I can see." Kim scanned the contents of both files without rushing. The headshots were recognizable, but Sylvia's photo reflected a rather plain female by comparison to the sophisticated woman Kim had observed yesterday at the crime scene.

Roscoe returned with new papers, and her old attitude. "So you're not interested in Sylvia Black, huh?"

Kim said, "You made it pretty clear that you won't help us until we help you with her. So it seems I've got two choices. Either I arrest you for impeding a Federal investigation, or I get your problem fixed so we can move on to Reacher. Let's try the easy way first. What were you looking for in these personnel files?"

"Sylvia's fingerprint records." Roscoe resumed her position behind the desk. She replaced the reading glasses on the end of her nose and turned her attention to the new documents she'd collected.

Kim passed through the file contents again. Every employee in any law enforcement capacity was fingerprinted. Lots of reasons. Standard practice, even before 9/11. Once in the system, prints were maintained forever. No exceptions. An existing fingerprint card and report were too distinctive to overlook.

"No prints in here."

"Exactly," Roscoe said, searching through the new pages she'd collected. She pointed to the personnel file with her chin. "Full work up before we hired her; no prints now." Her tone had lost its edge.

Gaspar sat almost upright in the chair and stretched out an open palm. "Can I take a look?"

Kim ripped the first page of Sylvia's file off its staple and handed both folders to him. She scanned the familiar checklist; she'd seen hundreds exactly like it. Everything that should have been completed was marked as done. "What was her job here, again? Dispatcher?"

Roscoe said, "Her title was Administrative Aide."

"Which means what?" Kim asked.

"She filled in where we needed her. Dispatch, scheduling, reports and databases, payroll, supplies." Roscoe stopped to think over Sylvia's duty list. "No public safety work. But we only have a ten-member team, including me and the Aide, so everybody pretty much does whatever needs doing."

"Unfettered access to records?" Kim asked.

"Yes, she could access personnel files, if that's what you're asking."

"So she could have taken the prints out of the file herself at some point after she was hired. She probably did."

"Why would she?"

"I have no idea." Kim brought the coffee cup to her lips with both hands and blew on the surface before she sipped. Really great coffee in this town. Was it something in the water? Maybe the brewing method? Steamed coffee was her favorite. A small stovetop Italian espresso maker. Freshly ground beans. Heaven.

Gaspar asked, "Was Sylvia issued a gun? Fingerprints would be required. The ATF would still have them."

"No. Not armed on duty."

"Allowed to carry?"

"She might have a concealed weapon permit. We can check. Hard to find a Margrave resident without one. Lotta snakes around here, both the two-legged and the four-legged kind."

"Okay," Gaspar said. "That's one possible source of old prints. Probably others. Is everything else that should be in the file actually here?"

"Seems to be." Roscoe nodded, preoccupied with the papers in her hand. If she thumbed through them too many more times, she'd rub the ink off the pages.

The clock showed 10:57 a.m. Maybe GHP would never call. Maybe the boss was wrong. He wasn't God, as Gaspar kept reminding her. But Kim's gut, what she'd come to recognize as her second brain, disagreed.

"What's involved in the background check?" Gaspar asked.

"Standard Homeland Security forms," Roscoe replied.

Kim was thoroughly familiar with those forms and the procedures they required. Smart choice. Presented several possible fingerprint record opportunities. Roscoe was a small-town top cop, but she was a good one. Kim would have enjoyed collaborating with a cooperative Roscoe under different circumstances. Maybe one day, they would actually be on the same team. Assuming Roscoe wasn't the dirty cop Gaspar believed her to be.

To confirm, Kim said, "So pre-hire, you checked criminal records, gun licenses, credit report, education and employment, drug tests, lie detector, physical exam, right?"

"Absolutely."

Gaspar said, "And all of that's still here, for both Harry and Sylvia. Sylvia's fingerprints and print report are the only things missing. No medical records?"

"Relevant medical records would be there if we had any," Roscoe replied.

Gaspar said, "Maybe we can get those from the insurance company?"

"We're self insured. She didn't get any medical care through us. I'd have known about it. I file an annual report," Roscoe said, inattentive.

Gaspar looked at Roscoe until she met his gaze. He raised one eyebrow; she grasped the point quickly. A woman Sylvia's age should have had at least some medical care in the five-year period. Sylvia herself looked well cared for and Gaspar lived in a house full of females, so he knew. Records existed. For sure.

The phone screamed silence. Twenty-six minutes. 11:01 a.m. What the hell were those guys doing out there, anyway? Kim's stomach snake thrashed around, fully alert. She gulped coffee to calm and distract, but coffee wasn't working any longer. She asked, "How about tax returns?"

She loved tax returns. She requested them on every case. Tax returns contained a gold mine of information if you knew how to read them. Predictable, comforting, recognizable digits securely held in proper boxes. Much better than dealing with people. Figures lie and liars figure, she knew. But Kim understood lies and liars; she liked numbers better.

Roscoe, it seemed, did not.

"No." She dropped papers on the desk. A few fluttered to the carpet. "No tax returns. No DNA. No cavity searches. No video of her mother giving birth. No goddamned place to look besides those two folders. No old fingerprints. Got it?"

Kim held both hands palm out in mock surrender. Roscoe bent down to collect the documents she'd dropped on the floor.

Gaspar asked, "How about tax returns for Harry after they married? If they filed jointly, that would be a start."

Roscoe straightened up. Without a glance, she stalked out and slammed the door behind her. But she didn't do anything worse.

"That went well, don't you think, Mrs. Lincoln?" he said lightly.

"Just great."

Gaspar stood, stretched, walked around the room as if he were mulling things over. Might have fooled someone else, but Kim recognized his pain relief routine. He said, "Don't worry, Sunshine. She's got to come back eventually. It's her office."

CHAPTER TWENTY

ROSCOE CAME BACK five minutes later, looking unconcerned. Kim said, "Beverly, we can figure this out. You're looking for fingerprints, but what you really want to find is Sylvia, right?"

"Duh," Roscoe said.

"Sylvia seemed out of place here, don't you think? You said she wasn't a local. So why did she come here? With respect, Margrave isn't exactly the town every sophisticated girl like Sylvia dreams about, is it? Surely she didn't just get off a bus and walk into town looking for a job in the local police station?"

Kim saw the briefest glint of surprise.

"What?" she asked.

Then the surprise softened to puzzlement. Roscoe leafed through the papers in front of her.

Gaspar said, "What?"

No answer. Kim waited to explain how to find Sylvia.

Tax returns.

Unlike fingerprints, tax returns weren't kept forever. The IRS normally held them for three years. Prior returns had to be somewhere, and Kim knew where they hid.

And tax returns knew where Sylvia hid.

The clock on the wall showed 11:06 a.m. What could the GHP possibly be doing with that Chevy for more than thirty minutes before notifying the correct homicide team? Sure, the first officer on the scene didn't want to make a mistake and set the wrong jurisdiction in motion. But this was GHP's beat. They had to know who to call. Even those two yokels from yesterday couldn't be *that* dumb.

Then Roscoe sighed and said, "Sylvia Black applied for her job here because Finlay recommended us. Sylvia had been living in D.C. and wanted to relocate. He told her he'd come from Margrave. Made it sound idyllic, she claimed. Peaceful. Just what she wanted."

And there it was. The connection. Under different circumstances, Kim might have cheered.

Finlay's name roused Gaspar pretty fast. He handed the personnel folders back to Roscoe and asked, "Did Sylvia say why she wanted to relocate?"

Roscoe hesitated before answering.

"Jealous boyfriend," she said.

"She give you a name?" Gaspar asked.

"I don't think so."

"Not Finlay himself, right?"

"No."

"How do you know, if she didn't give you a name?"

Roscoe didn't answer. Kim sipped her coffee, unsure. Even five years ago, Finlay was a long way up the food chain from an aspiring administrative aide. Unless he had some sort of personal relationship with her. But she couldn't see Finlay risking everything for Sylvia Black. He seemed too, well, *smart*, at the very least.

She asked, "Did you ever ask Finlay about Sylvia? For a reference, maybe?"

Roscoe considered that one for awhile, searching her memory. Her tone softer, sentences slower, she said, "I don't think so. We had an opening. Sylvia applied. We liked her. Her background checked out. There didn't seem to be any reason to go further, I guess."

Gaspar asked, "How did Sylvia know you had a job opening?"

"I don't know," Roscoe said. "Five years is a long time to remember details like that."

Gaspar asked, "How long have Sylvia's fingerprints been missing?"

"No idea."

"That's a lot of screw-ups on your watch, Chief. Your one and only prisoner escapes by walking out the door. With the full cooperation of your desk sergeant. Prints and print reports were removed from the accused's confidential file. You don't even know when that happened, let alone how. Awfully convenient, don't you think? "

"You think I pulled Sylvia's personnel file out today just to screw with you?"

Kim asked, "Why did you? Retrieve the file today, I mean? You booked Sylvia, right? Took prints? Why pull the old file? Looking for confirmation? Discrepancies? Or what?"

Roscoe ran her fingers through both sides of her hair. "Or what, I guess."

"Meaning?" Gaspar pressed.

Roscoe held up the papers she'd collected during her brief absence. "This is her booking file. We took new prints yesterday. Sent them in last night. Report from AFIS came back just before you arrived. They say no such person is on record."

She tossed the folder across to Gaspar. It landed in his lap and slid to the floor. He bent to pick it up, and winced. Something wrong with his right side. Not just his leg.

"Walk me through it," Kim said, and watched Roscoe's body language. She figured Roscoe had sound instincts. And she'd been on the job a good long time. Pride and anger and duty and uncertainty all crossed her expressive face. She liked her independence. She hated that help was required. Kim understood.

Roscoe said, "I've always been careful about fingerprints. Even with DNA now, fingerprints still solve cases. Early in my career, it was my job to take prints, and handle the reports."

"I hear a 'but' coming," Gaspar said.

Roscoe smiled. The first genuine smile they'd seen from her today. She had a nice smile, Kim thought. Kind. Like a nurse in a dental office, maybe.

"But," Roscoe said, drawing the word out and mocking Gaspar a little, as she stared directly at Kim, "I learned how important fingerprints really are when I met Jack Reacher."

The statement startled. Not what they were expecting. Not at all. Roscoe smiled. She enjoyed the upper hand. Who didn't?

"How so?" Kim asked.

"You know about Joe Reacher's murder now, right?"

"We have some open questions," Kim said. "But we know Jack was mistakenly accused and later released when his alibi was confirmed."

"Yes," Roscoe said. "Jack Reacher was innocent."

Kim said nothing. She doubted Jack Reacher was innocent, whether he had an alibi or not. Jack Reacher hadn't been innocent since Moses was a boy. But Kim needed to kill time until the call came. Reacher was a better topic than the Chevy.

Roscoe took another breath, and held it, then let it go. She said, "Joe Reacher's fingerprints weren't processed correctly. We got a false negative. And we didn't know that until after Jack's alibi had been confirmed. So we lost a lot of valuable time." Her voice trailed off into memories. Whether good or bad, Kim couldn't say.

Gaspar said, "Not to mention you accused and arrested the wrong dude."

Roscoe flushed crimson. "If you're trying to provoke me, Agent Gaspar, keep it up."

Gaspar gave it right back. "You did accuse Jack Reacher of killing his brother, didn't you? And you were wrong. You're telling me you did that based on a false fingerprint report?"

Roscoe shoved back, rapid fire. "I didn't accuse Jack Reacher of anything. Chief Morrison accused him."

"And then Chief Morrison got killed. So let's see: Bad fingerprint work, two murders, one false arrest. All coincidence? Or Margrave PD incompetence?"

"There was no incompetence."

"Who was dirty, then? Finlay?"

Silence in the room. Bewilderment in Roscoe's eyes.

She said, "Finlay? Dirty?"

Then she burst out laughing. Genuine laughter. She laughed like a kid watching cartoons. Tears rolled down her cheeks. She held her stomach in pain as the laughter kept on coming. She was still laughing when Brent knocked and opened the door.

Was the woman mentally unbalanced?

Kim looked at the clock to mark the time. It was 11:22 a.m. Forty-eight minutes since the GHP arrived at the scene; five to ten minutes to call in the plate, exit the cruiser, get over to the Chevy, and look inside to find the body. Two to five minutes to call and wait for backup. Talk it over before choosing first responders and making the call. Total lapsed time forty-one to forty-six minutes.

Way too long.

Which meant the Chevy was not Roscoe's case.

So why were they calling at all?

The stomach snake already knew.

"Chief?" Brent had looked fresh and clean the day before. Now weary eyes and sallow skin marked him a man who knew he'd screwed up. Maybe he was the one who released Sylvia to the impersonators last night, after all.

Roscoe picked up a tissue and wiped away the tears of laughter from her eyes.

She said, "Yes, Brent, what is it?"

She was still almost giggling. Odd behavior, to say the least.

"We've got a situation," Brent told her, as if another problem was the very last thing he wanted to report. "GHP just notified us. They've found another body."

"Homicide?"

Brent nodded. "Likely. On the interstate, by the cloverleaf at the county road.

"Who is the victim? Do they know?"

Brent squirmed. Squared his shoulders. Lifted his head. Confessed perhaps the second worst possible news in his world at the moment. "It's that lawyer. L. Mark Newton. The one that picked up Sylvia Black last night."

Kim and Gaspar looked at each other. Gaspar raised his eyebrow. *The imposter is dead already?* Followed quickly by, *Why would the boss care about him?*

"Any sign of Sylvia?" Roscoe asked.

"Long gone," Brent said. "Looks like she killed him too. He was shot just like Harry. Two in the back of the head."

CHAPTER TWENTY-ONE

Margrave, Georgia
November 2
11:39 a.m.

ROSCOE LOOKED SHELL-SHOCKED. Kim judged the reaction genuine. Mostly because she wanted it to be.

"Our jurisdiction?" Roscoe asked.

Brent said, "GHP turf. They only called because we'd put our BOLO out there for Newton and they say it's him."

Kim thought Brent seemed upset and relieved in equal measure. Upset, because the guy wouldn't be dead if Sylvia had been properly kept in jail. But what accounted for the relief?

Roscoe asked, "Who's there now?"

"Four GHP cruisers, more on the way. Paramedics just arrived. Coroner's ten minutes out. Guess he had another call. Can't move the body until he's done. I don't know who else. Crime scene will be there, if they're not already. GHP traffic, probably. This time of day, rubber-neckers won't be bad, but somebody will need to handle it." He looked down at the carpet as if he didn't want to deliver the last piece of news. But to his credit, he did, eventually. He said, "Media maybe. Got the first notice over the GHP radio. We're checking the TV news channels."

"Who's GHP on scene? Archie and Jim Leach?" Roscoe asked.

Brent nodded yes.

Swell, Kim thought. Just what she needed. Another encounter with the Leaches.

Roscoe felt differently.

"Good," she said. "Did Archie tell you what's going on?"

"I called him on his cell. The guy is dead. No need to rush, Archie said. They haven't even opened the car yet."

"Anything else?"

Brent looked down at his shoes again. "Not that I know of, Chief. Archie said they have it all under control. He said you can take your time."

"Call him back. Tell him I'll be there as soon as I can. Tell him to wait until we get there to open the car. I'd like to see the body before they move it."

"Will do."

"Tell him I'm about twenty minutes out."

"Ten four."

"Ask him if that's okay. Let me know if it's not."

"Will do."

"Before you make the call, can you cue up the edited video from last night?"

"Already done," he said. "View on camera three."

Roscoe pulled her cell phone off the desk and held it out to him. "And put two or three good stills on here of Newton, Marshal Wright, and Sylvia." He crossed the room and collected the phone and went away to do her bidding.

After the door closed behind him Roscoe turned her computer monitor around. She seemed to change direction and headed there directly. She said, "Take a look at this video. These two guys aren't who they claimed to be; there was no order and nobody sent here from the Marshal service. The short guy is an imposter too. L. Mark Newton died last year. Obituary is posted on the Internet. Give me a positive ID on these two so I can find their asses."

Roscoe pressed a couple of keys.

"What are we looking at?" Kim asked, admitting nothing. She wanted to trust Roscoe, but Gaspar could too easily be right about her. There was more going on here than Kim could fathom. She moved her chair closer to the monitor. Gaspar's viewing angle was already good enough.

Roscoe's demeanor was all business. No hysteria now, if that's what it was before. "We have constant security video inside the station, including last night when Shorty and his sidekick took Sylvia. The whole thing lasted 32 minutes. This edit is the total six minutes of action."

"Any audio to go with it?" Gaspar wanted to know. "I'm pretty good at voice identification, if you've got a reasonable recording."

Roscoe said, "There's full audio, but these guys didn't say much and they were careful not to speak loud enough for the microphones. We've punched the sound, which distorts the quality."

"So they were familiar with the limits of your equipment," Gaspar said.

"That's my guess," Roscoe said.

Kim asked, "Can we get the full video? Maybe our people can apply some forensics you don't have access to."

Roscoe nodded. "We sent it to the FBI Atlanta Field Office early this morning. But I'll have Brent get you a copy when we're done here."

They watched in silence for six minutes, straight through.

Kim saw the date on the tape was November 2.

Initial entry time was 12:01 a.m.

After which: Two men come in. They have a brief chat with the desk sergeant. Not Brent after all. Kim was glad. And she wondered now what he was so worried about since he wasn't at fault.

The fake Marshal hands over a folded paper. The desk sergeant makes a phone call at 12:06 a.m. lasting less than one minute. Another brief chat at the desk. The sergeant makes another phone call at 12:11 a.m. lasting less than one minute. He shakes his head. A briefer chat follows. The sergeant puts the paper on the desk and walks to Sylvia's cell. Sylvia is sitting as she had been in her own kitchen that day, hunched over, head down, forearms resting on her thighs, fingers pressing together rhythmically in sequence.

Sylvia looks up when the sergeant unlocks the cell. She stands, hands in front. He cuffs her, holds her right bicep, and walks her to the front. He presents her to the Marshal, who grabs her left bicep.

Sylvia and the two men walk out through the front door.

Outside, all three get in the Chevy Kim and Gaspar had seen on the interstate median. The one with the dead body in it. The one Roscoe called Shorty, still alive at that point, is driving. The fake Marshal is sitting in the navigator seat. Sylvia is in back.

The car drives out of frame at 12:33 a.m.

Roscoe said, "Recognize them?"

Kim shook her head once. Negative. Like Roscoe, Kim knew only who the guys were not.

"Roll it again," Gaspar said. "We've got questions."

Roscoe pressed replay without taking her focus off the screen.

Kim studied details this time.

Two men stood outside, pressed the call button, waited for the door to unlock, entered the station, and approached the desk. The shorter one was dressed in a dark business suit and tie. He carried a briefcase.

He looked familiar.

The taller one was wearing a U.S. Marshal uniform, complete with hat and equipment belt. Hat shadowed his face; uniform enveloped his body. Nothing visible enough to identify.

Both men wore leather gloves.

It was November.

Costumes.

Meant to convey normalcy and conceal reality. Well done.

The desk sergeant was the other guy Kim had seen with Brent at Sylvia's home yesterday.

"Who is that?" she asked.

"Officer Frank Kraft."

"He's new?"

Roscoe didn't look up. She must have seen the video a hundred times already, but she remained focused. "About a month, I guess."

"Break any rules about buzzing visitors in here at night?" Gaspar asked.

"Federal officers pretty much come and go as they please around here," Roscoe said.

Touchy, like small-town cops everywhere.

The shorter guy was the first to speak. His voice was husky in an abnormal way.

"Sergeant," he said, "I'm L. Mark Newton, attorney for Sylvia Black." He handed Kraft a business card. "This is Marshal Wright."

Kim registered the words. They seemed rehearsed. Had she heard the voice before? A tenor. Midwestern. Maybe.

The second guy also presented a business card to Kraft, but said nothing.

Kraft looked the cards over and placed them on the desk.

"What can I do for you?" Kraft asked. Deep baritone with a lisp.

"We have a federal court order for Sylvia Black," Shorty said. "We're here to collect her."

Marshal Wright reached into his breast pocket and pulled out a tri-folded white paper. No envelope. He handed the paper to Kraft. Kraft opened the paper and read it.

"I didn't know Mrs. Black was being released tonight," Kraft said. Was there any surprise in his tone? "I'll need to check with my Chief."

Shorty said, "There's nothing to check. It's all there in black and white."

The Marshal said, "We have to get her to Chicago by 3:30 a.m. We miss that flight in Atlanta, we'll all be in a world of trouble, you know?"

Kraft nodded. "Sure. I understand. It'll only take a minute." He picked up the phone and placed the first call. At 12:06 a.m.

Gaspar asked Roscoe, "Did he actually call you?"

She said, "What the hell do you think?"

Gaspar said, "I think he tried and didn't get you. Why not?"

"I was involved in something else at the time."

Gaspar didn't press her. Good. There would be a time for that, but not now.

Kraft didn't leave a message. He said, "I'll need to call again."

And the short man got a little nasty at that point, while keeping his voice down. Kim recognized the trick. She'd seen it before. Very effective for confounding voice identification. The end of his sentence was: "If your Chief has any questions, she can call us. Remind her that federal judges can't be challenged on matters of national security."

Kraft nodded, as if the statement was as obvious as wet water. Still, to his credit, he made the second call. Same result.

Gaspar didn't ask Roscoe why she failed to pick up the second time. Nor did Kim mention that Shorty was flat wrong on the law and Kraft should have known better.

On the tape Shorty looked at his watch and spoke again. Insistent words, nastier tone, but still controlled. Definitely rehearsed. He said, "We can take you into custody, too, son. Anybody here with you?"

Kraft said, "No. Just me."

Gaspar actually groaned. Roscoe shot him a withering stare.

Shorty's practiced coercion got heavier. "You don't want to leave your station unattended, do you?"

Now Kraft seemed unsure, and worried.

Shorty changed his tactics to the reasonable approach. "Look, officer, you have our cards and our numbers. You have the order. Your chief can follow up when you reach her. What's the problem?"

Kraft wavered, undecided. Body language conflicted, but leaning toward refusal.

The Marshal broke the deadlock. He stood tall and conveyed a simultaneously threatening and brothers-in-arms posture. "We're on a deadline, officer. We can't wait until your chief gets her shuteye. Shall we take Mrs. Black alone, or do you want to come along? Either way is fine with me."

Kraft spent four more seconds thinking it over before he said, "I guess I'd better stay here."

The Marshal pulled his handcuffs off his equipment belt and held them out. "Do you want me to come with you?"

Kraft said, "I can handle it."

He snagged the cuffs, left the desk, and headed toward Sylvia's cell.

Kim asked, "Any conversation between these two while Kraft is gone on the full recording?"

"None at all," Roscoe replied.

Kraft walked into the cell block. He pressed the release button on the wall and Sylvia's door popped open. She looked up, faced the camera, and flashed her model's smile.

"Time to go, Sylvia," Kraft said. Sylvia stood, smoothed her clothes, patted her hair to be sure it remained in place.

Gaspar asked, "These two know each other?"

Roscoe replied, "Of course."

Kraft said, "I have to put the cuffs on."

Sylvia held her hands out in front, palms together. Kraft put the cuffs on her wrists. They walked together out of her cell.

Sylvia showed no surprise.

And she asked no questions.

"Did you edit any of Sylvia's responses?" Kim asked.

Roscoe met Kim's gaze for the first time since the video began. She said, "No."

"She expected this, then."

"That's how I figure it," Roscoe said.

On the tape Kraft walked Sylvia back to the desk in silence and handed off his prisoner to the Marshal. Sylvia's face lit up. The Marshal's answering expression remained concealed by his hat. He took Sylvia's left arm without comment.

Shorty said, "Again, sergeant, have your chief call us if she has any questions. We'll be out of touch, off and on, until we land at O'Hare. After that, we'll be continuously available."

Kraft was clearly unhappy, but he said, "Okay."

Hat on, head down, the Marshal led Sylvia toward the exit. He pressed on the door with his forearm, but it didn't open.

Shorty, five steps behind, turned back to Kraft and said his last words, "Can you buzz us out?"

Kraft returned to his desk and pressed the lock release.

The Marshal's gloved hand pushed the glass door open. He herded Sylvia through the gap. Shorty followed.

The green Chevy was parked at the curb, engine running. The Marshal opened the sedan's back door. Sylvia looked back at the station and raised her cuffed hands and waved. Then she ducked into the back seat. The Marshal reached into his pocket and pulled something out. He handed it to Sylvia and closed her door. He turned away and got into the Chevy's front passenger seat without showing his face to the station's outdoor cameras.

Taking probably his last steps, too, Shorty walked around the trunk and got into the driver's seat.

The car pulled away from the station at 12:33 a.m.

Kim figured they felt elated at first. Maybe at 12:34 a.m. they were whooping it up inside the Chevy, with a bigger celebration planned for later. When they reached their destination. Which was probably not Atlanta and most certainly not Chicago.

They'd have reached the cloverleaf between ten and fourteen minutes later. Say three minutes to pull the car off to the side of the road, intending to switch to a replacement vehicle. No reason to park there otherwise.

Shoot the short guy in the head, get out of the Chevy, raise the hood, get into the second vehicle, and leave the scene.

Maybe five minutes.

Which put Shorty's time of death between eighteen and twenty-two minutes after the video ended.

Call it 12:51 a.m. to 12:55 a.m.

Almost exactly the time Finlay should have shown up in the JFK Hudson Hotel.

But hadn't.

Which, of course, the boss already knew.

CHAPTER TWENTY-TWO

Margrave, Georgia
November 2
11:54 a.m.

THE RECORDING ENDED for the second time and Roscoe waited for a reaction. She didn't get one. So she stood up and patted her equipment belt to confirm all her stuff was there, then she grabbed her car keys, and she moved toward the door.

At the threshold she turned back to Kim and Gaspar, both still seated.

She asked, "Are you coming?"

Kim looked at Gaspar, felt the fatigue in her bones and saw his exhaustion. She knew what he was thinking. Why go back out there? He'd already seen the body; she'd already seen the car. They could get full reports later. No need to traipse around in the weeds again. What they both needed was sleep. Decent food. Time to figure this thing out. Before they made a mistake they couldn't fix.

All of which would have to wait, Kim realized. She said, "We'll follow in our own car. We'll be there in twenty."

Roscoe said, "No, you'll ride with me. We'll talk on the way."

She left the room before either Kim or Gaspar could protest.

"So, Boss Lady, do we obey?" Gaspar asked. He stood, yawned, stretched. Eased his pain. He wasn't fooling her. His leg, and his side. He'd been sitting too long. He had to be hurting.

"Apparently, there's more than one boss lady here," Kim said. "And you heard her. So move your ass." She put a smile on her face. And in her voice. She was Number One. It was up to her to set the tone. Admitting exhaustion wasn't the way to start. Or defeat. She walked out, following Roscoe, Gaspar behind her for once.

Gaspar said, "I don't suppose we could stop at Eno's Diner on the way? For pancakes and country ham?"

"I'm guessing not."

"In that case, wait up." He ducked into the break room and came back out carrying two donuts.

"For me?" Kim asked, and grabbed one from his hand before he could stop her. "You shouldn't have."

"I didn't," he said.

Roscoe was waiting at her reserved parking space, next to her navy Town Car. She got in and started the engine. Kim took the navigator's position, leaving the back seat for Gaspar. She fastened her seat belt and used her right hand to hold the shoulder harness away from her neck.

Roscoe drove with the precise assurance of a woman who knew every chink in the local asphalt. She used her bubble light, but no siren. Other vehicles moved respectfully aside and she left them in her wake. She covered half the distance without speaking. Kim waited. Gaspar waited, too, for once.

Then seven miles from the cloverleaf, Roscoe asked, "What time did you find the body?"

Kim said nothing.

Gaspar said, "What?"

"No more games," Roscoe said. Her tone was level and determined. She lifted off the accelerator and the big car slowed. "You must take me for a complete moron."

"I wish you were a moron," Kim said. "You'd be easier to handle."

Roscoe glanced at Gaspar in the rear view mirror. "We all know Harry Black wasn't shot two hours before Sylvia called 911. Plenty of time for you to clean up that crime scene too. Good job, by the way. We didn't find much."

Gaspar said, "You're on the wrong track, chief. We don't know anything about Harry Black. We saw his body for the first time when you did." He raised his right hand, palm out, first two fingers up, last two held down by his thumb. "Scout's honor."

"Oh, please," Roscoe said. "You wouldn't know a boy scout if he ran up and bit you on the leg."

"Wrong," Gaspar said. "I *was* a boy scout. An Eagle Scout, to be exact. Matter of public record. Check it out if you don't believe me."

Roscoe slowed the car to a crawl and then stopped on the shoulder of the county road. Miles of emptiness stretched in all directions. She put the transmission in park, unbuckled her shoulder harness, and turned toward her captured prey.

What is she up to?

Gaspar yawned, stretched, lay down on the cushy bench and closed his eyes. "Wake me up when we get there."

Within seconds he was breathing evenly and his face was relaxed. Kim thought he'd actually fallen asleep. Maybe he was fresh out of amphetamines. Maybe they were what he kept pulling out of his pocket and sticking in his mouth when he thought she wouldn't notice.

"Now what?" Kim asked Roscoe. "Are we going to the crime scene, or did you have something else in mind?"

Roscoe said, "We'll continue on our way as soon as you tell me what you know."

Kim shrugged. Tried a new tactic. "Okay, I'll play along, Beverly. I'm guessing Jack Reacher killed Harry Black and cleaned up the mess, and the tall guy impersonating the U.S. Marshal on your videotape was Jack Reacher too. We already called it in. It won't help you to shoot us."

Roscoe's mouth fell open. Kind of comical really, Kim thought. She watched until Roscoe realized where her jawbone was and clamped her mouth shut, holding her lips in a stiff line.

Kim poked her again. "Oh, come on. It's got to be him. That's what Reacher does, right? Rescues damsels in distress? Sleeps with them? Saves their lives?"

A red flush crept up Roscoe's neck and over her face. "So that's the way it's going to be?" Then her cell phone rang. She answered and listened and said, "Can he wait ten minutes? I can be there in five, and I need five to look. Tell him I appreciate it."

She ended the call and buckled up again and pulled the heavy slow Town Car onto the road.

"Don't think we're finished with this conversation, Agent Otto," she said. She put the bubble light on top of the car this time and turned on the siren before she hit the gas. The big Lincoln accelerated faster than Kim expected. Gaspar didn't sit up. Maybe he really had fallen asleep, as unlikely as that seemed. The ride was smooth and quiet. Even at high speeds it felt like they were gliding over the bumpy old road wearing ear muffs.

Roscoe said, "They've got to move the body. Crowd control is becoming a problem. They've closed the interstate both ways and there's four miles of traffic already. Two fender benders so far and more to come if they don't get unsnarled before rush hour. Coroner's arrived and he's got another case after this one." Roscoe covered the remaining miles to the cloverleaf in less than four minutes and then slowed half a mile out. She didn't know the Chevy's precise location. Kim could have helped with that, but she didn't. Fifteen hundred feet from the east side of the cloverleaf, Roscoe slowed to a crawl, searching for the best place to park amid the official vehicles already present.

A rainbow of pulsing hazard lights was flashing in uncoordinated rhythms. Interstate traffic was backed up as far as Kim could see in both directions. GHP cruisers were blocking entrances and exits at each point of the cloverleaf. Officers were directing vehicles to move along instead of gawking, but drivers weren't complying.

Kim counted two fire department vehicles, a truck and a paramedic bus, three GHP vans with "Crime Scene Technicians" stenciled on their sides, two tow trucks, and an unmarked black sedan which must have belonged to the coroner. Three Crime Scene techs were working on the car. They had the trunk open, and they had cameras and markers and other equipment running. Then two techs left and walked back to their van while the third waited to document the body's removal. Most of the remaining work would be done when they examined the car later.

Uniformed first responders stood near their vehicles waiting their turn to work. No one seemed to mind the delay. It was a nice fall day. Warm enough. Slight breeze. No urgency.

Two news helicopters circled wide above the chaos. Three news satellite vans parked on the opposite side of the road. Two sets of photojournalists and stand-up reporters were taping live shots.

"What a circus," Roscoe said, quietly.

Kim saw three men, two wearing GHP uniforms and the third in a dark suit, approaching the Chevy. One Leach brother stood five feet southwest of the car; legs braced wide apart, arms folded, holding his shotgun precisely as he'd pointed it at her yesterday. He noticed the men, too, and walked to meet them.

Roscoe found a strip of grassy land off the shoulder a short hike from the focal point. She said, "I could get closer, but we'd get blocked in. If we park here, we can leave when we're ready."

The three men met up with the Leach brother and all four stopped next to the Chevy, exactly where Gaspar had collected the hound dog earlier.

Roscoe settled her Town Car into the place she'd selected.

Leach lowered his shotgun and extended his arm toward the Chevy's door handle.

Roscoe reached toward her keys.

Leach opened the Chevy's door exactly as Roscoe clicked off the ignition.

The click triggered Kim's reptilian brain and the training memories embedded there.

Instantly, she saw, heard and understood.

"Get down!" she screamed.

And the Chevy exploded.

CHAPTER TWENTY-THREE

THE HIGH-PRESSURE BLAST wave hurled the Leach brother and the coroner and the two GHP officers across the weedy grass like boneless scarecrows, dead before they hit the ground, and then a monstrous orange fireball filled the sky. White flames swallowed the Chevy in a blinding hot flash. Black smoke plumed up, then out, erasing normal daylight.

Kim closed her eyes, covered her ears and ducked her head. Smaller shock waves bounced Roscoe's Town Car on the grassy shoulder and squeezed Kim's breath from her chest. Pain seared as if her lungs had collapsed.

Muffled sound far away.

Kim squeezed her eyes tighter and curled as far into the foot-well as the shoulder harness would let her. Her chest hurt. She gulped shallow breaths.

Another explosion, smaller, followed quickly by a third.

Unnatural silence.

Kim waited, struggled to breathe, finally felt her lungs working again. She gulped air, hungry for it.

How much time had passed?

She opened her eyes again. Saw Roscoe still belted in her seat, conscious. Okay. Kim struggled upright in her own seat. Took her hands off her ears.

There were fires outside the Town Car. There were muffled noises. There were pieces, chunks, slabs of things scattered everywhere. There were burning vehicles. There was smoke too thick to see through.

The Chevy was still burning.

Kim's brain was processing data like slow-falling dominoes, one thing leading to the next. Both tow trucks were covered in flames. Tow trucks usually carried extra gasoline. Hence the second and third explosions? Two GHP cruisers also burning. One rested on its roof, the other in the ditch, lying on its side. Thrown there by the initial pressure wave?

Several uniformed personnel were down, injured, but likely alive. Gawkers might be hurt, too, inside vehicles closer to the Chevy than Roscoe's Town Car.

On-site rescue workers mobbed the scene. Firefighters rushed to put out the flames. Helicopter blades fought to disperse the blackness. The noise must have been outrageous, but everything remained muted by the Town Car's body and the cotton that filled Kim's head.

Behind the wheel, Roscoe seemed dazed, too, but conscious and not bleeding.

"Gaspar?" Kim asked. But how loud was her voice? She couldn't tell. And she heard no answer. "Gaspar?" she called, louder. No response.

She unhooked her seatbelt. She took stock of her body, which seemed to be unhurt and functioning. She turned in her seat but couldn't see him over the high seatback.

"Gaspar?" she said again. She raised up as far as she could without kneeling, craned her neck and looked down into the deep foot well.

She saw him, face down, prone.

She remembered he'd been lying on the bench seat, not wearing his seatbelt. Had he been thrown to the floor when the car bounced? Was he hurt?

Kim scrambled out of the sedan and pulled open the back door. "Are you okay?" she screamed, reaching in to him.

He didn't scream back. Instead, he nodded, lifted himself onto his hands and knees, and crawled backward out of the floor well onto the grassy red ground. He leaned against the door to steady himself upright. Kim thought he looked unharmed. But percussion injuries could manifest hours or days later, hard to detect and potentially devastating. They patted themselves down, checked for broken bones, or blood. Found none.

Kim and Gaspar moved away from the vehicle. Roscoe stared forward, pale, rigid, horrified. Kim understood. The dead, the injured, were Roscoe's friends and colleagues. She could have been among them. All three of them could have been standing at the Chevy when it exploded, had Roscoe not stopped back there on the county road.

And then the shaking started. Kim felt it, but was powerless to stop it.

Gaspar wrapped his arms around her, holding her close to his body.

"What is it? Are you hurt?" he yelled, patting her down, looking for anything, everything.

Kim shook her head and mouthed without sound, "No, I'm fine."

Then she thought: *Gaspar might have opened the Chevy's door this morning when he first found the body.* And her shaking intensified. Her teeth chattered. She couldn't stop.

But she had to stop.

She had to help those people. She knew combat first aid. They all did. She was fine. She wasn't hurt. She had to go help.

She pushed Gaspar away and walked three steps on spaghetti legs toward the carnage. Gaspar grabbed her arm, pulled her around to face him.

"They've got enough help," he said. "There's more coming. Better that we stay out of the way."

Kim heard him as if he was at the end of a very long tunnel. She looked ahead at the scene. Medical personnel, first responders, firefighters, sirens, helicopters. She shook Gaspar's hand away, put one foot in front of the other, determination as wobbly as her steps, but she kept on going. Her next thought was foolish nonsense. She said, "No way to keep the media away now, Roscoe. No way in hell."

She smiled. How silly was that? She giggled. She covered her mouth with her hand, pressed hard until only stifled silence remained.

Hysteria was the last thing anyone needed.

CHAPTER TWENTY-FOUR

KIM FELT GASPAR'S hand on her shoulder again after she'd walked only twenty feet. She glanced at him, noticed his limping, and slowed her pace. Maybe he was hurt after all? Roscoe had stayed behind. She'd moved the Town Car and parked it across the county road, bubble light flashing. Kim saw her talking on the cell, probably calling Brent for roadblocks. Preventing more chaos was a good plan.

Gaspar put weight in his grip on her shoulder. She turned her head toward him. He leaned closer, squeezed her shoulder tighter, stopped their forward momentum. He tapped his watch and spoke slowly to make her understand words she was unable to hear.

"We can't stay too long," he said. "We need to get out before our presence is recorded or questioned. Keep your head down. Talk to no one."

She nodded agreement. He squeezed her shoulder once more before they moved deeper into scenes resembling a war zone. Roscoe jogged over and met them at the outer perimeter of the most serious damage.

The November air was now blackened with sooty pollution. Kim tasted the stench; smoke burned her eyes. Explosion debris blocked all normal paths. Hot spots glowed in weed patches, threatening to reignite. Noise levels continued to rise around her as vehicles and personnel overwhelmed.

"Holy Christ," Gaspar said, crossing himself in the traditional Catholic way when they saw the Leach brother's charred corpse pass by on a stretcher. He reached into his breast pocket, pulled out a linen handkerchief and handed it to Kim. "Here. Cover your nose and mouth. You don't want to breathe this stuff any more than you have to. It's toxic."

He bent his left arm at the elbow and covered his own face with his sleeved forearm. Roscoe did the same.

"Let's split up," Kim said, through the fine linen filter. Was she whispering or shouting? She raised her voice anyway, just in case. "Meet back here or call me. Okay?"

He nodded through the crook of his elbow and peeled off to the southwest. Roscoe melted into the crowd of responders.

Kim moved north, making slow progress toward the smoldering Chevy. Along her route she helped where she could until the last of the victims was hustled into rescue vehicles. Then finally she reached the center of combustion. For a good long time, she stood away from the knot of investigators and simply stared at the debris.

Kim had recognized the blast for what it was: a VIED. A Vehicle Improvised Explosive Device. The idiot's weapon. She had learned in specialized FBI training that car bombs were easy to build and always effective and indiscriminately murderous. A nearly perfect disaster machine. No prior experience required.

Except everything she'd observed had confirmed that the Chevy bomber was an expert. He had demonstrated abilities idiots do not possess.

Kim pulled out her smart phone, running video and clicking stills as she surveyed the scene. A circle of burned grass surrounded the Chevy's blackened chassis. The vehicle and all forensic evidence it might have contained were obliterated. Perhaps charred fragments of the dead man would eventually be located here and there, but probably not.

Before the blast, when Roscoe was parking the Town Car, Kim had seen the trunk lid open while crime scene techs calmly processed the trunk's interior. Meaning there had been no explosives in the trunk. The Chevy hadn't been packed with low-grade explosives, as idiots' car bombs often are. Something more powerful in smaller quantities had been used.

Judging from the explosion's properties and the significant amount of damage, Kim figured the bomb was most likely PETN. An odorless, powerful military grade plastic explosive, PETN had become the first choice of serious terrorists. It was stable and it produced maximum damage employing a minimum amount of product. Quite effective.

The difficulty should have been obtaining access to PETN. In theory, unauthorized personnel couldn't acquire it. But laws are for the law-abiding and where there's a will, there's a way. Supplies were not as well controlled as Homeland Security would have the populace believe. Kim's team back in the Detroit field office collected PETN from radicals too often.

The Chevy's placement had been exact. Not only did the vehicle explode, the blast took out two flanking GHP cruisers. Tow trucks parked in front of the Chevy provided the secondary explosions. Five vehicles destroyed with one bomb. Either the Chevy bomber knew precise details of local procedures or he'd been blessed with dumb luck.

Kim didn't believe in luck.

She decided the bomb had been carefully designed to damage or destroy interstate travel north and south for miles. Which meant the bomb's designer was not only knowledgeable about local traffic patterns, but also ruthless. He was willing to kill cops, roadside crews, and innocent travelers as well. Kim shuddered, noticed, and forced herself to stop before the shudder escalated to violent shaking again.

Engrossed in her assessment and her self-control efforts, she didn't immediately notice the phantom cell phone's vibrations in her pocket.

CHAPTER TWENTY-FIVE

HOW LONG HAD the phone been ringing? Hard to say. She fished it out, opened it, and it nipped her thumb again. She juggled the two phones long enough to remove the cracked plastic's hold on her skin, then she lifted it to her left ear. She snapped photos as she talked. Two more black vans had arrived.

"Agent Otto," she said, into what sounded like silence. Maybe a satellite delay, or maybe her hearing was more impaired than she thought.

"Damage report?" her boss asked. Was there concern in his tone? Perhaps he was relieved to hear her voice. In which case, he should have said so. What would he have done if someone else had answered because she'd died in the blast? Dumb question. If she'd died, no one would have answered. The phone would have died too. Its vibrating insistence would have been permanently stilled. And the phantom cell was untraceable, dead or alive. If someone found its parts eventually, it would have made no difference; the boss would never have been officially involved. She was under the radar. She could be dead now. Did he care?

"Agent Otto?" he asked again, louder. More insistent this time. "What is your status?"

"No physical damage," Kim said, answering the question he should have asked.

"And Gaspar?"

"Gaspar's fine too. Thanks for asking." Cheeky response. Too defensive. Maybe she was just tired. Or still a little hysterical.

"No damage at all?" She thought he sounded relieved. So he had known. About the bomb. When he ordered them away from the Chevy this morning.

"Not to us," Kim said.

"That's good," he said, as if he actually believed it.

Uniformed teams approached from vehicles parked on all sides of the disaster site. She had to move. She put her personal phone back in her pocket and walked away from the Chevy, still holding the phantom cell to her ear.

"What else is going on out there?" he asked.

"It's difficult to hear you, sir. The noise is overwhelming. Fire's controlled. Injured transported. Casualties processing. Local professionals doing their jobs. Federals moving in on schedule. Atlanta FBI either here on the way, most likely." She added the last sentence to make him sweat.

"How long before you can get out of there and finish your assignment?"

Finally, he gets to the point. With something like curiosity, she observed her detachment morph to anger. A normal reaction? Odd in context, she realized. She asked, "Which assignment is that, sir? The Reacher file? Or the Sylvia Black case?"

"Both," he said, but the admission cost him.

She smiled to herself. "Tomorrow," she said. "Maybe longer." *Oh, what the hell,* she thought, before plowing ahead. "We could use some help."

"What kind of help?"

"We need background. Access to FBI databases, at least. Someone inside to get information to us as we need it. For now, send me Sylvia

Black's tax returns, both before and after she married Harry. Include all the attachments too."

"I'll see what I can do." He paused, but he didn't promise. "When will you have a report for me?"

Flash point. Her simmering hurt triggered like another VIED. She felt the familiar millisecond sequence in her head: click, blast wave, percussion, shrapnel, massive fire, billowing black smoke, unbreathable air.

Darkness.

She pulled the phone away from her ear. Snapped it closed. It bit the skin it had damaged twice before. She held the beast away from her body. She squeezed hard to release its grip. The crack separated, pinched and pierced her skin, refused to release her. Blood trickled across the phone's surface and down her wrist.

She threw the damn thing down and crushed it with the heel of her FBI regulation footwear. She left its pieces on the hard ground and walked away.

She was through the barrier, to where she stopped worrying and did what needed doing. She had been there before. She welcomed the feeling, slipped into it like an old leather jacket.

Gaspar was waiting for her twenty yards ahead. Behind him were the four old burned-out warehouses that Reacher had somehow wrought.

Death begets death.

More was coming.

She picked up her pace.

CHAPTER TWENTY-SIX

Margrave, Georgia
November 2
1:40 p.m.

GASPAR MATCHED KIM'S pace stride for stride. He said, "Eyes and ears everywhere. We've got to go."

Chemical smoke poisoned the air, burning their eyes. Whapping helicopter blades raised the decibel level to painful proportions. News media swarmed, multiplied like wasps. Ambulances, fire rescue, law enforcement, and tow trucks rushed inbound and outbound from all directions. Arriving vehicles slammed to quick stops, sirens wailing, flashing lights bouncing off every solid object, occupants dashing through the chaos. The gathering crowd of civilians provided more cover and confusion.

Kim and Gaspar walked away unnoticed, down the ramp, along the county road's shoulder, farther and farther from the Chevy's blackened husk. He breathed hard, but he didn't slow. Nor did she. They made it to Roscoe's car. Gaspar pressed the key fob, released the door locks. He went one way and she went the other, peeling apart like wide receivers, and they yanked door handles and slid into the front seats.

Gaspar started the engine, three-point turned, flipped on the bubble light. Kim pulled the power connector to the dash-cam mounted near the windshield. Front audio-video disconnected, but this was a wired state-of-the-art law enforcement vehicle recording every moment. Other devices might still be powered. No termination switch on the instrument panels.

Only one choice. For now. Least said was soonest mended. She put her finger to her lips. Gaspar nodded agreement. He drove south in silence. She held out her hand, palm up.

Gaspar shrugged and fished out the boss's phantom cell.

She disabled the GPS before shutting it down. She repeated the process on both their personal smart phones. They'd have maybe five to ten minutes of extra breathing room if they needed it. No more.

Plausible deniability was always good.

She saw the sign for the washboard dirt ribbon: Black Road.

She pointed.

Turn here.

Gaspar turned. Rain had tamped down the dust since Monday. They saw the pulverized mailbox that marked the driveway entrance.

Gaspar ignored the house and parked next to the car shack, nose out, for a quick exit.

Gaspar opened Roscoe's glove box and rooted around. He found four packs of peanuts. The console storage compartment yielded chocolate peanut butter cups. He tossed a half share to Kim and dropped his own share in his pockets. They moved away together and stood under pecan tree canopies in the weedy side yard.

Gaspar poured half a peanut pack into his mouth. Kim ate slowly from her palm. She said, "I want a closer look at that mailbox. Something not right about it."

Gaspar limped and she walked along the rutted two-track driveway. The quiet of the November country afternoon was punctuated only by nearby bugs and distant crows and scraping soles on gravel. Sunshine warmed the chill.

Gaspar said, "Five minutes on foot to reach the destroyed mailbox."

"Less if you're mad and chasing vandals."

He asked, "Why are we here?"

"I want a private look at things. Hands on."

He said, "It worries me that I'm beginning to understand you."

"How's that?"

"You talked to the boss, didn't you? We're working the Black homicide now, and Reacher's involved. We need to find Sylvia. I can see it in your twitches."

"Sylvia confessed to killing Harry, but the confession's hinky. At least as to chronology. Roscoe knows that. And where's the motive? Not spouse abuse, for sure. No evidence of any kind to support that."

Gaspar reached into his pocket and pulled out a fragment of scorched paper. "I found this in the grass not far from the Chevy. There were pieces all over the place."

"No shit, Sherlock," Kim said. She showed him identical burnt fragments from her own pocket. "They were hundred dollar bills."

Gaspar examined them. "Ragged edges, fibers, rough texture. The real deal. But they're old. Ben's face is bigger on new ones."

"Reacher blew up a Chevy full of cash? Doesn't make much sense."

They stopped at the end of the driveway, under a stand of trees all choked by kudzu, and looked at the battered mailbox. Kim swiped her palms together to dust off the peanut salt, and hooked her thumbs in her back pockets. She said, "What's bugging me about this mailbox is the repeated pounding. Had to make a hell of a racket in all this quiet."

"Who's gonna complain? The locusts?"

"Destroying the box is a felony and Harry's a cop, right? Slugger knows he'll get prison time and big money fines if Harry catches him, so he makes sure Harry's not home somehow. Doesn't make sense."

"Why not?"

"Takes planning. Slugger's going to a lot of trouble to piss Harry off and all he does is beat the mailbox. Why not burn the house down or at least trash the place?"

"What if they were cooking or dealing at the house, which is how they get a Chevy-full of hundred dollar bills? Slugger was a meth-head?"

"Crazy junky beats mailbox to hell?" Kim shook her head.

"Don't like it?"

"Why didn't Harry replace the box?"

"God, I'd hate to live inside your head, *Cosette*. Does everything bounce around in there like that?"

"Pretty much, la Mancha. It's a curse." She shrugged, mocking his favorite physical response.

"So what's your best guess?"

"I think Sylvia destroyed the box and Harry didn't care."

"Why?"

"I don't know."

He shrugged. "I'm not sure it matters. Why do we care about their mail? They didn't."

Kim said, "Exactly. They cared enough at one time to have the mailbox, though. So what changed? Their connection to the postal service was destroyed and neither Harry nor Sylvia fixed it for months, judging by the rust in those cracks. How do they get their mail?"

"Several options, I guess. P.O. Box. Forward to Harry's office. Whatever."

"Neither rain nor sleet nor gloom of night stays mail couriers from the swift completion of their appointed rounds."

He raised his eyebrow. "You were a mail carrier? You memorized the creed?"

"The postal service doesn't have a creed," she said, smiling for the first time since the Chevy exploded. "That was in a Kevin Costner movie. Man, you Chicanos are slow."

Gaspar laughed out loud and the sound made her feel normal. Almost.

She said, "How about this? The mail is delivered come rain or come shine, but only if there's a place to leave it. And people aren't *required* to provide a box or accept delivery."

He finished the thought. "So what mail was Sylvia avoiding? Maxed out credit card bills for her high-ticket fashion habit? Wouldn't be the first woman to spend her husband into bankruptcy. Might explain why she killed him, too, if he found out."

"Find the mail, find the answer."

"And how do we do that, Mrs. Einstein?"

She heard helicopters in the distance, pressing her. "We've got to get moving, Cheech." She'd taken a couple of steps along the driveway before she realized he wasn't following. He'd stepped closer to the box, balanced on a mossy limestone rock, and was peering down into the muck. He said, "I keep telling you, Cheech is Mexican, not Cuban. God, you Germans are dumb."

"We have to go," she said. She tapped his arm. And regretted it immediately. The moss on the rock and his bad leg and his poor balance all came together and he slipped into the weedy ditch, on his butt, legs flailing, arms in the air.

"Oh, man," he said, as the water soaked his trousers.

He looked embarrassed.

She shook her head in mock despair. "You're hopeless, you know that? Quit screwing around down there. Hubba hubba. We've got to go."

He reached up. "Help me out of here."

Kim secured her footing. Saw a fat stick floating toward him over the tops of murky ripples. Driftwood, maybe.

Not driftwood.

Gaspar reached up, ready to grasp her wrist.

Kim pulled her Sig and aimed an inch from Gaspar's heel.

He covered his ears a split second too late.

She fired once. A sound like thunder. Then again. And again, to be certain.

He jerked his right foot back and sat up straight and crossed himself rapidly.

He said, "Jesus, Mary and Joseph, are you out of your mind?"

The rattlesnake's bloody head dangled from a still-wriggling body as big around as Gaspar's ankle. Precisely three inches from where his right foot had been.

"Pray later," she said. "That guy's got friends and family nearby. We have to go."

CHAPTER TWENTY-SEVEN

Margrave, Georgia
November 2
2:15 p.m.

HARRY BLACK'S HOUSE was practically empty. Nothing that could be vacuumed, picked up or bagged remained. The mattress was gone and the linens were gone.

Harry Black's body was gone.

But his blood was still there. It had oxidized to rusty clumps on the wall pine. Dresser drawers were open and empty. Limp curtains were gone from the frosted jalousie window. The miniscule bathroom and the bedroom closet had been stripped of their meager contents.

There were seven new additions.

Seven perfect round holes, each three inches in diameter, had been made in the pine paneling by a hole cutter saw to collect intact the seven bullets lodged there; two behind the bed and five underneath.

Kim paced the room, as if brisk movement guaranteed fast solutions. "Let's see if we can figure out what was going on here and get the hell out while we still can, okay? You thought they might be cooking or dealing. Talk to me about that."

Gaspar said, "It's not a great theory. I was probably wrong. Bad as it was, this place was way too clean for a meth lab. And meth labs burn down. Average life expectancy is about a month."

"Agreed," Kim said. "Better idea?"

He shrugged, said nothing, leaned back, and watched.

Kim reached the room's corner, turned, and paced the next wall. "Somebody killed Harry Black. We know that. Was it Sylvia?"

He nodded from his fixed position. "She admitted she shot him. I can see it. Pop a guy in the head twice while he's sleeping. Not too risky. But cold. Sylvia was as calm as any killer I've ever seen." His gaze sought comment; she nodded agreement. "I figure Reacher did the other five post-mortem to cover-up, make it look more like passion."

"Possible." She reached the opposite corner, and turned, and increased her speed. "The boss knows Harry's dead, probably knows how and why. He dispatches us on a pretext? Reacher's an excuse?"

Gaspar shrugged. "He knows Reacher's here and involved. Wants to know what's going on without revealing himself."

Perhaps. "He knew we'd get here before Sylvia called in the homicide. How?"

He lifted his eyebrow, stuffed his hands in his pockets. "Too complicated."

"We confront Roscoe about Reacher and she's relieved to know he's alive. Means she hasn't seen him. She's astonished when she receives the homicide call. So she's not part of killing Harry." She reached the next corner and turned to face him across the long diagonal divide. "Do you agree?"

"Maybe," he said.

Kim said, "Sylvia, as you described it, was too hot for Harry and too hot for this place and had been for years. So why kill him now?"

"Beats me."

"You're really not helping, you know that?" She stopped pacing, and then started again. Gaspar approached the three TV tables, examined the recliners positioned at optimum viewing distance, stuffed his hand between the cushions, scanned the rough walls and barren floors.

"What are you doing?" she asked.

"I'm thinking maybe hardcore porn. Big potential with a star as hot as Sylvia. Maybe the big screen was for checking the product. Do you see the TV remote?"

"Nothing here. I'll check the bedroom." She returned almost instantly. "No."

There were loud helicopters in the air, coming and going from the cloverleaf. There were sirens in the distance. How much time did they have? She said, "Maybe forensics took the remote. They took everything else that wasn't nailed down."

Gaspar moved to the TV, felt around its edges. "No buttons." He looked behind it. "Articulating wall mount." He grasped the screen's edges, and pulled it away from the pine paneling. A scissors-like mounting device allowed the entire television to extend three inches. He said, "Harry's building skills sucked. Total hack job back here."

After a minor struggle he disconnected the cables. He peered inside the hole in the wall. "Too dark to see anything."

"Where's the video source?" Kim asked.

"There isn't one."

Kim glanced at her watch. Forty-five minutes already gone and nothing accomplished but a dead snake.

"I'm working as fast as I can," Gaspar said.

"Work faster."

He examined the wall all the way from the front of the house to the bedroom. He checked the bathroom and the closet. He tapped the paneling every six inches.

"Okay," he said.

"Okay what?"

"This wall is too wide."

"Is it?"

"Internal walls are normally four to five inches, depending on the width of the paneling on the studs. This one's at least twenty-four, maybe thirty." He tapped the rough pine paneling here and there with his knuckles. "False wall. Runs the entire length of the living room. Maybe twenty-six feet, give or take."

Kim said, "And I've used roomier port-a-johns than that bathroom."

Gaspar nodded. "The hidden space runs through the bathroom too. And the closet." He stepped inside the tiny space. He tapped the walls with his knuckles and knocked with the flat of his hands. "It's hollow back here. But there's no access. No hinges or sliding doors. Not even a finger hole."

Kim squeezed in beside him. Looked at the single shelf. It ran straight across the meager width of the space, maybe twenty-four inches below the ceiling. It was maybe fifteen inches deep. It was anchored to the back wall. There was a sturdy clothes bar solidly attached to its underside. The entire closet was constructed the same as the rest of the home's interior. Pine paneling, uneven boards, unfinished gaps, poorly made joints between floor, ceiling, and walls.

She said, "I know this sounds dumb, but what if we yank the whole back wall of the closet out? Maybe by hauling on the bar?"

Gaspar looked at the ragged joints which should have been closed seams. "Be damned heavy. No way Sylvia could have done it alone." He shrugged. "Worth trying, I guess."

Kim stepped out of the way. Gaspar grabbed the bar with both hands. When he pulled, the back wall flexed. He grunted and pulled twice more before the paneling came away. He tilted the assembly to free it. He breathed hard and heaved the solid pine to one side.

There was a dark expanse behind the wide opening.

Kim felt for a light switch and didn't find one. She pulled her phone out of her pocket, turned it on, and used its flashlight application to navigate the darkness.

About four feet ahead, a single bulb hung from a white, flat cord fixed to the ceiling. Two more bulbs hung at intervals deeper in the darkness. She approached, pulled each string, and turned the lights on.

She sneezed.

Behind her Gaspar said, "It would have been nice to find something more than dust."

"We have," Kim said. "There's more here than dust."

CHAPTER TWENTY-EIGHT

THE CEILING HEIGHT in the secret space was the same as in the rest of the house, a standard eight feet. The width was narrow. The TV cables were stapled to the wall. Connectors hung free of whatever electronic devices had once fed the screen. A closet organizer held empty garment bags, padded hangers, and transparent boxes perfectly sized for Sylvia's shoes. Hermès luggage had left dust-free squares on the floorboards.

There were four identical freestanding shelf units. Each was maybe five feet wide and six feet high and twelve inches deep. Each had six shelves set a foot apart, and provided seven stacking places, including the floor. On each flat plane rested two rows of six cardboard shoe boxes. Eighty-four boxes on each unit.

Two empty spaces must have held the two empty boxes she'd seen the day before.

Kim counted twice to be certain before she slipped a pair of latex gloves out of her pocket, pulled them on, and lifted a few random lids. Dust clouded up her nostrils; she sneezed again. After ten tests, she simply lifted each stack from the bottom to confirm its emptiness, while Gaspar sneezed through the same process from the opposite end.

When they'd finished, Gaspar stepped back into the bedroom, stripped off his gloves and swiped the perspiration from his brow; red grime filled the crevices.

He said, "There's only one thing Harry would have stored in those boxes."

"That much cash from porn?"

Gaspar shrugged. "Twisted. Kids, maybe. Or animals. We're in the countryside here. Regardless, we've got a solid motive that'll nail Reacher."

Kim blinked. *Reacher?* She asked, "You're saying Joe and Jack Reacher were involved in some money-making scheme together fifteen years ago? Joe's dead but Jack carried on anyway with Harry and Sylvia?"

"Works for me," Gaspar said. "Or Joe was legit back then so Jack killed him to avoid arrest. That works for me too."

Kim said, "So Reacher waits fifteen years? Comes back to collect his cash, and kills Harry, cleans up, and gets away, leaving Sylvia to take the heat. That's how you figure it?"

"Something like that," Gaspar said. "No legitimate way for Harry to accumulate that much money. You don't have to act like I'm stupid. It fits as well as anything you've come up with."

They both heard the unmistakable sound of helicopter blades headed their way. Kim figured maybe five minutes to touchdown. She pulled out her smart phone.

"What are you doing?" Gaspar asked.

"Covering our butts," she said. She started the video and started dictating. "Tuesday, November 3, two thirty-five p.m. Harry and Sylvia Black's home. Bedroom. FBI Special Agents Carlos Gaspar and Kim Otto entered the house through unlocked doors seeking evidence in support of a homicide and suspected terrorism investigation begun yesterday. Upon closer examination of the bedroom closet, we located the hidden storage compartment depicted here, containing

336 empty cardboard shoe boxes and a space sufficient to hold the two boxes collected from the crime scene previously by local officers."

She paused and changed her shot. "Also present are eight empty garment bags containing sixteen satin padded hangers, and twelve empty plastic shoe boxes, all believed to have contained Sylvia Black's fashion wardrobe."

She taped the entire row of shelving units and opened several of the cardboard shoe boxes to reveal their empty interiors. "Based on remains observed and samples collected at the scene of a related car bomb incident this morning, it appears these boxes contained U.S. currency. In particular, one-hundred-dollar bills more than a decade old. Calculations based on standard FBI protocols for cash volume suggest each box held approximately $200,000. If so, more than $67,200,000 was hidden here." She ended the video recording and took several still shots of the boxes.

Gaspar asked her, "Why didn't you say something about Reacher?"

"We're still under the radar on that. And besides, as we lawyers say, there's no evidence to support your wild ass guesses."

"You know I'm right though," he said.

"What I can prove is the important thing, Zorro. You want to stick your neck in that trap, go right ahead. I'm waiting to see those bright blue eyes before I say Reacher is responsible." She turned off her phone again. She ducked into the closet and collected one of Sylvia's transparent shoe boxes, and one lid.

"Prints," she said.

He nodded.

They snugged the panel back into place.

"We need to call the boss," Gaspar said.

The choppers were right on top of the house now.

Kim said, "No time."

CHAPTER TWENTY-NINE

Margrave, Georgia
November 2
2:50 p.m.

THE GHP AVIATION Unit UH-1H Huey settled on Harry Black's front lawn in a storm of noise. The ground was too wet for dust, but pine trees bent and waved. Uniformed personnel ran doubled over through the downdraft and fanned around the house. All local. No federal agents yet.

Roscoe and two others were the last to come through from the whipping wind. Then the Huey lifted off again. One of Roscoe's companions was the surviving Leach brother. He looked all wrung out. His hands were sooty. His face was lined by smoke and sweat and horror. He had big patches of dried blood on his filthy uniform.

His brother's blood.

Roscoe nodded the introductions. "FBI Special Agents Otto and Gaspar, GHP Officers Archie Leach and Sam Friesen."

Archie Leach stared holes in Gaspar's chest. Kim felt the showdown simmering. She understood a brother's need for vengeance. She didn't know why he directed that need toward them. She planned to steer clear of Archie Leach. She figured Gaspar should do the same.

Kim said, "We picked up charred scraps of hundred dollar bills at the site of the explosion. We figured they were in the car and might have come from here."

Roscoe nodded.

"Kliners," she said.

"What are they?" Gaspar asked.

"It's what we call them."

"Call what?"

Archie Leach said, "Stop screwing around, G-man. You know what we mean. Counterfeit hundreds. From the old Kliner operation. Find any here or not?"

Kim blinked.

Harry's stash wasn't porn money.

It was counterfeit money.

Made sense.

As if he had known all along, Gaspar said, "We found the storage spot, but no Benjamins, which is what they call them where I come from. This way."

They followed him to the bedroom. He pointed, then stood aside. Leach and Friesen yanked out the back of the closet revealing the black hole. Leach pulled his flashlight. He twisted sideways to get his bulk through the narrow entrance. He pulled the light cords as he went.

Roscoe stared as if he had exposed the lost city of Atlantis.

At the far end Leach turned back to face them, shaking his head slowly, like he couldn't believe it. His buddy Friesen whistled, long and low. He said, "Could Harry Black have kept this place full of Kliners? All these years?"

Kim thought they were genuinely surprised. She glanced at Gaspar for confirmation. He shrugged, unwilling to abandon his suspicions. Harry Black was a cop and had $67 million in dirty money. Hard to make that happen as an independent operator.

Gaspar had a valid point.

Then Roscoe took charge.

Kim followed her outside. Roscoe lined up her subordinates and said, "Get on the horn to GHP. Tell them we need forensics out here again. A full team to collect evidence. Properly this time. Tell them to bring a twenty-four-foot truck if they have it, a hand-truck, and a tool box. They'll need food and coffee. They're going to be here a while."

Sergeants Brent and Kraft were there. They exchanged quizzical looks. Brent said, "What's up, chief?"

Roscoe ignored his question. "You talk to me alone. No one else. And we need this place secured. No one goes in or out or past you except law enforcement with full ID. Any questions, you call me and only me for authorization. Set up at the driveway entrance and log every visitor, including the vehicles they arrive in. You keep doing that until I personally tell you otherwise. Each person asking to enter, you take a picture of them and their ID. Send it to me immediately. Got all that?"

"Got it," Brent said, but he made no move to do her bidding. Kraft took his lead from Brent and stood still. "Who are we looking for?"

Roscoe said, "Make those calls. I'll update you as soon as I can."

Brent and Kraft jogged toward the end of the driveway. Kim hoped Roscoe was wondering whether they were trustworthy. She needed to.

Kim asked, "Why are they called Kliners?"

Roscoe swiped her hair away from her face with a grubby palm. Soot had settled in the starburst crevices around her eyes. Fatigue freighted her shoulders. She said, "Because of the Kliner Foundation."

"What was the Kliner Foundation?"

"A charitable foundation based in Margrave, long ago."

"What kind of charity?"

"No kind, as it turned out. It was a front."

"For counterfeiting?"

"On a massive scale," Roscoe said. "Bad hundreds were floating around Margrave like leaves off the trees."

"How much total?"

"Joe Reacher estimated four billion a year. For five years or more."

"That's twenty billion," Kim said.

"Could have been more. We never got an accurate count. But it was enough to destabilize the currency, potentially. Which is why Joe Reacher was involved. Plus murder, intimidation, kidnapping, bribery, theft, embezzlement, bank fraud, and trafficking. You name it. Anything and everything except printing money. They didn't print the bills here as far as we know. Joe thought the printing was done in Venezuela."

Pieces of the puzzle crashed together. Joe Reacher's treasury job was to bring counterfeiters to justice. His death in tiny Margrave in the line of duty must have been caused by the Kliner Foundation. The waitress's freak-out at Eno's Diner when Gaspar paid the check with his crumpled hundred happened because she must have thought it was a Kliner fake.

And Jack Reacher lived so far off the grid because with that much cash and some ingenuity, he could easily erase his paper trail forever.

Roscoe said, "I really thought this mess was behind us. But Kliner spread the cash pretty thick. He was buying silence. And I guess people being what they are, bills got stashed. And pulled out on a rainy day here and there."

"But?" Kim asked.

"There could have been more than fifty million hidden here."

Kim said, "We figured sixty-seven million and change. Assuming each box was full. Including the two boxes worth that must have been in the Chevy."

Roscoe nodded. "It's unfathomable to me. Harry couldn't have acquired that many Kliners fifteen years after we squashed the operation. Where the hell did he get them from?"

Kim watched Roscoe and said, "And where are they now?"

Roscoe just shook her head.

Kim knew Roscoe was the key to building the Reacher file. Whether she was trustworthy enough to help was the big issue. Now Kim decided the answer to one simple question would make up her mind.

She asked, "Will you lose your job over this, Beverly?"

"Yes," Roscoe said.

"Are you sure?"

"I'm sure."

"Whose decision is it?"

"The mayor appoints the chief of police."

"Why won't he let you keep the job?"

Roscoe's shoulders slumped; she squeezed her eyes shut for a moment. "Long story. Family rivalry. Goes back a hundred years. Teales think they own Margrave."

"How'd you get appointed, then?"

"Finlay insisted. Mayor Teale's been looking for a good excuse to fire me since the second I was sworn in."

"Why didn't he fire you before?"

"No cause. But look at the facts here. Harry Black was operating right under my nose. Even folks who believe I didn't know what my sergeant was up to will judge me incompetent. You know how hard it is to pass counterfeits these days. The banks have taken old bills out of circulation. Harry's stash might have been equal to all the old hundreds still existing in the entire country. Every time he tried to spend one, it would be rejected by the scanners. People will figure he couldn't have passed those bills anywhere in Margrave, hell, anywhere in Georgia, without my knowledge. Even I can't believe it. This is definitely the end of my career. Even Finlay won't be able to help. Can't imagine our little asshole mayor will let such a prime opportunity go to waste. In his shoes, I wouldn't. Would you? I mean, it's not so much losing the job. When you serve at the pleasure of a weasel, that's always hanging over you. It's going out in shame that hurts. My entire family has been so proud of me. After a hundred years of obscurity, we'd finally become something in Margrave again. Might not mean much to you, but in our little corner of the world, to my kids and my husband, my parents, it means a lot."

Roscoe shuddered, and Kim watched her.

Now or never. Life or death. Yes or no?

She took the plunge.

She said, "I can help you, chief."

Roscoe raised her head, looked deeply into Kim's face, wary and weary.

She asked, "In exchange for what?"

Kim said, "Reacher."

Kim said, "Think about it, chief. We were sent here because of Reacher. And think about the two shots in Harry's head. That's how Joe Reacher died, too, wasn't it? It was a message. Reacher killed Harry. He killed the guy in the Chevy. Maybe vengeance for his brother. Maybe money. Maybe Sylvia. Maybe something else."

Roscoe was listening.

Kim continued. "Then Reacher rescued Sylvia. You saw her face on that video. She was expecting him. She was happy to see him."

A flicker of something else crossed Roscoe's face.

Jealousy?

Kim pressed on. "A clever jailbreak, easy enough for an ex-military cop, right? He knows where the weak points are. He's got Harry's money now too. He can go underground forever if we don't find him soon."

She wasn't pleading, but her argument was solid even if she couldn't prove it all. Roscoe had to recognize that. "Help us find him. And you've got my word. I'll help you navigate your way out of this mess. Finlay's not the only guy in high places. You've checked me out. You know I wouldn't offer if I couldn't deliver."

Roscoe studied Kim for what felt like a long time. She breathed in, and breathed out. She shook her head, slowly, and maybe with regret. She said, "Even if I knew where Reacher was, I wouldn't tell you. Even though I'd like to see him again, myself."

Kim shrugged, one bad habit she'd already picked up from Gaspar. She'd tried. She'd given Roscoe the best she had to offer. Sad. She'd come to like the woman. There would be no pleasure in bringing her down.

There were helicopters again in the distance, getting louder. Two, maybe three.

Roscoe said, "The GHP isn't going to accept all those shoe boxes were empty when you found them. You won't be able to leave Margrave tonight." She took out a card and a key. She said, "Make yourselves at home. I'll join you as soon as I can."

She walked away.

Kim read the card in her hand. It said: *Mr. & Mrs. David Trent, 37 Roscoe Place Drive, Margrave, Georgia.*

CHAPTER THIRTY

Margrave, Georgia
November 2
4:30 p.m.

THEY USED ROSCOE'S car as far as the Margrave Police Station, and then they changed to their own Crown Vic and drove south toward town. The county road ran straight through Margrave. Now labeled Main Street, it was nothing more than potholes connected by multi-layered asphalt patches.

The GPS found a satellite. Gaspar said, "The directions look pretty simple. We stay on Main Street to Roscoe Place Drive."

"Who knew Margrave was such a lovely place?" Kim said. Slow progress let her study peeling paint, broken windows, and ragged awnings. Small buildings faced each other on opposite sides of Margrave's four-block commercial district. Vehicles waited for angled parking spots along both sides of the street as patrons came and went. Graffiti defaced walls and sidewalks sprouted hearty weeds from their cracks. Pedestrians simply walked around them.

November twilight meant store signs and interior activities were illuminated.

Teale's Barber Shop was lined with benches where clients waited inside and out. Teale's Pharmacy had a flashing neon sign promising that flu shots were still available. Teale's real estate office windows were papered with colored flyers offering homes for sale or rent.

Teale's Mercantile & Sundry filled most of the storefronts in the center block. Its stenciled windows boasted discounts and closeouts on everything from baby clothes to toilet paper. Shoppers rooted through bargains piled on long tables, pushing and shoving as they competed for the best deals.

"Easy to see why the Teales might think they own Margrave," Gaspar said.

"Roscoe's right," Kim said. "Surprising she's lasted this long on the wrong side of anybody named Teale."

In the third block, Kim recognized a standard construction single story brick U.S. Post Office, circa 1960. Vehicles lined up to park as folks filed in and out before closing. A tall flagpole out front flew the stars and stripes as required, with an illuminating floodlight at its base, but the other poles along Main stood bare of colors.

"Want to stop and check out the P.O. Box question?" Gaspar asked.

"They're too busy right now. Let's put that on tomorrow's list."

"I was hoping you'd say that."

At the south edge of town a village green similarly in need of an increased maintenance budget sported a statue of a long-dead city father on a flat patch of long-dead brown grass, dandelions, and overgrown hydrangea bushes. Birds had defaced the statue in the usual way making it difficult to identify the bronze under the white slop.

"Roscoe should take a lesson; the birds know how to handle those Teales," Kim said, and Gaspar laughed.

Off one side of the statue's roost, a residential street ran west. Beckman Drive, its barely visible green sign asserted. A tired white church with an empty gravel parking lot filled a larger unkempt circle between Beckman and Roscoe Place Drive, the opposite residential street pointing east, where a convenience store serving coffee and conversation adorned the corner.

When the GPS instructed, Gaspar turned left into near darkness brightened only by the moon. This had been farmland once. Roscoe said her family had lived in Margrave a hundred years, probably here on the farm once upon a time.

Roscoe Place Drive opened up to a quiet residential lane unbounded by hedges or fences. Lawns rolled from the pavement up to red brick homes settled on multi-acre parcels. Built within the past twenty years. Not ostentatious, but stately. Well kept.

Kim counted three driveways as they passed. Each with solar lights along the drive to mark the way, and mailboxes enclosed by brick housings at the road. Each box was numbered. 7, 17, 27.

The Crown Vic's headlights revealed the house at the end of the road. Same vintage, similar construction. Number 37. Nobody home. Gaspar said, "Nice shack. A step up from what I can afford on my paycheck. Still think Roscoe didn't pocket some of those Kliners?"

Kim said, "Lets get connected. Let's find out what we can before Roscoe gets here."

Gaspar popped the trunk and stood aside while she collected her bags. He stretched like a cat. Bent over at the waist in three directions. Walked around a little. Retrieved his stuff and plopped it down by the front walk. "You've got the key, Sunshine. Turn on some lights. I'll stow the car."

Roscoe's key unlocked the double front door, which opened into a wide carpeted hallway. Kim flipped light switches as she moved through. Fifteen feet in, French doors faced each other on either side. A formal dining room on the left, guest bedroom on the right. She placed her travel case just inside and continued through the archway entrance.

A staircase leading to the second floor rested against the guest bedroom's wall, open rails and spindles on the great room side. The rest of the first floor was spacious openness.

Even uninhabited and chilly, the room was an inviting place to nest. On the right, a family room with hardwood floors, fireplace, and comfortable furniture. On the left, an expensively appointed kitchen. The two living spaces separated by a ten-foot cooking island containing a fashionable sink and pricey accoutrements. Big bay window on the front.

"Let's meet back here in twenty?" Gaspar suggested. "I'll make coffee. Whoever gets back first finds some food. Okay?"

"Perfect." By the time Kim pulled out her toilet kit, fresh clothes, and entered the guest bath off the kitchen, brewed coffee's heavenly aroma floated everywhere. A shower, and the promise of coffee, food and sleep. She almost swooned in ecstasy. Ten minutes later she was dressed in black jeans, red sweater and ballet slippers, wet hair loose around her shoulders, holding a cup of black coffee and working at her laptop on the kitchen table. She barely registered Gaspar's return.

"You're fast for a girl," he said. He opened his own laptop.

"So I've been told." She didn't look up from her work.

"My suit's a goner," he said. "We'll have to stop for a new one somewhere in our travels."

"How about Teale's? They have a closeout, don't they?" He'd dressed in casual clothes similar to hers, but lighter weights acquired for his Miami life.

"Find anything to eat?"

"Didn't look. Got distracted."

"By what?" He poured his coffee, opened the sub-zero fridge for cream and searched amid the neatly organized pantry until he found a bag of sugar and a measuring cup.

"Sylvia and Harry's tax returns. We also have the Roscoe/Finlay Kliner Foundation testimony. And images of whole Kliner bills."

"Where'd that stuff come from?" He continued searching cabinets for dinner, moving Roscoe's staples around.

"I'm guessing the boss made it happen. I found them waiting when I opened up my secure connection."

"So he's got a guilty conscience?" Apparently, Gaspar found nothing to his liking among the foodstuffs because he'd now returned his attention to the refrigerator.

"Or something," she said, sourly.

"You know we can't finish this job without his help. You don't have to like it, but prepare yourself to make that happen."

"That's what I have you for, number two." She returned to the screen, absorbed again.

After a while, enticing aromas. Her nose began to twitch. Stomach flip-flopped in happy anticipation. But she didn't look away from her work until he put two plates on the table, refilled her coffee, and sat down beside her.

"I hate eggs," she said.

"No problem." He picked up her plate and scraped the eggs off onto his own, barely stopping the shovel to his mouth. "How's that?"

She grinned. Snatched up his toast in one hand and hers in the other. Put the ham between the buttered bread. "Excellent. You're a good cook."

"I have many talents you've yet to discover," he said between bites. He polished off the entire batch of eggs and returned to the fridge for more ham. "Tell me while I cook."

"For starters, Sylvia's prior name was Kent. Not the one she was born with, maybe. I'm running that down. And Mr. & Mrs. Harry Black's joint tax returns are beyond silly. They even filed the short form because they didn't have enough deductible expenses to itemize. Claimed only themselves as dependents."

"Which means?" He remained at the stove, pan frying ham and eggs and working the toaster.

"Harry and Sylvia are practically begging to be prosecuted. Handing the IRS such an obvious fraud case doesn't make sense."

"Not everything makes sense, Sunshine. I've told you that before. Even when the crooks are cops, they're not as rational as we give them credit for." He winced slightly.

"You're not listening. Harry and Sylvia, like all smart crooks, filed tax returns because they knew not filing is the quickest way to jail."

"I'm aware. So what's the problem?"

"Second quickest one-way ticket to Uncle Sam's hotel-for-life is filing fraudulent returns. Might pass undiscovered for years. Harder to prove when suspected."

"As I said, I'm aware." He narrowed his eyes, watching something outside the bay window, but Kim barely noticed.

"Smart tax evaders make a plausible attempt to avoid obvious fraud so they can pay the fines and stay out of prison longer and maybe forever, even if they get caught."

"I'm not sure how smart Harry was. He's dead, right? Most of us smart people try to avoid that condition."

She said, "He and Sylvia were clever enough to collect sixty-seven million in counterfeits and move them out of that house right under everybody's nose."

He moved to the window and lowered the translucent shades; stood to one side, lifted the shade from the frame slightly to see out. "So they laundered the Kliners somehow. We figured that."

"Not as easy as it sounds. Especially for that much cash. Our financial world is too complicated. Computers make tracking and reporting too easy. Ever heard of Superdollars? The best counterfeits ever? Even better than the real thing?"

"I work in the Miami Field Office, Sunshine. We get briefed there too."

"Well, thousands of Superdollars have been snagged through mundane paperwork."

"You bean counters are gonna kill us all."

"Basic money laundering usually requires three pretty complicated steps because you've got to get the bad money out there, pass it through several legitimate places to clean it up, and then get it back and do something with it that makes the proceeds look legitimate so you'll have ready access."

"Right." Preoccupied.

"But I'm thinking Harry just found a good placement exchange plan and stopped there. In other words, he places the Kliners into the financial system somewhere and takes back genuine money, which he stashes someplace else. Not in his closet hidey hole."

"That's the simplest plan."

"But impossible for Harry to execute." She noticed he hadn't moved from the window. "What are you looking at?"

"Maybe nothing. Keep going. Why couldn't Harry execute the simple plan?"

"He couldn't place the old bills here in Margrave or anywhere close. Everybody around here would at least suspect they were Kliners, like your waitress. All the usual options for moving small amounts of money would take the rest of his lifetime to complete, given the volume. He's got a job, so he's not free to be traveling around the state or the country to buy a little of this and a little of that and get real money in change. No bank is going to take them. Any business that takes in a lot of cash, like a horse track or a theme park or casino, is going to have good anti-counterfeiting procedures in place."

"So what's left? Offshore banking?"

"Not so easy these days. Even the Swiss are turning in tax cheats now. He'd have to smuggle the fakes out of the country for starters. And how would he access the real money when Sylvia wants a new outfit?"

Gaspar seemed to think about it. "The dead Chevy guy and Reacher were in this all along. They helped Harry and Sylvia with the laundering."

She heard inattention in his tone. "That's how I figure it too."

"Why kill Harry now?" He still hadn't moved from the window.

"That's the sixty-seven million-dollar question, isn't it?" She looked up to receive his answer, annoyed. "And what the hell are you watching out there?"

"Headlights. Coming this way."

Her heart skipped uncomfortably. "Roscoe?"

"Smaller car. Pulling into the driveway."

Reflex. Hand slipped under the table to pat her gun lying on the seat next to her in its holster.

She heard the car stop out front. Car door opened. Slammed shut.

Gaspar said, "Tall male. Front door."

Too late to turn off the kitchen lights without signaling where they were inside the house. Kim grabbed her holster and slipped into it. Stood back to the wall beside the open hallway arch.

Stillness. A key in the lock. The front door opened.

A deep voice. "I'm in! Thanks for the ride!"

Front door slammed. Footsteps approached along the carpet.

The same voice, louder. "Hey! I'm home!"

Kim glanced her question to Gaspar. He nodded. Gestured that the car had departed. She remained vigilant.

"In here," Gaspar called out, while there was still time to appear normal.

A dark-haired boy dressed in sweats and unlaced running shoes came through the archway, tossed his backpack onto the sofa, flashed his multi-colored braces, and bee-lined to the refrigerator. The kid said, "I'm Davey Trent. You're Mom's friends, right? She texted me."

Kim relaxed slightly, but her voice was stuck somewhere. Davey Trent. Roscoe's thirteen year old. He looked like a foot-taller version of his mother. Same amazing brown eyes.

Gaspar said, friendly, "That's right. Carlos Gaspar and Kim Otto."

Davey collected a large bottle of blue beverage from the fridge and ducked his head by way of acknowledgement, "Mom said not to bother you. She'll be home later. Yell if you need anything. I've got homework." The kid grabbed his backpack and headed up the stairs.

Kim and Gaspar exchanged nods. For now, all strategic conversation was over. She returned to her seat, but didn't remove her holster. Gaspar collected his cold toast. He opened up his laptop and sat opposite her at the kitchen table.

"Transfer that testimony over here," he said. "I'll go through it and whatever else the boss sent me while you follow up on your stuff."

"Study the images of the fakes too. They're very good," she said.

For several hours, they worked like that until finally, Gaspar stood, and stretched, and glanced at the wall clock. "I need a beer."

Kim said, "I need a nap."

"That too."

"When do you think we'll be able to leave Margrave?"

Gaspar twisted off the top of the beer bottle he liberated from Roscoe's fridge, took a long swallow. "Without some assistance from the boss, never."

"I didn't peg you for a quitter."

"What's your plan?"

"Right now, I'm sleeping," Kim said. "Roscoe comes in, you can charm the answers out of her. Maybe this stuff will make more sense later. It can't get a lot worse."

She picked up her laptop, gathered her scattered possessions and moved to the guest room. Ten minutes later, she'd sunk into blissful oblivion.

CHAPTER THIRTY-ONE

Margrave, Georgia
November 3
12:45 a.m.

SHE WAS SUBMERGED in deep slow-wave sleep, like a dolphin, maintaining only enough consciousness to remain wary of predators. She bobbed gently, down and up, each soft bounce tugging her higher until at one apex her eyelids fluttered. An orange glow inches from her nose showed 12:45 a.m. She'd been asleep three hours.

But now she was awake.

Because: there was hushed shouting in the house. Echolocation placed two women safely distant. One older, one younger, both angry. She recognized Roscoe's voice.

Roscoe's guest room was cozy. The temperature was perfect. Quilted goose down enveloped in fine cotton created a warm cocoon. She snuggled deeper, drifted lightly on sleep's surface, still aware. She sighed.

Return to nirvana demanded a glass of water and a pee. She listened, heard no silenced screaming, concluded quick stealth was now possible. Where was the bathroom? Down the hall, she remembered, near the kitchen.

Vision limited through eyelids too heavy to lift, she moved toward the door, turned left, and shuffled along the carpet. A computer screen's soft night-light glow guided her progress. There were warm aromas she couldn't identify. Wood smoke, maybe? And something sweeter.

She reached the archway and stepped into cold open space. She recalled the kitchen on the left, a den on the right, the guest bath straight ahead.

Then the whole room lit up. Instant blindness. Kim's forearm flew up to shield her eyes. A tall, slender blonde girl had opened the refrigerator door. That was the light. The girl was holding a bottle of beer. She turned, saw Kim, and cocked her wrist, ready to throw the bottle.

"Who are you?" she asked. "And what are you doing in my house?"

The girl was very pretty. She was dressed in ragged jeans and a sloppy sweater and heavy mud-covered boots. She was backlit by the refrigerator. She was a foot taller and thirty pounds heavier than Kim, and she looked very capable. Kim figured the bottle would hit her dead center in the head, if the kid got around to throwing it.

Then from the shadows on Kim's right, Roscoe said, "Cut the drama, Jack. Does she look like a home invader? Bare feet? Red silk pajamas?"

The girl didn't stand down even a smidge.

Only one choice.

Kim prepared to run rather than hurt the girl.

Roscoe said, "Kim, this is my daughter Jacqueline, known to all as Jack for short, which as you can see, she isn't."

Jack? Kim felt like she'd been punched in the gut. *Reacher's kid?*

"Jack, this is my friend, Kim. But you'd know that already if you'd met your curfew."

Still Jack didn't stand down.

Roscoe said, "I'm sorry we woke you, Kim. We don't normally assault our houseguests. Jack apologizes as well. Don't you, Jack?"

The girl relaxed, loosened up, shrugged, and put the beer back on the shelf.

"Whatever," she said, like a fifteen-year-old.

She closed the refrigerator door.

Darkness.

Instant blindness.

"Another friend is sleeping upstairs," Roscoe said. "Don't wake him. Or your brother."

The girl said nothing.

Roscoe said, "Goodnight, Jack."

The girl walked upstairs with a heavy tread, grinding mud into the carpet. Roscoe must have been too exhausted to notice.

A door opened. A door closed.

The house went quiet again.

Kim shivered. High-tech microfiber pajamas packed flat for travel, but were not warm enough for November in Georgia.

"Hot chocolate?" Roscoe asked.

"I'm fine," Kim said.

"Translation: You've got questions and I can't sleep."

"I'm dead on my feet. I won't be very good company."

Translation: Or sharp enough to learn anything from you that I don't already know.

"Archie Leach wants to question you. I held him off tonight, but I had to tell him where you were. I've had other calls too. This may be the last chance we get."

Kim dropped into an oversized chair and tucked her bare feet beside her on the seat. Roscoe handed her a mug. Kim recognized the sweet aroma unidentified during her somnolent wandering. Sipping chocolate, spiked with something stronger. Whiskey, she thought.

"Jack's a pretty girl," she said, after the silence stretched a while.

Roscoe smiled. "You didn't see the sign out front flashing 'smoking hot girl inside, bad boys wanted?'"

Kim smiled too. "My dad threatened a ten-foot fence around our property to keep the boys away when my sister was about Jack's age."

"Did it work?" Roscoe sounded hopeful.

Kim sipped the warm chocolate, laid her head back against the chair. "Keeping the boys out wasn't the problem, actually. The problem was keeping my sister in."

"Exactly," Roscoe said. "She misses her curfews. She doesn't return my calls. She texts until all hours. She won't get up for school. Her grades are a mess." She ran splayed fingers through her hair cut. "And now she's sneaking out in the middle of the night."

"To do what?"

"I don't know."

"You could lock her in a closet until she's twenty-one. You could hire a crone to bring her bread and water."

"Don't think I haven't thought about it. When Jack was born, every moment away from her was torture. And now, after five minutes in the same room I want to slap her. But what would I do if she hit me back?"

"Shoot straight?"

Roscoe laughed.

Kim said, "Makes you want to call your mother and apologize, doesn't it?"

"Every single day."

"You know it's a phase, Beverly. A necessary rite of passage." She sighed. "If I'd gone through the bad boy thing at fifteen instead of twenty, my life would have been a lot different. I wouldn't be sitting here now, at the very least."

"Did he straighten up? Your bad boy?"

"You know the stats as well as anyone, chief. Bad boys get worse, not better. If you really want an update I guess I could check the prison database. Or the morgue."

"Kids?" Roscoe asked.

Kim shook her head in horror, hard enough to make her vision swim. "With him? Tied to him forever? Seeing him every time I looked at the kid? Always, always, wondering if his sorry genes would win out no matter how hard I worked to be sure they didn't? Definitely not."

Roscoe stared into the fire. "Wise choice, Agent Otto. Good cop is a lot easier than good mother."

She lifted a slim remote, pressed a button, and Mozart's *Piano Concerto No. 21* filled the room.

Kim asked, "Would it be so bad? If you lose the job over the Harry Black thing? It's not easy to be the boss, even in a sleepy small-town cop shop. You could move into something less demanding. Spend more time with Jack. Get her straightened out."

Roscoe replied, "Don't worry about me, Kim. Old man Kliner made my career fifteen years ago. Before that, Margrave wasn't even on the map. But when Kliner blew up, I became a star around here. Never would have happened without him. Maybe he's about to do it again. Ever consider that? I've got no regrets." She hesitated slightly. "I just liked my kid better before."

"Before what?"

"Before she grew boobs."

"And she was late coming home tonight?"

Roscoe sighed again, as if she carried Atlas-sized burdens on a frame much too small. She folded both hands together and brought them to her chin. Leaning her head forward, she rubbed her lower lip with one knuckle as she said, "The sneaking out started three nights ago."

Which had been the night before Harry Black's murder. Timing might not be everything, but opportunity leads to crimes and suspects. No wonder the momma hen was so upset about her chick. "You're worried that Jack is somehow connected to the Black case?"

Roscoe seemed relieved that Kim had finally caught up. "I know Jack had nothing to do with what happened out at Harry's place Sunday night."

"How sure are you about that?" Kim's gut said Roscoe wasn't as certain as she'd like to be. Worried cop, terrified mom. Simple equation.

"Very sure," Roscoe said. "I checked. Personally."

"Gaspar thinks Harry and Sylvia were into porn. He thinks that's how they collected and laundered the Kliners. You think Jack's been participating in that?"

Instant alarm widened Roscoe's eyes. "No! Of course not!"

"You think she helped Sylvia cover up the murder and escape?"

"No."

Less volume, but more worry. Getting closer.

"You think she's been out with Jack Reacher for the past three nights?"

Roscoe took a breath and held it. Her hands fell limp into her lap. Bingo?

But then Roscoe relaxed. She grinned. "Of all the possibilities I considered when Jack didn't come home the night my sergeant was murdered, Agent Otto, I never once worried that my daughter was cavorting until the wee hours with Jack Reacher."

Kim thought Roscoe was telling the truth.

Too bad.

She asked, "How do you know?"

Roscoe actually giggled. Maybe it was the whiskey. "Honey, you are so far off the mark you can't even *see* the bulls-eye."

Kim sat straighter in her chair. "Okay, I get it. You don't think Reacher's involved in the Sylvia Black case at all. At least tell me straight out. Why not?"

"To begin with, if Reacher was in town, I'd know it. He'd have contacted me, or someone would have seen him. He's a big guy. He's obviously not from around here. He'd stand out. That's how he got arrested fifteen years ago. He couldn't sneak in and out of Margrave without someone knowing."

Wishful thinking. The guy was a ghost. He'd slipped into and out of tighter places without any trouble, whenever he wanted to. "And?"

Roscoe took a big gulp of liquid courage. "When you mentioned the possibility that Reacher was involved with Sylvia, I'll admit, you threw me."

Now we're getting somewhere.

"And rescuing women like Sylvia is exactly the kind of thing he might do. So I checked your theory out. And it wasn't him."

"How do you know?"

"I just know," Roscoe said, sounding like her daughter.

"You're clairvoyant? You have a crystal ball? Tarot cards?"

"Have you learned nothing about the man, hot shot? Reacher wouldn't do any of it."

"Really? You're saying Reacher wouldn't kill anyone? Because twelve people died when he was here fifteen years ago and I'm thinking that was no coincidence." Kim knew she should have stopped right there even as she barreled on. "Don't try to sell me that line of bull, Beverly. Makes you look like Bonnie to his Clyde." Brief pause. *Oh, what the hell.* "Again."

Roscoe said, "You know, Kim, even Reacher would hurt you for that remark."

"Because it's true?"

"Because it isn't. You don't know Jack. At all."

"So enlighten me."

"His brother Joe died because of that money. Jack would never profit from Joe's death like that. He wouldn't shoot a sleeping enemy instead of taking him face-on. And he'd never spend his time cleaning up like that. Not his style."

"No?"

"Definitely not."

"What would he have done, then?"

"If he'd killed Harry for the Kliners, which he didn't, he'd have destroyed Harry's place completely. He didn't blow up the Chevy, either. So don't even start with that idea."

"And you know this because?"

The music changed to Chopin's *Nocturne No. 2* and filled the room with discordant peace.

Roscoe seemed to reach a decision. She wiped her face again. She settled her shoulders. She said, "Reacher left here bound for Chicago back then and I've never heard from him since. What I wanted to tell you tonight is that it wasn't him. On the videotape. Springing Sylvia last night. The fake Marshal Wright. Not Jack Reacher. Definitely. Not. Him."

"Evidence? Facts?" Kim asked. "And don't tell me you just know, Beverly."

Roscoe stood, moved to the fireside, turned her back toward the room. "Reacher's taller. Bigger build. Boxier shoulders. Straighter posture. Longer reach. Deeper voice. Different walk."

"Maybe he's changed in fifteen years," Kim said.

Roscoe paused again, and turned to face Kim from across the room. She made her next observations in a softer tone, confirming Kim's instincts about her relationship with Reacher in every respect. She said, "Reacher's wrists are thicker, and his hands too broad for the gloves in the video. He's kinder to women. He wouldn't grab Sylvia's arm or push her into the car like that. He displays more finesse. He's much smarter. It radiates off of him. And he's a very cautious guy. If he had collected Sylvia Black from our jail, no evidence would ever connect him to the escape, just as there's no evidence he was ever here fifteen years ago. Simply put, if Reacher had been here that night, we'd have no video to analyze."

Kim was quiet for a spell. She'd made too many assumptions. The assumptions had led to false starts and wasted time. She *didn't* know Jack Reacher, and the not knowing frightened her more than anything else. But Roscoe had known Jack Reacher in every conceivable way back then. That was clear. So unless he'd changed more than a man is capable of changing, Roscoe was right.

Dammit.

"So who was the guy on the tape?" Kim asked.

"You tell me."

"I would if I could," Kim said. Then she heard Gaspar coming down the stairs.

CHAPTER THIRTY-TWO

Margrave, Georgia
November 3
2:15 a.m.

GASPAR DROPPED HIS bags on the hallway floor and stepped into the room fully dressed, wide awake, and ready to go. "Our flight leaves Atlanta in ninety-five minutes. We've got to run. What's the best route outta here, chief?"

Roscoe said, "You can't leave. GHP wants to talk to you."

"They can send me an e-mail. Or kiss my ass. My badge is shinier than theirs." He moved into the kitchen, located the coffee pot, loaded grounds and water. He pulled out mugs and rooted around for sugar and milk as if he was competing for speed records. Way too much energy. Kim closed her eyes.

"Hey there, Sunshine," he called. "You might want to put some clothes on. It's a little chilly out there for pajamas."

When she didn't move, he said, "Get in the shower. Wake up. I'll pop a coffee in for you when it's finished. Come on. Shake and bake. Hubba hubba. Got to move it." Talking a mile a minute. Maybe he had located more amphetamines.

He said, "Before we leave, Chief Roscoe, I need you to answer a couple of questions about bringing down the Kliner Foundation. I read the transcripts. Several times. Couple open issues in my head."

"Such as?"

"Your testimony covered the highlights. I need to know the things you left out. Reacher was the heavy lifter, but how, exactly, did he do it? Forewarned and forearmed and all that. And tell me what happened after. Especially after old man Teale died. The mayor now is what? His kid?"

Kim believed in preparation. It had saved her life more than once. She tried to concentrate.

Roscoe said, "We answered everything relevant back then. Testimony took weeks. Every state and federal agency you can imagine got involved, and even a couple of foreign governments."

Kim didn't believe she'd answered everything; Gaspar wouldn't either.

"And afterward?" Gaspar asked.

"Nothing afterward. By the time the whole mess was sorted out, Reacher was long gone. I ran for mayor and lost to Junior Teale. He never forgave me. We all went back to the way we'd lived before." She shrugged. "The human condition, I guess. Hard to break the bonds of inertia."

"Not everybody went back, obviously," Gaspar said. "Otherwise, Harry Black couldn't have accumulated those Kliners."

The coffee was done. He poured a big mug of strong black energy sufficient to run a small train and carried it across the room. Waved it under Kim's nose like smelling salts. She reached up; he pulled away like pulling a puppet string.

Enticed to her feet, he rewarded her with the mug, pointed her toward the guest bath and lightly shoved between her shoulder blades. "Get going. You don't want me to come in there with you, but I will if that's what it takes."

She wrinkled her nose at him and moved slowly out of reach. "Yeah, yeah, yeah, Batista. Just try it. See what happens."

He grinned, nodded. "That's the spirit. I'm leaving in fifteen minutes. If you're not ready, I'll come in there and get you."

"You and what army?"

As if she'd dashed away at his request, he simply picked up with Roscoe where he'd left off while he mixed coffee for himself "Lotta cops killed during the Kliner fiasco too. Nobody prosecuted. No way to make that happen unless deals were made, even if Reacher was long gone."

Roscoe said, "Above my pay grade."

Liar, Kim figured as she walked away. Roscoe was too far down the chain of command to have been involved, but she'd have known what happened. Everybody would.

Gaspar let it go. "Was Harry working with Margrave PD during the Kliner days? Could he have been on the inside, gotten hold of the fakes back then?"

Roscoe said, "He was a cadet over in Calhoun county."

"But?" Kim called from the hallway.

Roscoe's thoughts seemed years away. "Reacher said at the time, the only safe thing is to assume everybody is involved."

Gaspar had said almost the same words to Kim a few hours ago. About Roscoe. And Finlay. And the boss too. She suddenly understood she had a secret weapon. Which was Gaspar. *Reacher thinks just like Gaspar.* Men. Cops. Veterans. Same foundation. Same training. Same experience. Same prism.

Instantly Kim knew why she'd been chosen. And understood how she would win.

Simple yet profoundly easy: *Reacher doesn't think like me.*

Kim turned to face the kitchen.

Gaspar had poured a mound of sugar and a river of milk into his mug, then added a dash of coffee, took a swig, smacked his lips, carried his mug over and settled into the seat Kim had just vacated.

Roscoe said, "I thought I knew Harry and Sylvia. Clearly, I didn't. I went to school with Harry. Sylvia worked for me. I'd have sworn they were both as honest as the day is long."

Kim was still in the hallway.

Gaspar looked up and said, "Ten minutes. And I'm not kidding."

"All right, already, I'm going." From inside the guest bathroom, she couldn't hear the remainder of their conversation.

CHAPTER THIRTY-THREE

Margrave, Georgia
November 3
2:40 a.m.

A HUGE HARVEST moon showed Kim the buildings growing smaller in the side mirror along the county road through Margrave, the post office, the police station, and finally Eno's diner. She watched them slide behind her without regret.

Roscoe had advised them to travel through the peanut farms, to stay away from the highway cloverleaf, which would still be lousy with government agents from many different jurisdictions. The advice suited Kim just fine.

Gaspar turned west on a wandering road that led toward some place called Warburton. It took them through miles of arable land. They passed bumpy side tracks that looped around and led back to the road again, suitable for dropping farm equipment and workers. Otherwise, nothing but uninterrupted middle-of-nowhere.

Then seven or eight miles from town, on the right, Gaspar pointed out a stand of trees. A little oval copse. The only visible cover amid acres and acres of plowed red dirt. He said, "Finlay testified three bodies tied to Kliner were found hidden behind those trees in a burned-out Buick. Stuffed into the trunk. About a week old, he figured. Males. Two shot with the same gun. Different weapon on the first."

They hadn't seen a single moving vehicle since they left Roscoe's place. Therefore Kim understood how the bodies could have lain there for days without being discovered. But hadn't anyone missed them? Come asking? She shivered. Gaspar misunderstood. He turned up the heat.

"Who killed them?" she asked.

"Never proved, but you know who my money's on."

"Reacher?"

"Pretty convenient scapegoat, seems to me," he said.

"Meaning what?"

"You're always demanding evidence. Except for Roscoe's kid, where's the proof Jack Reacher was ever here at all? Nada. But Joe died here. We know that for sure. The kid could be Joe's. The brothers looked alike, they say. Did you consider that?"

She might have argued, but his theories were as plausible as hers. Maybe more so. *What would Reacher think?* She shrugged, communicating with him in his own silent language.

The Warburton Road continued west, but Roscoe had directed them to turn before Warburton itself, head north, and then enter the freeway about twenty-five miles from Margrave. Gaspar watched for ice patches deposited by frosty dew. Sunshine or traffic would warm the roads to melting point later. For now, in the moonlight, black treachery remained invisible.

At the highway, the Crown Vic merged with light traffic northbound and settled into a droning cruise. Several times, Kim saw Gaspar move in his seat, seeking a comfort zone she knew he would never find. Still forty-five miles from Hartsfield. Their schedule was too tight. Again. Her stomach was already churning. Dwelling on the upcoming flight wouldn't help.

She said, "You know, this would be a good time to tell me why we're going to D.C."

He knew she needed distraction. He said, "I wish I could tell you. But no. I spent about three hours on background data while you and Roscoe were dealing with the *malcriada* and didn't get to a conclusion."

"The what?"

"The malcriada? The badly-raised female brat. My sister would have been sent back to Cuba for that behavior. Yiyiyiyiyi." He shook his hand rapidly, loose wristed, like Ricky Ricardo.

"You have a sister?" Kim asked.

He didn't answer. He said, "All indicators point to D.C. It's our best lead."

"Or worst. Perhaps you noticed somebody's very good at misdirecting us in this case?"

He took one hand off the wheel and used his fingers to enumerate his points. "Sylvia said she came from D.C. when she applied for the Margrave job. The Chevy guy claimed to be a D.C. lawyer. Finlay's been headquartered in New York for the past two years, but before that, especially when he was allegedly providing Sylvia a reference, he was a D.C. resident. Could be an elaborate head fake, but it's hard to get that many stories lined up over a five-year time frame. Amateurs would try to broom all that out. Impossible. D.C's a big town, people coming and going all the time. Much smarter to work with true stuff in place."

He glanced over. She said nothing, thinking things through. Maybe sensing he hadn't persuaded her, he offered new facts. "I received one individual tax return for Sylvia. Same social security number as the joint returns sent to you and the same maiden name. I spent a while chasing those down. All D.C. all the time."

"OK," she said. "You win. D.C. is not only the best lead we have, it's the only lead. Is that what you're saying? When all roads point to Rome?"

He nodded. "One more thing. The social on her tax returns is a real number, and it was issued from D.C."

"Well, duh," she said, without rancor.

"Touchy."

Maybe he didn't know? "I meant it's obvious where the number was issued because it begins with 579. Means D.C."

"I'm aware," he said.

She explained the logic. "Matching numbers is what computers do best. If Sylvia and Harry didn't list easy numbers the same way on every return and match stuff already in the system, the computers would have spit everything out, see?"

"I phoned a friend. Asked for a closer look," he said.

She bristled. "You called the boss?"

He shrugged. "The birth certificate used to support the number actually belonged to a woman four years younger."

"Let me guess. You found her and she's living in D.C.?"

"Not exactly. She died in a car wreck in D.C. A year or so before Sylvia showed up in Margrave."

Kim said, "Wow." Then: "So we weren't too far off with our guesses about Sylvia." Witness protection programs created new identities; stealing existing identities was the more common criminal custom. "Pretty ballsy to use a stolen identity working in a cop shop."

Unless Roscoe knew.

"Sylvia is nothing if not ballsy," Gaspar said. "It gets even better, though. The dead woman's prior address is a Crystal City post office box. But no criminal records before or since her date of death in any of the FBI databases for Sylvia Kent in D.C. or anywhere else. Not a

Government employee. Not a veteran. No death certificate, even." He glanced over. "And don't ask me how I know all that. You won't like the answer."

Kim compared what he said and what she already knew. Identity thieves she'd investigated were unconcerned about the crime itself. The usual problem with stolen identities as a free ticket to a new life was that something was wrong on the front end: A mistake in the paperwork gets kicked by some computer; unscrupulous seller repeatedly retails the same identity; belongs to a criminal; owners turn up and make trouble. A thousand things can go wrong, and you never see the bullet that gets you. Kim had arrested thieves in all these circumstances, many times. Living five years undiscovered on a stolen identity was a remarkable achievement.

Perhaps impossible.

Unless everybody was in on it.

"So she knew Sylvia Kent intimately enough to impersonate her," Kim said.

He nodded. "Only the one glitch."

She ran through the logic line again. Sylvia Black's prints wouldn't match the dead Sylvia Kent. Fingerprints are unique even among identical twins. Sylvia Black's prints were submitted and confirmed in databases when Roscoe hired her. When a fingerprint record is created, it lasts forever. When a match request comes in, there's only one way the prints are gone.

Somebody pulled them.

There had to be an insider somewhere very high up. And a very subtle one. A suggestion had been floated that a new identity had been created for Sylvia. Inquiring agencies would inevitably assume she was in witness protection. Which was the province of the U.S.

Marshal Service. Which explained liberating Sylvia by impersonating a Marshal.

"Marshals are in D.C., too, by the way," Gaspar said, reading her mind.

She said, "The boss controls all those resources, one way or another."

"You think he's known Sylvia's real identity all along? That he's been using us? Setting us up for something?"

"Don't you?"

Gaspar shrugged.

An eighteen-wheeler howled past in the left lane, followed by a second and a third, displacing enough air to push the Crown Vic toward the shoulder. Ribbed noisemakers embedded in the pavement assaulted the tires. Gaspar hung on to the wheel at ten-and-two.

Kim asked, "What did Roscoe tell you while I was in the shower?"

"She said the Kliners were the Superdollars of their day. Better than the real thing, almost. Nobody could spot them as fakes."

"No tells, even if you knew what you were looking at?"

"None."

"What else?"

He said, "I asked her about Finlay. She's a fan. Called him brilliant. Especially over the Kliner mess. Stood up to the Teales, which made him Sir Galahad in her world. Claimed Joe Reacher was a genius about all of that too. Both Reachers, apparently, were admirable performers."

"And I'm Yo-Yo Ma."

He laughed. "You didn't ask if I believed her."

"Did you?"

"She was sincere, but no, not a chance."

"Still think she and Finlay are dirty cops?" she asked.

"Bet your ass." He signaled and floated into the interchange toward the airport. Black ice glistened under the streetlights. For a Miami dweller, he wasn't a bad driver under hazardous conditions. He completed the treacherous overpass before he asked, "Anything noteworthy from your late-night girl talk? Like maybe why Archie Leach is chasing us like a relentless Javert on steroids? Or who else is stalking?"

Kim popped an antacid onto her tongue. Let it dissolve a little. She said, "Reacher headed for Chicago when he left Margrave."

"She told me that too. That's where the Chevy dude said they were taking Sylvia, wasn't it? Can't be a coincidence. What else?"

"She swore blind the tall guy on the video isn't Reacher."

He was surprised. "Did *you* believe her?"

"Yes."

At the time.

"What about Jacqueline?" he asked.

"What about her?"

"Did Roscoe admit she's either Joe or Jack Reacher's kid?"

"What do you think?"

They pulled into Hartsfield's monitored air space and shut down confidential conversation. They entered the short-term lot.

"We've got to hustle. No time to return the rental," Gaspar said. "And the way this case is going, we might need it again, anyway. We might have to come back."

"God, I hope not," Kim said.

Fifteen minutes later, they were in the plane. Gaspar leaned against the window shade and was asleep before the cabin door was closed. Skies were clear. Didn't mean they were in for smooth sailing, but Kim could hope.

She opened her laptop once the plane reached cruising altitude. Door to door, Hartsfield to Reagan National was posted as 134 minutes. Fifty minutes in, she heard the familiar bell tone from overhead speakers that never meant good news. Her stomach was already a cauldron of acid. Now, it bubbled up like it might explode. She pulled two antacids from her pocket. She chewed them for quicker dissolve.

"Folks, this is Captain Shaw speaking. D.C. air traffic control just told us we're going to be circling here for a bit. We've got gorgeous air this morning. Beautiful sunrise off to starboard. Our flight attendants will bring you another cup of coffee. We'll update you as soon as we have more information. For now, sit back, relax, and enjoy the flight."

Enjoy the flight?

Who was he kidding?

Gaspar remained sound asleep, oblivious.

Kim squeezed her eyes closed, visualized her favorite outdoor meditation haven in the north woods. Tried to breathe. After awhile, when the plane remained aloft, she managed to release her claws.

Distraction. The only available remedy. She spent some time composing e-mails to three tax accountant colleagues.

The real Sylvia Kent would have filed tax returns every year, with luck. The IRS wouldn't have those returns any more; returns were deleted after three years. But the data should be there in some form, and maybe that data would lead somewhere. Maybe she could finally catch a break.

The overhead bell chimed again. Kim's hands flew off the keyboard and gripped the armrests; her head jerked up. She turned.

Stared wildly out the window. The plane remained level. No smoke from the engines. Both wings intact.

"Folks, this is Captain Shaw again. We've just been rerouted to Baltimore. We should have you on the ground at the gate in about thirty minutes. Ground agents will be available to handle your connections. We're sorry for the inconvenience."

When the plane landed, Kim leaned in to shake Gaspar awake. He collected his bags and followed. When they emerged from the jet-way into the terminal, he looked around and asked, "Where the hell are we?"

CHAPTER THIRTY-FOUR

Washington, D.C.
November 3
7:55 a.m.

GASPAR SIGNED UP for another Crown Vic at the rental counter. Objections were futile; Kim made none. She bought a fountain Coke over crushed ice to chase the chalk from her mouth and calm her stomach. She followed him to the car. She settled into the passenger seat and blinked sleep from her eyes. He navigated around traffic knots.

First stop was at a convenience store. Kim laid out private cash for six pre-paid cell phones and six pre-paid gift cards. Burners. Forty minutes later, Gaspar parked at a strip center. Mailing address Crystal City.

"This is it," he said, checking his notes to confirm.

American homogeneity at its finest. One long cinder block building divided into five storefronts, with an adjacent parking lot. Beige painted exteriors, matching store name plates affixed to the brown hip roof atop each entry door. Bookended by a coffee shop and yogurt store; computer shop, liquor store, and their destination centered between.

Winter threatened here as everywhere they'd traveled. Clear skies at 30,000 feet invisible through the low gray clouds immediately overhead. No snow flurries yet, but Kim could smell them in the air. She flipped up her collar and huddled into her blazer. Wished for a coat. She hated cold almost as much as she hated flying.

There was only one person inside the mail drop. Manning the counter was a spiky-haired dude, late twenties, dressed head to toe in black. A clunky nose ring rested in the groove above chapped lips. Quarter-sized round holes elongated fleshy earlobes. A botched tattoo replaced the guy's right eyebrow. Permanent black coal eye rims completed the effect.

"How can I help you?" Husky timbre. Polite. Maybe a real human heart beating inside the frightening package.

Gaspar flashed his badge. "We need to see the contents of P.O. Box 4719."

Without rancor, "Got a warrant?"

"We can get one. Do we need to?"

The dude didn't move.

"Show me your ID," Gaspar said.

The dude held up the work badge hanging from the black lanyard around his neck. Gaspar maintained eye contact, took a photo of the face and the badge with his phone, sent it, and dialed a number.

"Jenny? Carlos Gaspar here. Can you run that mug I just sent? Alfred Lane, works at *Mailboxes are Yours* in Crystal City. Yeah, probably twenty-seven?" Alfred nodded. "Uh, huh. Right. That's the guy. *How* many? Yep. Okay. Thanks."

He clicked off the call and dropped the phone in his pocket and said, "Alfred Lane, you're under arrest."

Then he started in with the Miranda warning and got as far as *silent* before the dude shrugged and said, "I thought all that was cleared up. Sorry. Come over here."

A long row of mailbox doors was set into the wall. The guy stopped at one of the larger sized boxes, maybe eleven inches square, mounted about mid-collection. The guy pulled a small silver key from a ring of a hundred similar keys. Opened 4719's brass door. Inside, envelopes were stuffed tight as Cryovac sausage.

"Is this all of it?" Gaspar asked.

"More in the back."

Kim followed Alfred Lane's shuffle through a door into a well-maintained storage area. There was a clean cement floor. The space was brightly lit. The walls had been recently painted.

Lane pointed to a standard white cardboard banker's box stacked neatly among identical boxes. The number 4719 was stenciled in black on all four sides. The box below was numbered 4720. Logical.

"Is this all of it?" Kim asked. It seemed a small amount of mail for five years.

"If there were more, it would be here." The guy was breaking several federal laws by releasing mail without a court order. Kim wanted to arrest him on the spot.

Instead, she asked, "Take it out front for me?"

The guy bent down and grabbed 4720 and lifted it together with 4719, the proper way, with bent knees and a straight back. The exertion didn't seem to stress him. He shuffled past her and through to the lobby. He called back, "Check the lock on that door, okay?"

"Okay." Kim wondered how 4720 was related to 4719. But she didn't ask.

The guy put both boxes on the counter.

Gaspar said, "I'm going to need the rental information too. You have it on your computer?"

"Should be there." He pecked and clicked and pulled up an account page. He printed it. He pecked a few more times, located a scanned copy of the application form, which included a photo of the box's owner, Sylvia Kent. He printed that one too.

Gaspar found a packing crate, plopped down a ten dollar bill to pay for it, and filled it with the remaining contents of 4719.

"What about 4720?" Kim asked, holding out her hand for the key.

"Oh, right. Sorry." The guy handed the key over and returned to do the computer work on 4720, too focused to notice Gaspar's questioning glance, or Kim's quick shrug in reply.

She opened mailbox 4720 and found it packed just as tight as 4719 had been. She waved Gaspar over with his crate.

"Do you know when these boxes were emptied last?" she asked.

Alfred Lane replied while continuing his computer work. "We don't monitor the customers. They collect their mail when they want to and we store it for them until they do."

"How many customers do you have?"

"Varies. Max is 750. Full up right now. Sometimes we have vacancies."

"You demand the same proof of identity as the U.S. Postal Service to rent these boxes, right?"

"Required by law, we do it. Trust me, we don't want terrorists here."

"Can we get a copy of the list?"

"Why not?" he said. He tapped a couple of keys. The printer hummed.

Gaspar took the pages and dropped them in the packing crate. He said, "Thanks, Alfred. Now help me tote these out to the car, okay?"

"No problem," Alfred said, like he was helping paying customers, like it was all part of the service. Eager to see them go away happy. Or more likely, just go away.

Gaspar said, "I'd suggest you get those outstanding warrant problems ironed out. Otherwise, you'll be a guest of the Feds by early next week. Know what I mean?"

"I'm on it, man."

Kim figured what he'd be on was the next outbound bus as soon as their taillights disappeared around the corner.

Gaspar popped the trunk open, stowed the boxes and slammed the lid.

"You all set? Anything else I can help with?" Alfred asked, hands resting in low side pockets.

Gaspar pulled out his smart phone again, and brought up the fingerprinting app. "Put your right forefinger here."

Alfred Lane did what he was asked. No objection.

"Thanks." Gaspar sent the print. "But don't forget about those warrants. I'll check on you tomorrow. Everything's not fixed by then, they'll send me back to pick you up, you know?"

"No problem." Alfred Lane turned and shuffled back into the store, keys clanging on the chain hanging from his sloppy jeans.

"Warrants for what?" Kim asked, once Gaspar had the Crown Vic on the road again.

"He jumped bail in Jersey about three months ago. Twelve counts of grand larceny and aggravated battery."

"And you just ignored that? And left him there? Are you nuts?"

"You're so easy." He grinned and winked. "Locals are on the way. They'll get here before he scrams."

She punched his shoulder with her fist because he'd had her going. She felt better, though. "Some bondsman in New Jersey will be happy too."

"And thereby hangs a tale," Gaspar said.

"Why? Who was the bondsman?"

"Bernard Owens."

"Never heard of him."

"Me neither. Goes by Bernie, apparently. But we got a bonus. They sent me a picture along with his name." He tossed his smart phone into her lap. "He looked a little worse than that the last time I saw him."

Kim looked at the photo. And gasped.

She recognized the face.

Bernie Owens, New Jersey bondsman, was the rescuer of Sylvia Black.

The shorter guy on Roscoe's videotape.

The guy who wasn't L. Mark Newton.

Very likely the charred body in the Chevy.

CHAPTER THIRTY-FIVE

GASPAR DROVE ON and said, "And Alfred Lane, who owes Bernie Owens big bond money, just happens to be working in the very place where Sylvia's mail hibernated for five long years. Gets better and better, doesn't it? Go right ahead. You can call me brilliant now. Roscoe would."

Kim punched him again, harder this time, and he laughed harder too.

"Lucky is better than good," she said. She fired up her phone for an Internet search, and less than sixty seconds later, she said, "Guess what other business Bernie's got going on?"

Gaspar said, "Tell me."

"Privacy management."

"Which is?"

"A euphemism for helping people disappear."

"Enterprising guy. But apparently workaholism kills."

"Tax records will confirm or deny, but I'm betting Bernie owns the mailbox place too."

"Because?"

"Because the bond on twelve counts of grand larceny and aggravated battery must have been pretty steep. Bernie could have gotten his money back, and he didn't."

"If he knew where to find the kid."

"The kid wasn't exactly hiding. He had his name hanging around his neck. He was a walking investment. In Bernie's own business. The kid said he thought his outstanding warrants had been taken care of. He made a deal with Bernie. Who owns the mailbox store. It's the only conclusion that fits the facts."

He shrugged.

"Can't you ever admit I'm right?"

He shrugged again. She went to punch him again, this time with feeling, but he caught her fist in his right hand and squeezed it. Briefly. Not too hard, but hard enough to hurt.

A whisper-thin layer of civilization separates men from animals, her father had warned many times. When she let her guard down, she always regretted it.

Traffic snarls slowed them through two intersections. Gaspar said, "Bernie owning the place might mean there's more dodgy customers. Agents are already on the way to ask the judge for warrants on the remaining mailboxes. Doubtful they'll get a lead on Jimmy Hoffa, but you never know."

She took his concession as an apology for hurting her hand. Welcome, but insufficient. No matter. She'd long ago learned to mask her heart effectively. Kim understood the game, and played it expertly, even when she didn't feel like it. Nothing personal. Just business. Professionalism demanded no less.

She said, "The photo ID on 4719 is definitely Sylvia Black. But we won't find any usable prints. She never touched any of that stuff in the boxes. Face recognition?"

"Already in process."

"Maybe we'll find something when we sort through the mail."

Gaspar pulled the Crown Vic into a budget hotel driveway. They stacked a luggage cart with the contents of the trunk.

"I'll check us in," she said. She pulled the cart and left him to stow the car.

At the counter, she used the first of the pre-paid gift cards to reserve a second floor room near the side exit for two nights. She used Sylvia Black's name and address.

CHAPTER THIRTY-SIX

Washington, D.C.
November 3
1:05 p.m.

THE ROOM SERVICE menu offered limited options. Kim chose coffee and pastries, French fries, mixed nuts, and bottled water. She placed the order and left cash on the table and headed for the bathroom. She locked the flimsy hollow door and leaned back against it. She closed her eyes. She breathed the stale air and the faint antiseptic fumes in the darkness. She stayed that way for a good long time. She vaguely heard Gaspar accept the room service delivery, but still she didn't move.

Eventually she did what she needed to do, washed, dried, tucked her hair into a fresh chignon, and examined herself in the mirror.

Competent. Professional. Unyielding.

Perfect.

She squared her shoulders, opened the door, and rejoined her partner, for better or worse.

The curled contents of mailboxes number 4719 and number 4720 were dumped on one queen bed, and the surplus from the banker's boxes was on the other. Years of accumulated mail made surprisingly small piles. Gaspar had taken off his shoes and his jacket and rolled up his sleeves. He had eaten his pastry.

He asked, "Who keeps two P.O. boxes open for five years, but never collects the mail?"

Kim said, "Someone who doesn't want to be found. Everybody gets mail. Has to go somewhere."

"If she wasn't going to deal with it, why pay for storage?"

"If mail is returned, senders get curious."

"Why two boxes, then? One would do the job, wouldn't it?"

Kim picked up envelopes and thumbed through them. All were addressed to Sylvia Kent, at either P.O. Box 4719 or P.O. Box 4720, in Crystal City, Arlington, VA 22202. All were postmarked five and six years ago.

She said, "Maybe she planned to come back someday."

Gaspar did the eyebrow lift. Good. That point hadn't occurred to him. She needed to stay a few steps ahead, anticipate what he might do, make a plan B.

He said, "But if she planned to return, then why not just tell people she was taking a year or two off to live in France or something?"

Kim tossed the pile of envelopes back in the box. She stretched her back. She collected a black coffee from the tray, and returned to sorting. The letters were depressingly similar. She saw most of them repeatedly, with no variation aside from dates. "Maybe she was hiding from someone. That's what she told Roscoe. Could be true."

He shrugged.

They worked in silence.

Gaspar finished the packing box stack. "Looks like Bernie should have hired Alfred Lane years ago. The prior clerk wasn't as competent. The early stuff is all mixed up."

Kim found Alfred Lane's computer print-outs at the bottom of the pile. Eight pages. The printer was low on ink. The font was tiny. She sought brighter light to read.

Gaspar's phone rang. He walked his own kinks out as he listened. Then he said, "Okay, keep me posted. Thanks, Jenny."

Kim asked, "So is Alfred Lane in custody?" She opened the drapes and tilted the print-outs to the light. She scanned them.

She stopped on page two.

How could that be?

She flipped to page four. She barely heard Gaspar's reply to her question.

He said, "No, some genius got held up at the courthouse. Duty judge out to lunch or something. By the time they reached Crystal City, Alfred was long gone."

She asked anyway, "Did they get any data?"

He said, "The whole freaking place was on fire. They're still fighting the blaze. Jenny says there will be nothing left but the cinders."

Then there was a knock at the door behind her.

CHAPTER THIRTY-SEVEN

THE KNOCK SOUNDED like a rhythm. Like a pre-arranged code. Like Morse.

Dum-diddy-dum-dum; dum-dum.

Housekeeping?

Kim looked at Gaspar. The only name registered downstairs was female. So Kim called out, "Who is it?"

A voice said, "Sylvia? It's Elle. Gabrielle. Can I come in, honey?"

What the hell?

Gaspar shook his head, raised both palms to indicate he was equally clueless.

The knock code came again. *Dum-diddy-dum-dum; dum-dum.* Elle or Gabrielle sounded happy but urgent. And too loud. "I want to see you, Sylvia. You know that. Come on. Let me in."

Kim navigated around the bed, and looked through the peep-hole. Saw a woman about Sylvia's age, and well dressed.

"How'd you find me?" Kim asked, in a stage whisper, and watched.

Elle chuckled and said, "Some things haven't changed, honey. I still know every front desk clerk and every security chief in every hotel in D.C. I knew you were in town. I asked my friends to call me if you checked in anywhere."

No one else within the fisheye's range. "Are you alone?"

"Just me, myself, and I, honey. Open the door."

Gaspar pulled his gun and moved silently into the bathroom, and left that door open an inch. Kim folded Alfred's printouts and stuffed them in the back pocket of her slacks. She slipped on her gun and added her jacket to cover both bulges. She flipped the safety lever, turned the deadbolt, twisted the knob. She stood a little behind the door, where Elle wouldn't see her immediately. She swung the door halfway open.

Elle came in like a runway model, hips thrust forward, all angles and elbows. She was dressed in vintage Jackie Kennedy pink, from the pillbox hat and the pale lipstick all the way down to the tan hose and the pumps. She was wearing Chanel No. 5. She was giggling like a teenager.

"I can't believe you're back, sweetie. You've been gone so long! I thought I'd never see you again!"

Elle cleared the threshold.

Kim body-pressed the door and clicked the deadbolt.

Elle turned.

She blinked several times as if Kim would become Sylvia if only her emerald contact lenses would clear.

Didn't happen.

Elle said, "Who are you?"

Up close, she looked a few years older than Sylvia. Well-groomed, expensive style. A pink purse in white-gloved hands. Maybe wondering if she should pull out the pepper spray right now.

Kim said, "I'm a friend of Sylvia's."

Elle scanned the room. Saw the room service tray, set for two. Saw two suitcases. Two laptop cases. She saw Sylvia's name on the mail.

She called, "I'm so glad you picked this stuff up, Sylvia," clearly thinking Sylvia was in the bathroom. "I went over there like you asked me to and cleaned out a couple times. Some new guy started working there this summer. A real stickler. He wouldn't let me take any more."

Then Elle saw Gaspar's shoes and jacket. "Where *is* Sylvia?"

"She dashed out to pick up a few things," Kim said. "You know Sylvia."

Big smile from Elle. And a wink. "Forever, honey. We worked all around the world together. I mean, really, Zurich, Paris, New York. Me and Sylvia, we had some good times. She's like me. Loves the job. Loves the adventure. It's exciting, you know? Will she be back here before the party? I have *really* missed that girl. I'd love to see her before the crowd gets to her."

The boss's cell rang. Elle looked toward the source, which was Gaspar's jacket. She nodded knowingly, as if unanswered ringing from a man's pocket should absolutely always be ignored.

Why was he calling right this moment?

Split second decision. Kim said, "I'm meeting Sylvia in the bar in a minute. Why don't you come with me? It'll be fun."

Another ring.

She ushered Elle out to the corridor and closed the door firmly behind them. Gaspar could deal with the boss. In the elevator Elle said, "You don't look like a working girl." She scanned Kim's black suit and her work shoes. "Are you going as a cop? Is that what they want? You could be real FBI in that costume. Do you know Sylvia's FBI boyfriend? Was that him in the bathroom? Oh my God! I didn't interrupt, did I? You were done, right? All the cops ever want is oral, anyway."

Kim covered the jolt with what she hoped was just the right amount of salaciousness. "Her FBI boyfriend?"

Elle's unfazed babbling continued, as if now she and Kim had a great deal in common. "I only met him once. Tall. Built. Gorgeous eyes. High level job over there in the Hoover building. He's the one kept Sylvia out of jail when we all got jammed up a few years back. Set her up out of town someplace. She just couldn't say enough about him. Sounded like a boyfriend to me."

Elle saw Kim's sickened expression, and patted her hand. "But I maybe read it wrong. I'm sure they're just friends, honey. You don't need to worry. Sylvia's got her head on straight. She keeps her mind on the money. No silly romance for working girls like me and Sylvia. We don't want that. Gets in the way, you know?"

The elevator opened in the lobby. Elle waved to her friend at the front desk. They entered the bar, where Elle knew the bartender too.

"Jimmy, send us over two gin martinis, will you, honey? Bleu cheese olives? Just a little dirty, like me. Thanks, honey. But weak, okay?" She slid into the first booth. Giggled. Delivered another body slam to Kim's gut. "Don't want to get drunk before we get there. Marion Wallace throws the best parties in D.C. Booze flows like water. And the food! To die for, honey, just you wait."

Elle laughed as if free flowing alcohol at a Marion Wallace party was the height of luxurious joy.

Marion Wallace?

How could this be happening?

CHAPTER THIRTY-EIGHT

Washington, D.C.
November 3
5:05 p.m.

WALLACES HAD LIVED on Dumbarton street in Georgetown "since Eve ate the apple," as Marion Wallace often said. Gaspar parked down the block and Kim watched him limping back toward her, trying to hide the pain. She knew he'd walk it out. She wished her own anxiety was as easily dealt with.

She saw fall leaves and green spaces and tired jack-o-lanterns nestling on stoops. She was hunched into her jacket against the frigid wind. She was repeating her silent mantra on a constant loop: *One choice, right choice. One choice, right choice. One choice, right choice.*

Marion Wallace's place was a Colonial revival mansion, all red brick, white trim, Doric columns, eyelid windows, and keystone lintels. The exterior had been well maintained since the nineteenth century. Kings had slept there, and waltzed there. Diplomats. Presidents, senators, governors. A few other worthy celebrities from time to time.

"Where's your new best friend?" Gaspar asked, only slightly winded when he got next to her.

Kim nodded toward the house. He raised his eyebrow. She couldn't speak quite yet. But she would. She opened the white wrought iron gate. Preceded him along a red brick walk lined by tended hedges. Four steps up, under a canopy, a double entry door separated the past from the present. Kim pushed the bell and heard chimes pealing inside. She fought nausea.

One choice, right choice.

A liveried butler opened the door. "Welcome to Wallace House," he said. He indicated an open archway on his right. "Guests will be received in the ballroom."

"Thank you," Gaspar said.

One choice, right choice.

Kim stepped across the threshold.

The ballroom was alive with beautiful women. Champagne and hors d'oeuvres were delivered and removed by tuxedoed servers. A string quartet played lively classics in the far corner. Stargazer lilies and gardenias battled vintage perfumes.

"Wow," Gaspar said. "What's the occasion?"

One choice, right choice.

She cleared her throat.

"Hump day," she said.

"Say what?"

"Wednesday party. Every week."

Gaspar nodded. Looked around the room as if he'd never attended a prom. "Don't get me wrong. I love all these gorgeous women. But where are the men?"

"Too early. Events start at seven."

"What events?"

"All events. The ballets, the symphony, state dinners, the theater. Whatever is going on in D.C. tonight where diplomats and dignitaries need escorts."

"These gorgeous creatures are hookers?"

Gaspar seemed bewildered; she had no patience for silliness. Not now.

"This is *Wallace and Company*. Try not to be such a Miami rube, will you?"

Too harsh.

He snapped back, "Little Miss Detroit knows all things Washington?"

Softer reply. "Four years of Georgetown law school for my JD/MBA left me no choice. D.C. overwhelms you even more than New York. Seeps into your bones. Never leaves."

One choice, right choice.

Kim led Gaspar to a line of guests awaiting their hostess poised amid a gaggle of beauties at the receiving line's end. They shuffled forward after each guest was welcomed, ever closer to humiliation. Her heart pounded, and her breathing was shallow. Acid churned in her stomach. She wiped sweaty palms on her thighs. Her hands didn't get drier.

The final group moved past their hostess. Straight ahead now was Marion Wallace. Perhaps the most famous courtesan to power since Madame de Pompadour. Vivid beyond reason. Exquisite alabaster skin. Amazing violet eyes and inky lashes. Lush full lips perpetually upturned. Leonine mane loosely flowing from crown below taut chin. Diamonds and sapphires adorned lobes and clavicle above a perfect neckline.

Intimidating as hell.

And as poisonous as she'd been on Kim's wedding day.

"Welcome to my home," Marion said. A white-gloved hand was extended for a brief squeeze.

Kim's voice deserted her. She squeezed back, and was released.

Gaspar stepped up. He said their names and handed over two business cards, one for each of them. Marion glanced at the cards and placed them on a silver tray next to her throne with all the others.

Gaspar said, "We won't take much of your time, Mrs. Wallace. Maybe five minutes. After you've received your guests."

Marion exhibited the kind of grace under pressure that Kim had yet to master. "I'll be pleased to help you if I can. We will talk privately in my salon when I'm free. In the meantime, please enjoy yourselves."

Thus dismissed, an assistant waved them forward.

Was it possible Marion didn't remember Kim at all?

Thank you, God.

Gaspar shifted his weight, and clasped his hands and said, "Let's find a less conspicuous place to cool our heels. I feel like an underdressed prune in a loaf of angel food cake."

Kim moved toward Marion's salon. He followed, entranced by the spectacle.

She said, "Don't worry. Dressed in FBI ugly, people will think we're the security team. Totally ignorable."

"Where's our Gabrielle?" Gaspar asked, after putting his back to the wall. "She sounded fun. Maybe even affordable on a government salary."

"She'll find us, I'm sure."

He said, "I talked to the boss. I need to fill you in. And Roscoe's trying to reach you. Wouldn't say why. And while you were girl-talking with Elle, I went through the rest of Sylvia's mail."

"Find anything?"

"I found a batch of envelopes forwarded to Margrave and returned to 4719 as undeliverable. All dated about three months ago, when our boy Alfred Lane came on the scene. What did Elle call him? A stickler? Looking like you were right about the demolished mailbox."

"What else?"

"Forty-seven-twenty yielded more. I'll give you the blow-by-blow in the car later." He fished out his phone. Pulled up a picture. "But it led me to this old mug shot."

Kim examined the photo. The accused was identified as Susan Kane. She looked good. Classy. Well tended. Dazzling smile. Hair and makeup about the same. Like Marion Wallace, she hadn't aged.

At six o'clock Kim noticed a change in the noise level. The crowd was thinning as escorts with prior engagements departed to meet their dates. Two or three well-attired men talked near the entrance where the reception line would form again.

Gaspar said, "Criminal records came up pretty quickly once I had the right name. Three counts of prostitution. Right here in D.C., if you can imagine. Some big scandal. Pled guilty. Sentence suspended."

Kim handed the phone back, suddenly weary. Two years after Van's desertion. One year after her testimony. A senator and two Russian diplomats were caught having rough sex with hookers provided by lobbyists. Finally. But there were few arrests and fewer resignations. Sacrificial lambs only. Wright & Company closed, but only briefly.

Now six short years later Marion Wallace was conducting business as usual. Grievance was etched indelible on Kim's heart.

"Kimmy! Honey! Look who I found!" The voice carried above the party sounds from twenty feet away.

Kim opened her eyes to see Elle approaching as swiftly as she could in the tight skirt, babbling like a cheerleader the entire distance, arm-in-arm with the unmistakable Sylvia Kent Black. Or Susan Kane. Or whoever she was.

Kim instantly recalled Elle's bar talk.

"Kimmy, it's a great life, don't you think? Every night is like a drama; different names, different scripts. A stage where I'm the star. The phone rings, curtain goes up, the play begins. Always a little tension, Kimmy. The adrenaline never stops. When it's not so great, the money's still good. Sylvia's just like me. That's why we get along so well, you know?"

Elle was ten feet away now. Sylvia looked reluctant. Then as if the moment was elaborately choreographed, the salon door opened wide revealing tasteful furnishings in historic hues.

Unchanged, Kim thought.

Surreal.

Peach and ivory brocade, gold tassels, and spring green stripes, all blended to please. Plush carpets, cozy fire, Marion Wallace reposed in the same green brocade Louis XV armchair, at the same end of the same rectangular grouping. On each side of her, white brocade sofas faced each other. Even the same silver tea service graced the coffee table between. The entire tableau made Kim woozy.

"Mr. Gaspar, Ms. Otto, Mrs. Wallace can see you now." A well-coiffed assistant waved them inside using her entire body as if introducing another stage performer.

At that precise moment, Elle arrived, slightly breathless. She stopped at the open salon entrance and the assistant said, "Thank you, Gabrielle. Susan, Mrs. Wallace invites you to join her. This way everyone, please."

Elle grinned, and released Sylvia's arm. "Go ahead, honey. We'll all visit later."

What, Kim wondered now, was real about Sylvia Black? Not her name. Which was disorienting. Names mattered to Kim. They meant something. But this woman was never Sylvia Black at all. Had she known Van?

The assistant left the room and Sylvia approached Marion Wallace as a commoner might approach a queen, with obsequious smiles and air kisses, and no touching.

"You look wonderful, dear," Sylvia said. "I've missed you. I'm so sorry we've been apart such a long time."

Marion gave her the same official smile and the same gloved squeeze she'd given everyone else. As far as Kim knew, Marion Wallace never had any real friends and she never would. All business, all the time, now as then.

Sylvia perched herself on one sofa as young women learned to do in finishing school once upon a time. Skirt pulled down as far as it would reach near her pressed together knees; ankles crossed. She removed white gloves and laid them neatly beside her handbag.

Marion turned to Kim and Gaspar as if they were visiting diplomats, and extended her hand to each again. Gestured toward the sofa opposite Sylvia.

"Where's that handsome boyfriend of yours, Susan?" Marion asked, after pouring tea from the silver service into bone china cups.

"Work, unfortunately." Syliva did not lift the teacup. Nor did Kim.

Marion passed a small plate of shortbread. Only Gaspar accepted.

Marion asked, "Is his office still at the top of the Hoover building?"

The question startled Sylvia briefly. "Yes, of course."

"I suppose there's only one better address in the world," Marion mused. "Very helpful to you when that unfortunate business happened, though, wasn't it?" She glanced down at her watch as if she'd just recalled an important meeting. "Will you excuse me? I have something else I must attend to. Please carry on."

Marion stepped out and Sylvia was left facing Kim and Gaspar across the silver. Gaspar got up and planted himself at the exit as if to say Sylvia would not walk out of that room as easily as she'd walked out of Roscoe's jail cell.

"I should have known Marion wouldn't have time to visit on hump day." Sylvia smiled as she might have indulged an aged aunt. She replaced her gloves. "I am expected elsewhere myself. Was there something in particular you wanted to ask me?"

Gaspar said, "For starters, why don't you tell us your real name?"

"Elle told me you'd read my mail, Agent Gaspar. I'm sure you already know all about me."

"Why did you kill Harry Black?" Kim asked. A pretty blunt tactic.

"Kill Harry? My goodness, why on earth would I do that?"

Gaspar said, "Cut the crap, Sylvia. Or whatever your name is. What the hell is going on here?"

"I take it you haven't checked in lately," Sylvia said. "You might want to do that before you get too forceful with me, Agent Gaspar. Your bosses won't like your tone."

"You confessed to murder," he said.

Sylvia was amused. "Are you sure?"

"You called 911. You said you killed Harry Black."

"I did not. Have you heard the tape yourself?"

Which proved she wasn't merely foxy, but also sly. And informed. Neither Kim nor Gaspar had heard the actual 911 tape. Roscoe hadn't heard it, either. And Sylvia knew all that. But how?

What had Sylvia said at the time? Kim searched her memory. Recalled Roscoe's report precisely. *"I'm told Sylvia's exact words were 'I shot him. He's dead. I just couldn't take him anymore.'"*

A subtle difference. "I shot him." Not, "I killed him." Hair splitting? Maybe. But criminal cases fell apart for less. Harry had been killed by two bullets to the head, but he'd been shot a total of seven times. Five post-mortem. Sylvia might have shot him only after he was dead.

Nothing really tied Sylvia to Harry's murder. Repeatedly, Roscoe mentioned the crime scene was totally clean. Sylvia had escaped Roscoe's jail, but a good lawyer would argue she'd been falsely arrested and imprisoned in the first place. He'd sue Margrave and Sylvia would end up owning the whole town.

Was it really possible that Sylvia would walk away free? They had no warrant. And couldn't get one based on existing evidence.

Sylvia knew that too.

"We found the money, Sylvia," Kim said, quietly.

"What money?" Sylvia asked, deadpan.

"Bernie Owens is dead too."

Contrived alarm in Sylvia's expression. "You killed Bernie?"

"You know we didn't. Your lover blew up that Chevy with enough explosive to scatter Bernie for ten miles."

Slight reaction. Kim concluded Sylvia cared for Bernie, but not as much as she cared for the money. She was a hooker, after all. Kim said, "All that cash in Bernie's car went everywhere too. Couple hundred thousand, at least. Maybe more."

Sylvia sat still, unblinking, but Kim could see perspiration beading along her temples, gathering on her upper lip. Her hands were clasped tight in her lap.

Kim knew Sylvia's trigger point now. She said, "He stole Harry's money, and then he killed Harry. He stole Bernie's money, and then he killed Bernie. He's stealing your money now. But don't worry too much. You'll never be poor. Because as soon as he gets it, you'll be dead too."

"You're lying," Sylvia said, mouth so dry the words barely escaped.

"Think so?" Gaspar showed her the photo he'd taken when he looked in through the Chevy's window. "That's Bernie, right? Two bullets to the back of the head. Just like Harry."

He reached into his pocket and pulled out charred pieces of paper. He forced them into Sylvia's palm. He said, "And that's Bernie's money."

Sylvia looked at the burned scraps. She started to shake. Slightly at first. Then more. "That's not really Bernie. Or his money. You manipulated that picture. You burned these yourself."

"Your lover killed eight people and hurt dozens more." Gaspar was angry. "You knew Jim Leach, right? There's video. Want to see Jim Leach blown apart with your own eyes? Very entertaining."

Kim's tone was gentler. "We're so glad you're okay. At first we thought you were in the trunk. Can you imagine? Being in the trunk when the car exploded? That Chevy burned so hot there was nothing left but cinders. Everything in the back seat? Right where you were sitting? Toasted. Blown away. Ashes." Kim raised both hands and pinched her fingers and flashed them open. "Poof! Gone with the wind. Just like that."

Sylvia began to sob. Her shoulders heaved. Several minutes.

Acting? Or real?

Kim handed her a tissue box from Marion Wallace's side table. Sylvia pulled a fistful. Dabbed her face.

Gaspar said, "You help us, we'll help you. Otherwise, you're on your way to Leavenworth. If you're lucky."

"What do you want me to do?" A catch in her voice.

"Testify," Kim said.

"About what?" Sniffles.

"Everything," Gaspar said.

Sylvia's face brightened. She flashed a bright pixie smile.

"Is that all?" she said. "I can do that. When do you want me?"

CHAPTER THIRTY-NINE

KIM HEARD NOISE from the ballroom. More volume, lower tones. Men were showing up. The party was about to start.

"Okay, let's go," Gaspar said. "Right now."

Sylvia asked, "Go where?"

Kim wondered that herself. Margrave jail?

Gaspar opened the boss's phantom cell and pressed the call back button. "We have a witness to bring in," he said. "Sylvia Black." He listened to brief instructions and disconnected. He said, "Our boss wants to see you."

Sylvia smiled. A mega-watt blinder this time. "I'm so glad," she said. "Would you mind if I slipped into the powder room to, um, fix my face? You can check for escape routes first." She giggled. Flirtatious once again. A hooker.

Gaspar accompanied her to the small toilet at the back corner of the salon. She stood aside while he ducked in and back out.

"Don't lock the door," he said.

"Why would I want to do that?"

Gaspar stood guard, left hand clasped over his right wrist, his watch face visible, marking the time.

The salon's main door opened. Marion Wallace returned. "Was there anything else you needed from me before I return to my guests, Agent Otto?"

Kim's stomach snake thrashed violently. Acid bubbled up her esophagus. But she refused to flinch. She swallowed hard.

"No," she said.

"Call to schedule something with my assistant if you need to see me again," Marion said, and Kim watched her walk through the main door again.

"Agent Otto, Agent Gaspar."

Sonorous male voice. Like radio. Unmistakable.

Kim's skin crawled.

"Hello, Hale," she said.

Which was as curt as she dared to the boss's right hand man.

Michael Hale. Grandfathered in place before the boss recruited her or Gaspar. Binding ties between Hale and the boss ran from merely distasteful to downright disgusting. Kim avoided Hale whenever possible.

"Where is she?" Hale asked.

Demanding, as always.

"Primping," Gaspar said, pointing at the powder room door.

"Cooper sent me to assess and report." Hale's derivative power was enormous. He wielded it more overtly than the boss ever would. "Get her out here."

Gaspar rapped twice on the powder room door.

Sylvia came out. She recognized the new man in the room. She approached. She parted her newly glossed lips. She flashed her pixie smile.

"Mr. Hale, so nice to see you again." Sylvia extended her gloved hand, and touched his arm ever so briefly. Ownership. A lover's caress. "How is Mr. Cooper?"

They all knew each other. Mildly surprising. Maybe Hale had bedded Sylvia. Unremarkable. Hale was a notorious womanizer. Definitely not the boyfriend type.

But Cooper?

Elle had described Sylvia's FBI boyfriend. *Tall. Built. Gorgeous eyes. High level job over there in the Hoover building.*

Cooper. Self-described serial monogamist. Could he have been that dumb? Maybe Hale wasn't the only Hoover building occupant Sylvia had screwed.

Kim berated herself for being so stupid.

But everything's obvious once you know it.

Hale ignored Sylvia's greeting. "Otto, what's this about?"

Sylvia returned to her perch on the white sofa. She was more relaxed than anyone else in the room. Kim delivered by rote, "Susan Kane, a/k/a Sylvia Kent Black, has agreed to testify against her accomplices in matters related to the murder of Harry Black."

Hale looked straight at Sylvia.

"That so?" he said. "You're going to admit everything?"

Sylvia batted her eyelashes and raised her right hand and said, "The truth, the whole truth, and nothing but the truth, so help me God."

Hale flushed pink from his stiff white collar right up to his sandy hairline. His eyes narrowed, either in incomprehension or calculation. Kim couldn't tell. His tone was hard enough to cut diamonds. He said, "In exchange for what?"

"Dangerous people will be looking for me. You and Mr. Cooper can fix that, can't you?" Sylvia's tone was so sweet it made Kim's teeth ache.

Hale's face turned redder. "You agreed we wouldn't need to help you again. Yet, here you are, and it's not a minor prostitution charge this time, is it?"

Sylvia's breathless little voice begged, "I'm innocent, Mickey. You know I didn't kill anybody. Helping me again shouldn't be a problem for Charlie, should it?"

Mickey?

Charlie?

Hale looked like he'd swallowed a turd. His eyes bulged from his head. "We're not in the immunity business. But if your testimony is valuable enough, I suppose we might help. What are you offering?"

She said, "Who killed Harry."

Hale was unmoved. "That might be of minor interest to the Margrave Police Chief. It's of no interest to me."

Sylvia remained quiet for a minute. Then she looked at Kim, and Gaspar. Then her gaze returned to Hale. She said, "I suppose I could talk about *why* he killed Harry too."

Kim had to hand it to her. Men had followed women like Sylvia right off a cliff since the dawn of sex. Sylvia was smoking hot. And while not brilliant, she was undeniably clever. Harry Black, the poor bastard, had never stood a chance. Yep. Sylvia was a stone-cold bitch.

Hale's eyes were slits. "What do you mean? Exactly?"

Sylvia straightened her skirt and crossed her remarkably long legs, giving him a full shot view up her thigh. "I shouldn't say more until my lawyer is present, should I? Maybe we can get the whole truth recorded tomorrow morning? Would that work? I'm at the Hay Adams. These agents can escort me. I'll call my lawyer and we'll take care of everything tomorrow. How's that?"

Hale covered the short distance to Sylvia and grabbed her bicep and jerked her off the sofa and shoved her hard against Gaspar. "Bring her to Cooper's office in the morning. Eight o'clock sharp."

And then he stalked out.

Which was when Kim knew for sure. Hale was expendable. They all were. Except Cooper. Rank had its privileges. Cooper was the top dog. Untouchable without hard evidence. Suicide to try.

If the situation went sideways others would take the hit.

Gaspar had been right all along.

They were all involved in it.

Reacher, too. Had to be.

Cooper was the leader. Had Reacher crossed him somehow? Had Cooper sent them to find Reacher for some private purpose?

Possible.

There was plausible deniability all around if they succeeded. If they failed, everyone except Cooper went down. Cooper would make it so.

CHAPTER FORTY

Washington, D.C.
November 3
6:35 p.m.

KIM PACED THE room for a solid half hour, seeking solutions, but getting nothing except impatient and thirty minutes older. Gaspar waited quietly, butt in chair, long legs stretched out and crossed at the ankles, hands folded, eyes closed. He said, "We could follow orders for once. We could deliver Sylvia in the morning. And return to normal life."

His laconic style was familiar to her by then, but no less maddening. "But don't you feel like a first class patsy? And what do we tell Roscoe? Have you even thought about that? She's going down in flames and Sylvia walks free? Again? Sixty-seven *million* dollars richer? And Cooper too? Does that seem right to you? And what about Reacher? Do we leave him out there doing God knows what to God knows whom?"

No response.

Her hands balled into fists. "Well?"

"Tantrums never work on me," he said, unmoved. "But anyway, in answer to your questions, in order of asking, yes, I don't know, yes, sucks, sucks, sucks, sucks, no, don't care, sucks, deep subject."

She was not amused. "Are you going to help me or not?"

He stood and stretched. He limped around the spacious room. He stopped outside the door to Sylvia's bedroom and stared as if he had x-ray vision or supersonic hearing. He ran a hand through his hair. He limped some more. He returned to his seat.

He said, "Of course, I'll help you. But with what? There's something going on here, and it's buried deep. I don't even know what it is, let alone know how to prove it. We turn all this over to an internal investigations unit and they fail, too, and then what? Give me a stroke of genius and I'll be there. Otherwise, I don't see any options except deliver Sylvia in the morning."

She sighed.

He pressed. "Any bright ideas? Preferably something that won't get us fired? Did I mention I have a large family?"

She said nothing.

He said, "That's what I thought. You got zilch."

He was wrong, technically. She had one desperate, last-ditch option. But she didn't describe it. Maybe she would never need to. Maybe something else would come along.

She went back to pacing. She talked as she walked. "Roscoe said Archie Leach is howling because we left before he debriefed us. He wants vengeance for his brother."

Gaspar said, "We didn't kill his brother. So how is Archie Leach our problem?"

"Cooper called you after the fire in the mailbox store."

"Right."

"He asked you about Sylvia's mail. You told him everything. The smashed mailbox theory, forwarded envelopes, the list of box holders, and how you found her mug shot."

"Yes."

"He didn't ask to see the list?"

"No."

"That's weird, isn't it?"

"No."

"You saw the list just like I did. His name is on it. And so is mine. And yours. He wasn't even interested?"

Blandly, like he was calming a suicide, Gaspar said, "But I didn't know all that when I was talking to him. You took the list with you, remember? To the bar? In your pocket?"

"But he had to know, right? So it's weird that he didn't ask or deal with it somehow, isn't it?"

"You're wearing me out."

"Isn't it?"

"We've been over this, Sunshine. All we have is the list. Nothing else. If it comes to it, he'll say he has no idea why his name was on the list, and he'll say he didn't have a mailbox at Bernie's, and we'll believe him, because we have no idea why our names were on the list either, and we sure didn't have mailboxes at Bernie's."

"Cooper is involved with Sylvia."

"Sex is not illegal."

"Sylvia laundered the money and stole it from Harry and killed him."

"Maybe so. No proof, though. And nothing connecting Cooper to any of that."

When she didn't raise anything else, he said, "Can I go to sleep now?"

She patted herself down, checked her gun and her pockets, and walked toward the door.

Stretched out in his chair, eyes closed, Gaspar asked, "Where are you going?"

"To call Finlay."

He didn't move so much as an eyelid. But his tone conveyed every catastrophic consequence she'd already argued in her head. "If anybody asks, you're on your own. I've got a family to feed. Did I mention that? Twenty years left. Fit for no other work. Not even fit for this, to be honest. I'm a charity case. You can throw your career out the window, but please don't add mine to the landfill while you're at it."

"Cooper's not God, you know," she reminded him, in his own words.

"He's the God of my family dinner. And yours too. Whatever special relationship you think you two have, Sunshine, make no mistake. He'll throw you under the train in a Hot'lanta second and never look back."

Only one choice.

She opened the door. Looked back. He hadn't moved.

"I was wrong about you," she said. "Zorro, you're not."

"Sad but true," he said, and the door slammed behind her.

CHAPTER FORTY-ONE

Washington, D.C.
November 3
7:15 p.m.

KIM GOT A cab outside the hotel and sharpened her plan on the fly. It was cold, but she barely noticed. She thought through her counter-surveillance options but knew she was unlikely to hide much. Unmonitored transmissions in Washington, D.C., were as scarce as innocent felons. The very airwaves were alive with ears and eyes every moment of every day.

Best case: Cooper was otherwise occupied at that moment. He was covering a private operation solo and off the books. There would be inevitable windows of surveillance black-out. He wasn't God. He could find the pieces afterward, but he might not be observing in real time.

But he'd anticipate her call to Finlay. He'd be ready to intercept. The problem gnawed at her. She rubbed Finlay's card inside her pocket. She needed an unpredictable location. And fast. The Redskins' FedEx Field would work, but there wasn't enough time to get there and back.

Only one choice.

Which was: Verizon Center during tonight's hockey game.

Twenty-thousand-plus in attendance; most of them using electronic devices. On a pre-paid burner phone, she would be as anonymous as any hay straw in the stack.

The cab ride took eight minutes door-to-door in light traffic. The game was already in progress. She used the media entrance at 6th and G Streets Northwest. She flashed her badge everywhere she needed to. She found the best reception she was likely to get. She put a finger in her opposite ear to mute the screaming crowd. She called the number.

Finlay answered on the fourth ring. Boston accent. Rich baritone. He said, "How can I help you?"

"I was hoping you'd tell me," she said. "We've hit a snag."

"Your partner knows you're calling?"

"Yes. But he advised me not to."

"Because you've worked your way up the food chain to the killer whale?"

"Correct."

"And you want me to remove the obstacle in your path. Why would I do that?"

Trading favors. What did Kim have that Finlay wanted? "You tell me."

"Much has changed since we met. You're operating under a bright spotlight now."

But his price might be too steep. "Can you help or not?"

"Depends."

"On what?"

"How far you're willing to go."

Kim paused briefly. Reflex. *Only one choice.* "I think we understand each other, Mr. Finlay. One more thing. Roscoe's in trouble. Friendly fire. Fix it."

Silence. Had he not anticipated her demand? He said, "Agreed. I've left a package for you at the Swiss embassy. Offer expires in twenty minutes. Your taxi's waiting."

Connection terminated.

She checked her watch. Fifteen minute trip in the opposite direction under current conditions. She burned five extra minutes to dispose of the phone, exit on F Street, and flag a new cab of her own. "Twenty-nine hundred Cathedral Avenue Northwest. And I'm in a hurry."

The cab pulled up in front of an unimpressive building. Tan brick boxes joined by a brown mullioned glass structure all seemed deserted. A lone security guard waited inside the locked gate. Kim asked the cab to wait.

"ID, please," the guard said when she approached. She showed her badge. He checked his watch, examined the photo, compared her face. Returned her ID wallet.

"One moment," he said.

He walked behind a majestic maple tree and retrieved a shrink-wrapped Redweld accordion file. He handed it through the bars. He turned away. Kim ran back to her cab.

"Hay Adams hotel, please." No time for further counter-surveillance maneuvers; she'd been gone too long already. She ripped off the shrink wrap, removed the attached elastic, opened the Redweld's flap, and pulled out its contents. She held them up to the cab's window for passing ambient light. She stared. Flipped through. Too dim to read. Ink blurred on the pages.

Her smart phone rang. She answered without thinking. "Agent Otto."

Gaspar said, "We've been released. Where are you now?"

"On my way." She was maybe five blocks out, but traffic was barely moving.

"I'll meet you in the lobby."

Kim didn't understand. "What about Sylvia?"

"She's gone."

"Gone?"

"Cooper had Hale pick her up twenty minutes ago."

She saw the Hay Adams up ahead in the distance, but the traffic was stopped in all directions.

"Wait for me at the front entrance. I'll be there in five." She disconnected, grabbed cash from her pocket, paid the driver, and left the cab where it was.

She dialed the second pre-paid burner while she jogged along the sidewalk.

CHAPTER FORTY-TWO

Washington, D.C.
November 3
9:45 p.m.

KIM HAD WORKED at the Washington Hilton, one of the biggest and busiest hotels in D.C., during law school. She knew its eleven hundred guest rooms, its acres of function space, its forty-two meeting rooms, its four restaurants and bars. She remembered the service corridor, the loading dock, and the freight elevator. Tonight and every night, the hotel buzzed with crowd cover. The night manager was happy to help her. Returning felt almost like coming home.

Gaspar had asked no questions for the past hour while they collected Sylvia's mail from the Crown Vic and transferred to the Hilton. He'd felt her urgency, perhaps, but whatever his reasons, he had stuck with her and demanded no explanations.

She wondered how long he'd wait.

Kim picked up the banker's box containing Sylvia's newer mail from P.O. Box 4720 and dumped it out on one of the beds. She pushed envelopes with both hands, seeking recognizable logos amid the junk. Marketers were ever smarter. Separating the gold from the dross wasn't simple. Evidence was easily missed.

Five items looked promising.

She scooped junk mail into the box and shoved it aside. She carried possibles to the desk and rooted around for a letter opener. She unfolded contents and sorted them into piles.

Two senders: Jensen & Associates, C.P.A, and The Empire Bank of Switzerland.

Gaspar said, "Okay, Sunshine, I give up. What's all this about?"

Kim glanced at her watch. Seventy-three minutes of patience. She wondered if that was some sort of personal best. It probably was. She said, "I know why they killed Harry."

He shrugged. "Everyone knows why they killed Harry. For the money."

"It's more complicated than that. If I'm right, Sylvia and Harry were about to be on the wrong end of the IRS for back taxes, penalties and interest of $137 million. More than twice Harry's total Kliner stash. They'd have lost everything and gone to prison."

No reaction.

She said, "And they would have taken Cooper down with them. And they still can."

"How?"

She said, "You need to decide if you really want to hear this. It ain't going to be pretty. It's going to be a train wreck."

"But you're sticking with it."

"You don't have to."

"Because I'm not Zorro."

"You have a family. And twenty years to go."

"Tell me what you know."

"You sure?"

"You deaf? How many times do I have to say it?"

"Sylvia's mail tells the story," she said. Then she hesitated. She took a deep breath. "And Finlay confirmed it for me."

Gaspar said nothing. He just headed for one of the upholstered chairs.

"Don't get too comfortable," Kim said. "We've got an appointment in thirty minutes at the Swiss Embassy and a flight to Zurich at 1:12."

"Fill me in, Susie Q," he said.

She pulled the Redwell's contents, and divided them into three batches. "We were right about the laundering. Harry figured out a way to exchange the Kliners for real money. Caribbean casinos." She tossed the first group into his lap. "Photographs of Harry and Sylvia at blackjack tables in four separate establishments over four years. Tried and true. They bring the Kliners out of Atlanta in small batches. They buy chips, they gamble a while, they cash in the chips for real money. Pretty simple, even with Harry's full time job. Short flights from Atlanta to the Caribbean. Easy enough to confirm by flight records."

He asked, "But what did they do with the clean money? Stupid to bring it back and hide it in the closet."

Kim tossed him the second set of Redwell contents. "Bank records. Deposits to Caribbean banks."

Gaspar thumbed through the half dozen statements. "They run for slightly less than five years. Stop abruptly three months ago. Offshore, like we thought."

"But then they screwed up."

"How?"

"Two ways. First, they never claimed any of their gambling winnings on their income taxes to get the clean money into the paper trail. Fraud would have been a lot harder to prove when the IRS got on their tails. Bought them extra time."

He shrugged. Tax issues had never impressed him much. She figured he'd never been on the wrong side of the IRS. Those bastards were meaner than the FBI by a long shot.

"Second?"

She held paper in each unsteady hand. Raised Finlay's contributions in her left first. "The Caribbean bank statements are fakes too. Meant to comfort Harry, maybe. The money wasn't there. It was deposited somewhere else. Might still be there."

Gaspar lifted his eyebrow. Didn't reach out for the paper. Touching meant plausible deniability destroyed.

Kim raised Susan Kane's mail from box 4720 in her right hand. "These confirm."

"Where is the money, then?"

"Empire Bank of Switzerland."

Gaspar smiled. "Of all the gin joints in all the world."

She smiled back. "Poetic, isn't it?"

CHAPTER FORTY-THREE

Washington, D.C.
November 3
11:25 p.m.

THE SWISS EMBASSY was alight and active inside when they arrived slightly ahead of a developing storm. Temperatures had dropped and lightning flashed in the distance. The wind had picked up. No rain yet, but Kim could feel dropping atmospheric pressure in her bones. The cab driver said, "I'll wait, but if you want to make it to Dulles in an hour, you'd better hurry. They're predicting hail the size of golf balls."

Kim tried to ignore everything she knew about flying through thunderstorms as she rushed ahead of Gaspar into the glass enclosed center connecting the two brick wings. There was more lightning, followed by deafening thunder, and then wind-whipped rain started to fall. The effect of standing inside the storm while totally shielded and feeling none of nature's outrage was surreal.

They were escorted quickly to Finlay's contact, deep in the north wing. The office was decorated as if by ancient financiers. Teak floors, worn Orientals, ancient vases. Likely real. As was Wilfred Schmidt, according to his desk nameplate.

Schmidt offered two hard chairs on the other side of his desk. He clasped manicured hands together on a burgundy desk blotter. He had gold links in his starched white cuffs. He spoke precise English, clearly not his first language, and maybe not his second.

"Please excuse the necessary abruptness," he said. "My schedule is quite full as it is about to be tomorrow in Zurich. I have been instructed to disclose certain information. I am allowed to answer no questions. Agreed?"

Kim nodded because she had no power to demand more.

Herr Schmidt prompted, "Yes?"

Maybe there was an audio recording.

Gaspar said, "Agreed."

Schmidt launched into rote speech he'd likely delivered to countless customers over the past twelve months. "As you know, Empire Bank of Switzerland will provide a list of depositors and amounts on deposit to U.S. Internal Revenue Service pursuant to new treaties signed by our respective governments. Understand?"

Kim nodded. He waited. She said, "Yes."

Everyone knew the IRS was salivating like a starving Rottweiler before dinner. Negotiations with Swiss banks and treaties executed the previous year were well publicized all around the world. Looming deadlines for disclosing tax cheats had been preceded by a period of tax amnesty about to expire. Tensions on Wall Street and Main Street and in every criminal enterprise that touched the country had led to panic among legitimate and illegitimate alike.

If Kim's theories were correct, the same panic had led Sylvia Black to murder her husband. Panic that could lead to solid testimony against Cooper.

Schmidt noticed Kim's preoccupation. He cleared his throat to bring her back.

He delivered a rehearsed disclaimer next, with appropriate emphasis. "Swiss privacy laws demand *strict* secrecy. Penalties for privacy violations are severe. Accounts will be revealed *precisely* as required. Individual depositors are permitted six remaining days to complete satisfactory asset arrangements and agreements with respective governments. *We have no information on the status of such activities.* Understand?"

"Yes," Kim said. She understood. The Swiss remained as politically neutral as possible. A policy necessary, some said, to maintaining the most opportunistic country on earth. A friend to everyone is a friend to no one, in Kim's view, stacks of money regardless.

Schmidt reached the red meat. "Four individual depositors are relevant here. Four numbered accounts and two safety deposit boxes. Contents of boxes are not disclosed to the bank. Understand?"

Gaspar said, "We understand. Who are the four depositors?"

Schmidt passed another sealed Redwell across the desk to Kim.

She tore off the shrink wrap, removed the elastic band, pulled out four account statements and two small brass keys affixed to numbered tags. She checked the account names. Susan Kane's on one box made sense. But the others? She blinked. Again. The names didn't change. Charles Cooper, Carlos Gaspar, and Kim Otto. How could that be?

She felt the stomach snake begin to uncoil.

Nothing is ever what you think it is.

Gaspar asked, "Where are the safety deposit boxes located?"

Schmidt said, "Zurich. They've been alerted to receive you. Your taxi is waiting."

CHAPTER FORTY-FOUR

Zurich, Switzerland
November 4
4:00 p.m. local time

A DELAYED DEPARTURE at Dulles due to weather meant they missed their appointment in Zurich. But they had a chance to make it to the bank before it closed. She jogged and he limped through the spotless terminal, all the way to a spotless cab at a spotless curb. He asked, "Doesn't it worry you that Finlay is doing this?"

"Should it?" Kim asked back. She watched Zurich pass by out the side window.

"Cooper is a ruthless guy."

"Clearly Finlay is just as ruthless."

"Exactly. Two ruthless guys battle, other people die."

She shrugged. Useful gesture, she'd concluded. Conveyed everything and nothing. Economical too. "Everybody dies."

The cab pulled up in front of an imposing gray brick skyscraper thirty minutes late, but still thirty minutes before closing. They climbed out together into dry but overcast twilight. The EBS logo was prominently displayed on the building. It was identical to the logos on the envelopes they'd found in box 4720, and on the four bank statements and the two keys in the second Redwell.

There were patrons milling around inside the bank. Kim was slightly surprised. Who made personal visits to banks anymore? Kim's paychecks were automatically deposited, her withdrawals made at ATMs, and her bills paid online or by draft.

There was a very formal male receptionist in the lobby, seated behind a mahogany desk. He asked, "Do you have an appointment?"

"Herr Gartner is expecting us." Kim showed regret and her driver's license. "Our flight was a bit late, I'm afraid."

The receptionist looked down at a print-out with the day's appointments discreetly listed and unreadable from Kim's viewpoint. "Yes, I see," he said. He sounded like a bad guy in a bad movie. "Perhaps it is possible to accommodate you. Please be seated. I will contact Herr Gartner."

Five minutes later a middle-aged man entered the lobby through one of the heavy wooden doors on the left-hand side. He said, "This way, please." They followed him down a narrow carpeted hallway. There were gray steel doors placed ten feet apart on both sides. Twenty feet in, he stopped. He unlocked a door into a carpeted eight-by-eight windowless room. The room held a wood parson's table and four unforgiving chairs.

Inside, he asked, "May I see your identification, please?"

They produced badge wallets. He photographed their ID first, and followed with headshots. Then he extended his device to each of them in turn. "Please."

Both agents pressed an index finger onto the screen. A green light signaled success. The man seemed satisfied.

"Please wait here. The boxes will arrive momentarily."

Kim marked the time. Tested the lever when he left. They were locked in. A surveillance camera was mounted at the corner ceiling joint opposite, with a red light indicating that it was operational. Kim suspected clients turned their backs on the camera while other hidden lenses created indelible records. If they failed to follow instructions, consequences would be immediate and unpleasant.

Precisely eight minutes later, the middle-aged man returned with a sturdy cart upon which rested two bottles of water, two glasses, a silver-plated coffee carafe, two cups, two saucers, two spoons, and cream and sugar.

And two heavy metal boxes.

Maybe fifteen inches by twelve by fifteen.

Each box had two locks.

The man pulled two keys from his pocket and put them on the table. "You brought depositor keys, correct? I will collect those before you depart. You may not remove anything from this room. Your authorization permits viewing only. No photographs or recording of any kind. We close in thirty minutes."

He indicated a small rectangle on the wall. "Push this button and I shall return to escort you to the exit. Any questions?"

"No," Kim lied. She was overwhelmed with questions.

The man left without ceremony.

Kim used the bank's keys and Gaspar used the depositor keys Finlay had provided. They lifted heavy, hinged lids and let them rest fully open.

They peered into the boxes.

Susan Kane's was full.

Charles Cooper's was nearly empty.

Kim slipped latex gloves from her pocket. She said, "I'll take Kane, you take Cooper."

They worked quickly and followed standard protocols. They examined and sorted contents. They snapped photos surreptitiously with their smart phones, but used no dictation. Video capture by the bank's system was inescapable, but they'd provide no sound track of their own.

Gaspar finished first. He poured coffee and moved to a chair and studied Cooper's treasures.

Kim catalogued Kane's contents robotically. She'd worked vice raids enough times to recognize the common sex-trade tools. They were secured inside a small canvas duffel. Harnesses, body paint, paddles, rubber belts, spiked shoes. French ticklers, satin gloves, pleasure mitten, massage oil. Polaroid camera, but no film and no photos.

A red satin pouch held slightly more exotic items. There was an elaborate dual-control vibrator labeled "Busy Beaver." There was edible underwear. Ben wa balls were nestled in a velvet case. There was a silver egg filled with mercury. There was a matching two-inch silver band.

Underneath the nostalgic keepsakes were three obsolete flash drives snugged into a Cartier watch box: silver, gold, black. No labels.

When she'd finished, she saw Gaspar had long ago adopted his relaxed posture. She said in a level tone, "There's nothing remarkable here. Nothing has been added for at least five years, maybe longer."

He understood. His jaw clenched. He added this latest insult to his long list of Finlay grievances. He nodded, but didn't open his eyes. He said, "Ancient history here too."

Kim repacked and returned the Cartier box below camera surveillance angle. She replaced the red satin bag and the canvas duffel. Her right hand slipped her phone and concealed all three flash drives until she dropped them into her pocket while her left hand retrieved the depositor key. She relocked the box. She left the depositor key in place as instructed. She took a bottle of water.

Her watch said the bank had closed ten minutes ago.

"Don't want to get locked in," she said.

She assumed he was as ready as she was to escape the tiny space. Five minutes, if their watchdog was close by. She reached the doorbell and pressed it before Gaspar could react. She'd misjudged his signals.

Swiftly, he body-blocked the door. His expression was unreadable. He whispered, "Take a look at those pictures. Make some copies in case mine get lost. Be sure we've got several backups."

She saw four photographs from Cooper's box spaced out on the table.

The first was of a group of Marines dressed in fatigues. Hard to judge ages, but the setting and the picture were both old. Faded color. Maybe 3 x 5 instead of the more common 4 x 6 for later photographs. She flipped it. Kodak paper. Undated. Late 1960s?

The center Marine was a young and handsome Charles Cooper. Standing next to him was a giant. Couldn't be Jack Reacher. Reacher was much younger than Cooper. And Army, not Marine Corps. She didn't recognize the others. A crude hand painted road sign proclaimed 472 miles to Hanoi. Her Viet Nam geography was rusty. Da Nang, maybe?

There was a knock on the door.

Gaspar called, "One minute."

The second photo was from the same era. Similar location. Maybe the same camera and the same lab. The photo was of a man and two boys. The giant from the first, with what had to be his sons, one a couple of years older than the other.

Acid bubbled in her throat.

She pressed on.

The two remaining photos were much newer. Kim figured six months old at most. The third was Roscoe and her family.

Roscoe's stylish haircut, son Davey in basketball uniform, sulky Jack inexplicably smiling.

Fourth was a candid group shot. Outside. Picnic table. Summer. Beers and laughter. Roscoe, Brent, Kraft, Harry Black, Sylvia Black, Jim Leach, Archie Leach.

Another knock on the door. An insistent voice. "Please. We are now closed. You must return tomorrow if you have not finished."

Kim made her copies and returned the originals to the box. Closed the lid. Glanced to check with Gaspar, her hand on the key.

"Not yet," he said. He held out a white standard number 10 business envelope. Overfilled. She lifted the flap. Extracted a thick wad of hundreds. "Kliners?"

Through the door: "Please. You must go now. Or security will remove you."

Gaspar called, "Two minutes. We'll be right out." For her ears only he said, "I can't tell if they're fakes. Can you?"

She confirmed all standard markers of authenticity. Her phone application quick scan discerned no metallic strips. Older bills. Could be genuine. Could be fake. Could be Kliners. What she needed was an expert.

Sharp, doubling pain in her stomach.

Gaspar pressed. "Now or never. What's it going to be, Madame Prosecutor?"

"You're taking on Cooper as well as Finlay now, Che?"

He shrugged. "I'm no revolutionary. I'm a lawman, just like you. But I know a no-win scenario when I see one."

The assistant was pounding on the door.

Gaspar said, "I've got your back. I'll tell him you're sick; don't make me a liar. I'll buy you five minutes."

He slipped out into the hallway and closed the door firmly behind him.

Kim knew the right things to do. Either leave empty-handed, or stay with the evidence. She was an officer of the law and of the court. She'd taken her oaths with pride. She still had ideals. She planned to be the Director of the FBI one day. Bright lines divided her conduct from those less ambitious and less committed. Lines she'd never planned to cross.

Yet she looked around for a disposable container, just in case.

The hundred dollar bills were solid proof. They were the only hard evidence that Kliners still existed, and that Cooper owned some.

No warrant. No time to get one, even if she could.

If she took the envelope with no warrant, not only did she break the law, but the evidence became inadmissible.

If she left the envelope until a warrant was obtained, the evidence would disappear.

She might never find another Kliner.

Cooper might go free.

She might get caught in possession and be arrested and convicted.

No more time to think.

Do something.

Create a record, at least.

Gaspar was arguing with the assistant in the hallway. Voices were rising and falling.

Working as fast as possible, shielding her actions from the cameras as much as she could, Kim photographed the envelope and its stuffing. She counted 250 bills, all of them hundreds. She laid out several on the table. She photographed them front and back. She quietly dictated a list of serial numbers, careful to keep her voice below the volume of Gaspar's argument on the other side of the door.

Now or never. Take Cooper down or let him win?

What's it going to be?

Her trembling hand slipped four bills into her pocket. She returned the rest to the envelope and then to the box. She relocked the box. She left the depositor key in place.

She'd have controlled her stomach, but Gaspar's excuse made the effort unnecessary. She made it to the ten-inch plastic trash can in the corner before she heaved. Vomit splashed the wall and dribbled down her chin. She heaved again.

She doused her face with bottled water. Rinsed her mouth with Gaspar's cold coffee.

She squared her shoulders. She straightened her jacket.

She rang the bell.

Gaspar opened the door. Sour vomit fumes hung in the air. The security guard fled. The assistant turned green and marched them to the exit. All but shoved them out into the night.

"The vomiting was a bit above and beyond, don't you think?" Gaspar asked.

"Not at all," she said. She gulped exhaust laden air. She sipped the last of her water while Gaspar hailed a taxi. The four Kliners sat like nuclear waste in her pocket.

CHAPTER FORTY-FIVE

Washington, D.C.
November 4
9:45 p.m.

THEY LANDED AT Dulles. Caffeine and anxiety leveraged Kim vertical. She'd spent the entire flight working. She looked like hell and smelled worse. She felt subhuman. Nothing a long shower and a hot meal and red wine and two weeks in bed and a stomach transplant and a new career wouldn't fix.

Gaspar asked, "What's the plan?"

Her life was circling the drain. She grinned anyway. She said, "We attack at dawn."

He grinned with her. "I'd hug you, but you stink."

First phase: employ secret weapon. *Gaspar thinks like Reacher thinks.*

She said, "Tell me again what happened when Hale collected Sylvia last night."

"Not much to tell. Maybe ten minutes after you left, Hale showed up and took her away."

"How did she react?"

"She'd been talking to her lawyer. She expected it."

"How'd she look?"

"Like sixty-seven million dollars."

"What, all green and wrinkly?"

"No, perfect. Clean clothes. Fresh makeup."

"What did she take with her?"

"The Birkin bag. She's not expecting indefinite detention."

"Hale arrested her?"

"How long have you been doing stand-up?"

"What was he wearing?"

"Most guys only get dressed once a day unless someone pushes them into a ditch full of slimy water."

"You fell in."

"You touched my arm. Technically that was battery."

She asked again, "What was Hale wearing?"

"Trench coat. Gloves. It's cold out there, in case you forgot."

"What, precisely, did he say?"

Gaspar was tired of the subject. "The whole episode was a year shorter than this inquisition."

They shuffled with the airport crowd. Slow progress.

He relented. "Hale said Cooper sent him for her. He said the AG's ready. I said okay. He knocked on the bedroom door. She came out. I asked should we wait. He said not necessary, she said goodbye and they left."

"That's all?"

"Yes."

Ten minutes later they were in another taxi. Thick plastic separated the front seat from the back. Three nickel-sized holes permitted sound exchange. There was a cradle for cash payments and a swipe box in the passenger compartment for credit cards.

"Washington Hilton," Kim said, and the taxi joined the outbound traffic. Then she said, "I checked Sylvia's flash drives on the plane.

One contained copies of the Caribbean bank statements Finlay gave us."

Gaspar raised his eyebrow. "Chicken or egg?"

"Sorry?"

He slowed delivery as if addressing a dimwit. "Did Finlay *take* the statements *from* Sylvia's safety deposit box? Or *plant* the statements *in* the box?"

She shrugged; she'd come to love that response. "Either way, statements prove Sylvia and Harry laundered Kliners offshore. Statements add up to fifty-eight million over four years."

"Leaving nine million still unwashed?"

"Maybe. Or stashed in one of the other three accounts."

"We've only been on this case four days."

"Cooper could have made a long-lead plan, I guess. Knowing he was going to bring us in sooner or later?" Some things still made no sense to her.

He shrugged. "Unlikely."

She said, "The statements prove the box was accessed at least once after Sylvia's initial set up. Five years ago, she hadn't laundered any money yet. The flash drives were obsolete. Like the data was old too."

"Was it Sylvia who accessed the box at least once?"

"Maybe."

"When?"

"Can't say for sure."

He shrugged. "Anything on the other two flash drives?"

"Sylvia's memoirs on one. Nothing we couldn't guess."

"Boyfriend?"

"She called him 'My Man' or 'MM.'"

Gaspar noticed her hesitation. "What about the third drive? Anything about Harry? The Kliners? Cooper? Reacher?"

She pointed to the hotel just ahead. "I'd rather show you."

The taxi dropped them at the service entrance. In their room, she pulled the third flash drive out of her pocket. Tossed it to him. "Look at this while I shower."

What would he find that she'd misinterpreted?

CHAPTER FORTY-SIX

Washington, D.C.
November 5
1:15 a.m.

SHOWER, FOOD, COFFEE, talk. She felt fortified enough. Her plan was ironed out. Redundancies and backups were in place. Electronic evidence had been transferred to secure locations. She had two hours of work to complete later. Dawn was five hours ahead.

Sleep three hours.

Work two hours.

Implement plan.

Bingo.

Gaspar was in the room's only chair. She didn't ask why he wasn't stretched out on the other bed. She dressed in pajamas and the hotel's terry robe. She set her alarm. She punched her pillows. She turned her cell phone off. She snuffed the bedside lamp.

She stretched out.

She closed her eyes.

Gaspar said, "I forgot to ask. Did you recognize anyone on that last flash drive?"

She murmured before she fell off the cliff, "A toady guy using the *Busy Beaver* was the U.S. Ambassador to Switzerland until last year. And a guy wearing the silver band is pretty high up at the Attorney General's office now."

Then what felt a minute later room service delivered a 4:00 a.m. breakfast.

Gaspar was already showered, dressed, and packed. He dealt with the waiter. Seconds later he was chowing down on eggs, ham, and toast.

Revolting.

Kim arose groggy. Mainlined coffee before, during, and after her shower. Munched dry toast as she packed. Twenty minutes later they were on the road to Baltimore. It was still full dark. Traffic was light. It was cold. No precipitation.

"Did you check your voice mail?" Gaspar asked. "Roscoe called me again an hour ago. Looking for you. Seemed a bit frantic."

Kim pulled out her smart phone and fired it up and found three voice messages, all from Roscoe. She listened. "She says Archie Leach is on his way. Says he's out of his mind with grief. Dangerous, is how she put it."

"Something off about that guy. He was the cool head back at Eno's diner when brother Jim was holding his shotgun on us. Now he's so grief stricken he's chasing a couple of federal agents?"

Kim shrugged. "We've got plenty to deal with as it is. Let's put Archie Leach on the back burner."

Gaspar followed the directions they'd worked out. Forty-eight minutes later they pulled into the bus station. Kim hurried inside and located two self-serve lockers permitting sixty day pre-paid rentals. She stashed duplicate hard copies of the evidence she'd made last night in each. Dropped each key into a padded envelope, postage prepaid. Mailed one at the station. Mailed the second from a random roadside box.

She repeated the process at the train station and the airport.

She rejoined Gaspar at the curb outside Baltimore Washington International.

He asked, "Good to go?"

She said, "Our asses are as covered as they're ever going to get."

She checked her watch. Right on time. The sun was just peeking over the horizon.

Attack at dawn.

But the attack would fail unless Sylvia agreed to help them. Which she might. If they could separate her from Marion Wallace and Charles Cooper.

CHAPTER FORTY-SEVEN

Washington, D.C.
November 5
8:50 a.m.

KIM RANG THE bell three times before Elle opened the door wearing her bathrobe. "Goodness, Kimmy. It's awfully early. Is Marion expecting you?"

Kim stepped over the threshold and kept on walking. "Is she in the breakfast room? We can find our own way."

Gaspar followed.

Elle called out, "She's in the salon, I think."

Perfectly costumed, Marion glanced up from her morning paper. She had coffee in a bone china cup. French pastries filled a basket on her silver tray. "I wondered when you'd be back. It's Agent Otto now, am I right? Not Mrs. Nguyen anymore?"

Kim shrugged. Refused the bait. Essential work here didn't involve Marion, but her breakfast companion, Sylvia Black. She was right there. Cheeks bright. In expensive travel clothes. Jeans, silk shirt, leather jacket. Fashionably functional boots.

The costume worried Kim. Sylvia was all but gone.

"Agent Otto, Agent Gaspar," Sylvia said, rising, as if greeting old friends. "How may I help you?"

Kim selected her best opening. She touched Sylvia's arm, connecting. Gentle, lowered voice. "Cooper's cut you loose, Sylvia. He's setting you up. He sent us to Zurich for evidence against you."

Sylvia barely flinched, but Kim caught it. She said, "He sacrificed you last time. He's doing it again. You'll go to prison."

"That's not true." Faint whisper, quivering chin, dry mouth.

"You think he'll be your Main Man forever? Come on. You're smarter than that. Aren't you?"

"Smarter than you give me credit for."

Kim said, "I think you're a very smart woman. That's why I'm here. Come with us. It's all set up for real this time."

No response. Kim felt the clock ticking. Sylvia looked to Marion for guidance. For fifteen years Marion had mentored and protected her younger protégé. Sylvia trusted her.

Another betrayal.

Kim pushed as hard as she dared. "I thought Marion was my friend once. But believe me, her own hide always comes before yours."

No response.

Gaspar said, "Wake up, Sylvia. You were expendable five years ago and you're expendable now. Cooper would have killed you in that Chevy with Bernie Owens, but he still needed you. When he doesn't need you anymore, that'll be the end. And it's coming."

No response.

Kim said, "He's on his way here now to take you away, isn't he?"

Sylvia's expression was the only acknowledgement required.

Kim said, "You're leaving D.C. You're leaving the country. And when no one is around to watch him? He's going to kill you, Sylvia. You know that. *You know it.*"

Sylvia looked down at her hands. She was close to panic. Kim recognized the signs.

One last hard push.

"He's *using* you, Sylvia," Kim said. "He doesn't *love* you."

"He does too." Defensive and insecure, but defiant.

Kim considered telling the truth, that Cooper didn't love anyone. Was never loyal to anyone. Never had been and never would be. But Kim had read Sylvia's memoirs. She wasn't the stone-cold bitch Gaspar assumed her to be. She was bendable. Fragile. Somewhere under all that experience, the Iowa farm girl remained.

And Kim knew all about farm girls. She'd been one herself, once upon a time. Impossible to beat your DNA. Couldn't be done. Even after years of trying. In death, Sylvia's farm girl DNA would be precisely identifiable. No escape. Only surrender. Kim had to make Sylvia own it.

Sylvia loved Cooper. And she wanted to believe Cooper loved her. But she was as smart as she said she was. Or at least as cunning. Self-preservation was paramount. She knew the truth. So she'd work it out eventually, precisely the way Kim had planned.

But how long would Sylvia take to get there? Cooper was close. Kim felt it the same way she felt the temperature in the room.

She said, "You've been betrayed before, Sylvia. You know how it feels. Your heart hurts. Your mind warns you constantly, but you keep going, thinking you're going to get away, that it's only fear, that you can break through, you're really okay. But you know you're not. *You know.* Trust your gut, Sylvia. *Trust me.*"

No response.

Kim said, "We've got to get out of here before he shows up. We're sitting here like targets, Sylvia. Are you coming with us or not?"

She was so focused on Sylvia that Marion Wallace's voice startled her.

"You should think about it, Sylvia dear," Marion said absently, rustling the paper as she turned the page. "I mean, why don't you go with them? He's rescued you before. He'll do it again. And when he does, you'll know for sure that he loves you and everything these people are telling you is nonsense."

Translation: use the emergency plan. Working girls always had one. And these two working girls were smarter than most and they'd been in tight spots before. Sylvia raised her head and looked directly into Marion's eyes. Something passed between them. A bond forged in earlier times, and leaner struggles. Sylvia nodded slightly.

"Okay," she said. "Let me get my bag. I'll hurry."

And she headed up the stairs.

Marion returned her gaze to her newspaper. "Still too trusting, Agent Otto. She might escape."

"You told her to come with us. She will."

"You overestimate me. People do what they do."

But five minutes later Sylvia came back, with her bag.

Sylvia hugged Marion and said, "Until we meet again, sweetie." Then she led Otto and Gaspar through back hallways to a rear exit originally used for deliveries. They came out in a narrow paved alley running parallel with Dumbarton Street. There was dog manure and broken bottles and empty soda cans and trash and pale leggy weeds all over it. There were overfilled dumpsters awaiting pickup. Overhead, a low gray cloud ceiling masked visibility. Winds whipped around corners and through tunnels between buildings. They walked fast, with their hands stuffed into their pockets for warmth.

They were twenty feet from the end of the alley when Archie Leach stepped out of the shadows.

CHAPTER FORTY-EIGHT

THEY ALL STOPPED dead. Leach was at least six-three and two-fifty. He filled half the alley's width. An effective barrier. He was scowling hard but not speaking. He was dressed in jeans and boots and jacket.

Kim said, "What do you want, Leach?"

Leach moved his right arm and brought a shotgun out from behind his leg. Not the Browning A-5 his brother had used in Eno's diner. It was a Remington SP-10 instead. He pointed it directly at Gaspar. Kim slowed down into extreme high-alert mode. She saw every detail. She heard individual motes of dust jousting in the wind. She smelled garlic and pumpkin and rotten eggs and cat urine.

Leach took six deliberate steps forward, never dropping the shotgun's barrel a fraction. His eyes were on Gaspar. When he was close enough to be heard, he said, "You killed my brother, and I can't let that go."

Gaspar maintained eye contact, and pushed Sylvia out of the way. Kim reached out and pulled her close. But clear of her own right hand. Sylvia was shaking. It felt real enough.

Gaspar said, "You don't really believe I killed your brother, and no one else will, either."

Leach advanced, gritty steps loud on the asphalt. He said, "You should have opened that car door before Jim ever got there, asshole. You saw Bernie inside. He could have been alive. You might have saved him. You're an FBI agent. You should have checked him out."

That's crazy, was Kim's immediate thought. She understood what Roscoe had been trying to tell her. Archie Leach was armed, dangerous, and out of his mind. Kim thought: I could die today. Right here in this alley, among dog shit and weeds and rotting garbage.

What was Leach waiting for?

Then she heard footsteps behind her.

She glanced back.

Michael Hale was there.

Hale had come out of Wallace's back door into the alley. He was approaching with no hesitation. Could Leach not see him?

Hale walked right up to them and grabbed Sylvia's arm.

And Kim knew.

The grab, the gloved hand, the silence.

She'd seen that choreography before.

Hale had made the same moves the night he took Sylvia from Margrave jail.

Hale turned back, pulling Sylvia with him.

Gaspar never took his eyes off Leach. He called out, "Hale? Cooper will kill you, too. You know that, right? He's killing everyone."

Hale kept walking. Sylvia was stumbling alongside him.

Gaspar called, man to man, "Hale? It's not too late. You can still save yourself."

Hale stopped and turned. Classic moves Kim had practiced a thousand times. So had Gaspar. They were all FBI. They'd all had identical training. All three knew precisely what Hale was about to do.

What happened next unfolded in Kim's line of vision like stop-motion animation of an elaborate dance. A race in agonizing slow motion.

Kim shouted a warning to her partner. Gaspar snatched a quick look back. Kim reached smoothly into her holster as she'd practiced ten thousand times.

Muscle memory.

Gaspar was a fraction of a second behind her.

Kim took cover.

Hale fired first.

Four rapid shots, three deliberately high, one not.

Gaspar went down and rolled behind a dumpster.

Hale put Sylvia in the line of fire before Kim could get off a shot.

Archie Leach's focus on Gaspar made him miss Hale's moves. Gaspar's focus on Archie made him pull the trigger on his Glock. A double tap. Two hits in Leach's right shoulder. The big Remington whipped sideways and upward as Archie fell. The gun fired uselessly into the air. Kim looked back; Hale and Sylvia had disappeared.

Archie went down. Blood bloomed on his shoulder. On the ground, determined, hurting, slowed, he aimed the shotgun to fire again.

Gaspar put three bullets in his neck.

The shotgun clattered on the asphalt. Leach's giant body went slack. Collapsed. Blood spurted from neck holes. Mouth moved like a fish. No sound. Eyes showed awareness. Became glassy. Pupil reaction stopped while blood bubbled softly a moment more. Then a stopped heart stopped the bubbles.

Severed wind pipe, Kim thought. Severed jugular. Severed spine at the cervical vertebra. She ran across the alley to find Gaspar laying flat with his eyes closed. Blood was seeping through his shirt on his right side.

Distant sirens approached.

Someone had called 911.

"Carlos?" Kim said. "Are you okay?"

Gaspar looked up. He winced. He said, "We've got to go. If we stay here, there will be more red tape than either of us will ever survive. Help me up."

Kim helped him stand. He leaned heavily on her shoulder and several times she thought he might fall, but they made it back to the Crown Vic. He laid out on the back seat. She put some distance between them and Archie Leach's corpse, and then she stopped in a deserted Crystal City parking lot.

She reached back and found the phantom cell in his pocket.

She dialed.

Only one choice.

CHAPTER FORTY-NINE

Washington, D.C.
November 5
10:35 a.m.

COOPER ANSWERED ON the first ring. He asked, "How's Gaspar?"

Kim said, "You know about that already?"

"Of course I do."

"Gaspar needs a doctor."

"No doctor. Deal with it."

"How?"

"You've had training. There are drugstores open."

"It could be worse than that."

"If it is, call me back."

It wasn't worse than that. Kim treated him on the back seat of the Crown Vic. The wound was superficial. A tear in the flesh. Water and antiseptic and drugstore butterfly bandages did the job. He would be fine. Eventually. But he was hurting now.

He asked, "Hale?"

She said, "Still at large."

"Not for long."

"How?"

"You can figure that out, boss lady."

She called Cooper again. Adrenaline had worn off. Shame fueled her now. She was responsible for Gaspar's injuries. Cooper answered promptly. She gave him the full report without flinching. He said, "Sounds to me like Hale killed Leach. That works, right? And the shooting was righteous. I'll take care of Hale. Tell Gaspar not to worry. You either."

"Not good enough," Kim said. She didn't want Cooper to take care of Hale. She would do that herself. As soon as Gaspar was good to go. "You knew it was Hale all along, didn't you? He manipulated Sylvia. He killed Harry. He bombed the Chevy. You knew. We were all human targets. Now Gaspar is hurt and people are dead."

His voice remained low and controlled. He said, "I wish I had that kind of power. Believe me, the world would be a lot different."

"I don't believe you," Kim said. "I may never believe you again."

"Oh, come on. At least go with trust but verify. Good enough to bring down the Soviets. Should be good enough for you."

"Okay, let's verify," Kim said. "You knew Harry was already dead when you sent us to Margrave. True?"

"Yes."

"Who killed him? Hale? Owens? Or Sylvia?"

He said, "Does it really matter which one delivered the kill shots?"

Good point, Kim thought. Legally, morally, practically, it made no difference. She said, "Hale and Owens helped Sylvia sterilize the scene, and to steal and launder the Kliners."

He sounded disappointed. "I wanted your particular expertise. I expected you to learn who else was involved. Like Archie and Jim Leach, we know now, for sure. Probably others. I'd hoped you would figure that out. You let me down."

"You know Reacher. Personally."

"Never said I didn't."

"You knew his father."

"Again, never denied."

"You know where Reacher is."

"I wish I did. That's something else you didn't achieve."

She ignored the rebuke. "You have a significant numbered account balance and a stash of Kliners in a safety deposit box at Empire Bank in Zurich."

For the first time, he paused. The silence lasted too long. His tone was quiet.

He said, "That's good to know."

Half a beat later, she saw it.

She said, "Finlay hates you."

"The feeling is mutual. You've met the man once. Be careful. Roscoe doesn't know him as well as she thinks. The man's a stone killer."

"And you're not?"

"Takes one to know one."

She felt the pushback like a physical force. She said, "What about Sylvia?"

He said, "What about her?"

"You'll let Hale use her and then kill her?"

"I will if you will."

"What does that mean?"

"Whatever you want it to mean."

She didn't answer.

He asked, "Are we done here?"

"Hell no," she said. "Where is Hale?"

"On his way to Phoenix, Arizona."

"Reacher, too?"

"Maybe you should ask your pal Finlay that question."

"You're an asshole, you know that?"

He sighed. "So I've been told."

She said, "I've got a plane to catch."

CHAPTER FIFTY

Washington, D.C.
November 5
12:15 p.m.

GASPAR HAD EASED himself behind the Crown Vic's wheel. He was the number two, and the number two drives. Simple as that. He was on his personal phone, calling home. "I know. I'll be home soon. Don't worry. Kiss the girls for me." He paused to listen to his wife. He said, "Yeah, I love you too."

"Everything okay at home?" Kim asked, as she slipped into the car. She handed back the phantom cell. Until Hale was dealt with to her satisfaction, she had nothing more to say to Cooper.

"All fine at home," Gaspar said. "Where to now, boss lady?"

She recognized his attempt to normalize their relationship again after she'd failed him in the alley. He was more generous than she would have been.

She said, "Phoenix, Arizona."

"For?"

"Hale and Sylvia."

"What about Reacher? Is he with them?"

"Cooper says he doesn't know."

"You believe that?"

"No more than you do. He's sending transportation and instructions." She could see he was hurting. "Want me to drive?"

"I told you I'm fine."

"Hale won't deliberately wound you again when we find him. This time, he'll shoot to kill."

He shrugged. "What did you tell the boss?"

"I said you were fine."

"Thanks."

"Least I could do, don't you think?"

"Why's that?"

She looked away.

He said, "If you're harboring some crazy ass boss lady alpha female idea that you should have gotten Hale before he got me, then forget all about it. I didn't see it coming, either."

But you weren't looking. I was.

Kim blinked it back. "Maybe I've been spending too much time with Roscoe."

He said, "I'm tired, that's all. I'll sleep on the plane. I'll be right as rain when we get there. Don't worry."

She laughed. "Worry? Who, me?"

He smiled. "Right. What was I thinking?" He pulled out into the traffic. "What time's the flight?"

CHAPTER FIFTY-ONE

Phoenix, AZ
November 5
3:45 p.m. local time

FACTS WERE FACTS: Hale had a three-hour head start. And Phoenix was her last chance to get him before he left the country. She didn't want to chase him all around the world.

But she would if she had to.

By the time they landed at Phoenix Sky Harbor International she had her plan in place. Gaspar had slept all the way from wheels up to wheels down. He had denied being in pain, but the crevices etched deep in his face revealed the lie. His limp had gotten worse too. He'd refused to explain the extent of his prior injuries or how Hale's shots might have interacted with them. He'd waved away her concerns. But the stiff upper lip act wasn't fooling her. And it was making her feel worse, not better.

A small nerdy desk jockey agent from the Phoenix FBI field office waited with ground transportation, as Cooper had promised. "Agents Otto and Gaspar? I'm Agent Picard. This way, please."

They followed him out to the standard black SUV. He offered keys.

Gaspar held out his hand.

"I'm number two," he said.

Picard's eyes widened behind his glasses. He swallowed, and offered a quick rundown. "This vehicle is special-task-force equipped. Firepower in the back if you need it. Fully wired. Activate if you want backup. I'm assigned to you as long as you need me, but otherwise you're not being monitored. There are extra phones in the console for quick response teams. There's a cooler with food and water. The GPS is pre-programmed. Access it with your security code. Anything else you need?"

"That'll do it, thanks," Kim said.

Picard nodded. "Good luck." He returned to his own vehicle.

Gaspar opened the cooler and pulled out two sandwiches and two bottles of water. They settled in. Kim plugged in her smart phone to charge its dead battery. Within seconds, a text came in from Cooper containing a seven letter GPS security code. She entered it into the system. The pre-programmed map showed the fastest route to Coolidge Municipal Airport. An hour's drive time. Fifty-eight miles.

"We might not be too late," Gaspar said. "He's in a private plane. Private planes fly slower and have less fuel on board. The flight would have taken them longer. Maybe required a stop enroute."

She'd already figured all that out while he was sleeping, but she liked that he was starting to think strategically again. She said, "Be good if you're right."

"Check for private jets on the way in and which ones landed in the last half hour?"

She pushed a few buttons on the specialized GPS system and was able to locate airport radar. "Shows flight plans for a helicopter departure. Waiting for inbound passengers. Then nothing else for the remainder of the day."

He said, "Helicopter?"

She nodded. The only thing Kim hated worse than flying was flying in small planes. And the only thing worse than small planes was helicopters. They crashed. Constantly. People survived chopper crashes, but plenty died too. Survival rates were higher with water crashes. Unhelpful in the Arizona desert.

And Gaspar would never manage a chopper. She'd be on it alone. *Only one choice.*

She collected unjacketed hollow points from the SUV's supply chest and stuck them in her pocket. She couldn't risk more firepower inside a chopper. She wanted penetration sufficient to reach vital organs and stay there. Incapacitate. But not instantly. No head shots feasible.

The onboard radar beeped and identified a Learjet incoming westbound at 3,500 feet. Control tower access. Female pilot requesting permission to land. Cleared for final approach.

Kim met Gaspar's gaze.

He recognized the pilot's voice too.

Sylvia Black.

What?

Now Hale's reckless attack in the alley seemed less foolish.

Gaspar said, "Hale grabbed Sylvia this morning because he needed a pilot, not a hostage."

Which confirmed one set of suspicions Kim had flushed out inflight. Sylvia had never been a dispensable pawn in Hale's game. She was an integral actor in a long term criminal enterprise. She said, "Hale and Sylvia planned to meet Archie Leach at Wallace's place. They planned to kill us in their crossfire."

"How long have we got?"

"They're on final approach. Five minutes, maybe?"

Gaspar accelerated.

CHAPTER FIFTY-TWO

LANDING CONDITIONS WERE close to perfect. Winds were blowing straight down the runway at 10 knots. Clouds at 6,000 feet. Sylvia turned to line up with the runway. They would land, switch to the waiting chopper, and take off again. Maybe to a final destination in the mountains? Somewhere the Learjet couldn't go?

Gaspar put the pedal to the metal and raced the Learjet to the runway.

He didn't make it.

Too far.

Sylvia landed and taxied fast and came to a stop close to a waiting Huey. She and Hale walked from jet to copter. Just the two of them. No third party. No Reacher.

Kim was puzzled, briefly. From the air Hale must have identified the SUV as an FBI task force vehicle. He should have aborted the landing and flown on. He would have been out of U.S. airspace before Kim could have done anything about it.

Therefore, Hale knew who was on the ground, and why.

The Huey's rotor started turning.

Gaspar slammed the SUV to a stop.

Kim opened her door.

Gaspar asked, "Do you know how to disable a chopper?"

"I'll think of something," Kim said. "But feel free to chime in with ideas."

She slid out of the truck and ran through the downdraft from the whapping blades and the storm of noise from the turbine. Sylvia was in the Huey's pilot's seat and Hale was about to climb in on the navigator side. He had one foot on the ground and the other on the Huey's step.

Kim drew her gun.

She called, "FBI! Stay where you are!"

Protocol satisfied.

Legalities completed.

Hale didn't stop. He was too close to an escape planned over too many years. Or maybe Kim's voice had been swallowed up by the Huey's noise.

Gaspar had driven up very close to the front of the Huey, but the bird could clear the truck for lift off. That was the nature of helicopters.

Kim aimed and fired.

Bullets hit rotors and ricocheted.

Hale braced himself halfway into the cabin and returned fire. Covering fire. Not aimed. He was trying to keep Gaspar inside the SUV and hold Kim back until the Huey could get in the air.

The turbine spooled up and the blades increased their speed. Runway dirt whirled and danced. The Huey went light, and then weightless. It rose steadily. Hale was still on the step, one foot inside, holding on with one hand, and firing with the other.

Kim had no chance to get on board.

She did not feel relieved.

She aimed.

She fired.

Four shots directly at Hale's receding body.

Two missed.

But one hit him in the hip and a second in the thigh.

He fell.

Forward, into the helicopter's cabin.

Shit!

Sylvia lifted ever higher.

No target now except the chopper itself.

Kim emptied her clip into the tail. Solid hits. But no result.

Sylvia turned the Huey straight toward the SUV.

Gaspar's was at the SUV's weapons locker. He had a rifle. He braced. He aimed.

He fired.

Straight at Sylvia as she flew directly toward him.

The first shot hit the windshield and deflected.

The second shot deflected.

Bulletproof. The Huey was armored for war zones. The Learjet was not. They'd stopped for armored transportation.

Where were they headed?

Gaspar fired again. He hit the glass in precisely the right spot to take Sylvia's head off.

The bullet deflected.

The Huey raised higher and higher overhead. It turned south, toward Mexico, toward the mountains.

Kim took a sniper rifle from the rack. She steadied herself against the SUV. She aimed. She fired.

She hit.

No result.

She stared at the retreating helicopter.

She'd lost.

She'd failed.

They were gone.

Then the Huey's blades slowed.

The tail dipped low.

Kim's bullet had damaged the Huey.

Maybe just enough to force Sylvia to land.

Maybe not enough to make her crash.

She fired again, and again, and again. She hit the Huey every time. It started to swing and falter. It lost power. It started to come down.

"Get in!" she yelled to Gaspar. "Drive!" They scrambled into the SUV.

The Huey started to fall.

Gaspar closed the gap. The Huey lost its rotors. Began to dive.

Gaspar reached the runway's end and kept on going over the flat gravel apron. Kim watched the Huey fall and crash on the desert floor.

Fifty feet away, Gaspar stopped the SUV.

Kim jumped out and ran. Gaspar limped behind her.

Kim felt the heat. Smelled the fuel.

Sylvia was bloodied but alive. She was unbuckling her seatbelt, trying to rise. Hale had his pistol in his hand.

Sylvia opened her door and got her left leg out.

Hale shot her in the back.

CHAPTER FIFTY-THREE

AFTERWARD KIM FIGURED the standoff lasted less than ten seconds, but at the time it felt like ten hours. Hale was still alive, but he couldn't move. He was wounded in the leg, by her handgun rounds, and shaken by the crash. He stayed in his seat. Small tongues of flame were starting up. The desert air was shimmering with heat and vapor.

She walked toward the crippled Huey. Gaspar tried to stop her, but she shook him off. She said, "Hale, I can help you. Hang on. I'm coming for you."

Hale lifted his gun, like a great effort, and aimed it at her.

"Are you insane?" she called. "You can't get out of there unless we help you."

The flames bloomed bigger, twisting and racing, searching out air and fuel. Gaspar came after her, slowed by his wounds. He called out. She couldn't understand his words, but she knew he was warning her to stop before the Huey exploded.

The fire was roaring now. There was black smoke and the stench of kerosene.

Hale fell out of his seat, to the cabin floor, then to the step, and then to the ground. He tried to crawl away, but he was dazed and his hip and leg were too badly wounded.

He stayed where he was.

Kim rounded the tail section. Gaspar came up beside her.

"We have to get out," he said.

"Hale! Hale!" she called over the roaring flames.

Hale heard her. He rolled on his back. He stared at her.

He aimed his gun at Gaspar's chest.

Instinct.

Muscle memory.

Training.

Kim stopped, braced, and fired.

Once, twice, three times.

Hale lay still.

Gaspar pulled her back.

She stood a moment longer, looking at the first man she'd ever killed.

Washington, D.C.
November 6
5:45 p.m.

Twelve hours later they were sitting in a coffee shop across the street from the Hoover Building. FBI headquarters. Cooper's lair. They had completed their formal encrypted reports to Cooper, detailing all the news fit to print about the last five days. They had divided the paperwork into two separate halves: the Reacher file and the Harry Black investigation.

They would leave it to others to testify about Black. They themselves were under the radar, and would stay there. Their personal involvement in the Margrave mess, as they'd come to call it during private conversations, was completely redacted. They didn't know how Cooper had managed to spirit them out of the evidence trail, and they didn't want to know. Both agents were grateful, but neither said so out loud.

Kim's last task was to copy everything to her personal secure storage. *Paying my insurance premium,* she called it. She hit the send button and watched the upload and closed the laptop's lid.

She said, "That feels good."

Gaspar smiled. "Too bad about our numbered Swiss accounts, though. Could have made several little girls happy with all that cash."

Kim nodded and sipped her coffee. "Have you changed your mind about Finlay?"

"Should I?"

"Finlay sent us to the Empire Bank. That's how we discovered Hale had set up the accounts in our name and Cooper's too. Those accounts would have lived forever. Without Finlay, where would we be? Testifying in front of a Federal Grand Jury and dodging the IRS, that's where."

"If he gave us a heads up, he had his own reasons."

"I was wrong about him," Kim said. "And at least I can admit it. He hated Hale, not Cooper."

"Probably hated them both."

"Maybe."

Across the street a young man in a suit came out of the concrete fortress. A junior agent. Little more than a messenger boy.

Kim said, "Now what, *compadre?* Back to Miami? Hug the kids, say hi to the wife, drink sweet coffee and sit behind your desk for the next twenty?"

The young man in the suit was crossing the street. Heading straight for them.

"That would be a wonderful life," Gaspar said. "But I think someone has other plans for me. Reacher is still in the wind."

"He had nothing to do with any of this, did he?"

"He was in Margrave fifteen years ago. I bet he never went back. Why would he? So no, he had nothing to do with any of it. We wasted a lot of time."

The junior agent approached their table. He said, "Otto? Gaspar?" When they acknowledged, he handed each a small padded envelope. Unmarked. But recognizable.

Gaspar ripped his open. A cell phone. He shrugged. He slipped the phone into his pocket. Kim looked up at Cooper's office window. Was he standing behind the reflective glass? Right then? Watching? She saw the messenger boy head back toward the building.

And she saw a man, too, motionless in a shadowed doorway. He was looking straight at her. He was tall, easily six-five, and broad, easily two-fifty. A giant, really. He wore jeans and a leather jacket. Work boots on his feet. He had fair hair and a tan face and big hands. Sunglasses hid his eyes. He looked infinitely patient, just standing there, self-possessed, self-confident, simultaneously alert and relaxed, both friendly and dangerous.

She turned to Gaspar, to point the guy out. When she looked back, he was gone.

THE END

ABOUT THE AUTHOR

Diane Capri is an award-winning *New York Times, USA Today,* and worldwide bestselling author.

She's a recovering lawyer and snowbird who divides her time between Florida and Michigan. An active member of Mystery Writers of America, Author's Guild, International Thriller Writers, Alliance of Independent Authors, and Sisters in Crime, Diane loves to hear from readers and is hard at work on her next novel.

Please connect with her online:

http://www.DianeCapri.com
Twitter: http://twitter.com/@DianeCapri
Facebook: http://www.facebook.com/Diane.Capri1
http://www.facebook.com/DianeCapriBooks